To Walk The Night

E.S. MOORE

KENSINGTON PUBLISHING CORP.
http://www.kensingtonbooks.com

KENSINGTON BOOKS are published by

Kensington Publishing Corp.
119 West 40th Street
New York, NY 10018

All Kensington Titles, Imprints, and Distributed Lines are available at special quantity discounts for bulk purchases for sales promotions, premiums, fund-raising, and educational or institutional use.

Special book excerpts or customized printings can also be created to fit specific needs. For details, write or phone the office of the Kensington special sales manager: Kensington Publishing Corp., 119 West 40th Street, New York, NY 10018, attn: Special Sales Department, Phone: 1-800-221-2647.

Kensington and the K logo Reg. U.S. Pat. & TM Off.

ISBN-13: 978-0-7582-6872-3
ISBN-10: 0-7582-6872-6

First Mass Market Printing: January 2012

10 9 8 7 6 5 4 3 2 1

Printed in the United States of America

To Lena, for suggesting I go back and work on "that vampire book" again.

1

Blood dripped from the edge of my blade, falling soundlessly in the deathly quiet room. Bodies lay strewn about the floor, heads separated from torsos, holes punctured through temples. Every last one of them died by my hand. Now only one remained.

I crouched motionless behind an overturned table. My gun, a modified Glock 17, was empty, had been for a while. Most of the kills had been clean. One bullet to the head, one slash with my sword, and it was over.

Werewolves and vampires couldn't handle silver. It was poison to them. It attacked the taint in their blood, burned in their veins, paralyzing them so that they were helpless for the killing blow.

Everything I fought with was made of silver. My bullets, my katana blade, the blades of my knives, they were all crafted from pure silver.

And thanks to vampire regulations, they were all illegal.

A faint slither of cloth over skin caught my ears, but I remained hidden. The gentle tap of Count

Paltori's boots on the wooden floor seemed to come from right behind me. I held still, knowing it was a lie.

Paltori was a Count of some moderate ability. Given time, he might have turned his Fledgling House into something of a power. He could throw sounds, make his voice seem to come from anywhere in the room, and make the sound of his footfalls echo down empty hallways. If I hadn't done my research on him, I never would have known, and this entire battle could have gone the other way.

"I commend you," Paltori said. His voice slithered through my head. "It's obvious this isn't your first time. It's a shame it will be your last."

A droplet of blood slid down the blade of my sword, then hung from the tip. It quivered there, elongated, and then dropped with a faint *plink*.

I scarcely dared to blink. While I had the advantage of silver, Paltori was still dangerous. His wolves had gone down relatively easy. There had only been five of them, which was impressive for a Fledgling House. He had two vampires to call his own as well, and they lay among the corpses of the wolves, dead just like everyone else. Even his Pureblood servants— men and women who had chosen to live as food and slaves rather than to suffer the more violent end most Purebloods faced when captured by a vampire Count—were among the dead.

A werewolf's body lay only a few feet away. She had been pretty before shifting. My knife had taken her in the throat, paralyzing her seconds before a silver bullet to the brain finished her off for good.

"I would have your name," Paltori went on. "You aren't like the others. You are special. I want to know who it is I kill."

I tried to ignore the false sounds of his movements and instead tried to focus on what was really there. I knew he was somewhere on the other side of the table, probably close by. There was a reason he was stalling. He was scared. No one walked into a vampire House and did what I just did.

No one but me anyway.

I shifted my weight and the leather of my coat groaned ever so slightly. All sounds in the room abruptly cut off. There was a heartbeat of silence. I held my breath, knowing I had allowed him to pinpoint my position behind the long banquet table. The low chuckle that came next sounded as if it had come from right behind my ear.

"I can hear you." Underneath the silky-smooth sound of Paltori's voice was a harsh edge. I had ruined him. He knew no matter what happened here, whether he lived or died, he would never regain the power he had lost. His House was done.

His anger gave him away. I tensed and sprang to my feet just as Count Paltori leaped over the table, his own sword swinging down in a deadly arc.

Our weapons met with a clang, my softer silver giving way to his much sturdier steel. His blade gouged my own, and I jerked the sword back before he could damage it further. He smiled, exposing blood-smeared fangs.

"Where did you get the silver?" he asked, falling back into a fighter's stance. "It isn't exactly common these days."

I smiled, exposing my own teeth. He probably already knew who I was but wouldn't want to believe it until he had proof. I was happy to oblige. The blood oozed from my gums as my fangs elongated.

Paltori's eyes widened. "Lady Death," he said. His hand shook where he gripped his sword.

I ground my teeth at the name but didn't say anything. I hated that name. It was the name the vampire Houses had given me, one that was spat like a curse by every Count in the city. It was the only name they knew me by. No one who heard my true name, Kat Redding, lived to tell about it later.

Paltori feigned to the left and then darted to the right.

I was ready for him. I spun past him, reaching into my coat as I went by. My hand closed around a small square packet; I used the edge of my blade to cut into it as I came to a stop, facing Paltori. His face was red with rage.

"You killed my House," he said. "I have nothing left."

I smiled at him but didn't answer. I simply waited.

Count Paltori growled low in his throat and raised his sword for another charge. I ripped the packet the rest of the way open and threw it in his face.

Silver dust burst from the packet as it struck him. I ducked out of the way, closing my eyes to the poisonous cloud. Paltori screamed and his sword fell from nerveless fingers. A moment later, the heavy thump of his body followed.

I waited a few minutes for the dust to settle. Getting it into my eyes wouldn't kill me outright, but it would put a pretty big damper on my night. It would paralyze me just as it had Count Paltori, not to mention the fact that it would hurt like hell.

When I rose and turned, Paltori was lying facedown on the floor, twitching. I rolled him over with my boot. I wanted him to see who it was who killed him.

"I would ask you if you had any last words," I said.

My eyes were stinging from the remains of dust in the air. "But unfortunately, you aren't in much of a condition to speak them." I raised my sword.

Paltori's red-tinged eyes widened. His lips peeled back and a low moan issued from between his clenched teeth.

Then his head rolled away as I severed it from his neck.

I looked around at the mess around me and my stomach did a flip. So much blood. All of it was on my hands now.

Turning away from the massacre, I began making my way from room to room, making sure I had killed every last person loyal to House Paltori. I never left anyone behind, not even the Purebloods who loyally waited on the vampires. Leaving a single loyalist alive could easily bring down my ruin.

It wasn't until I reached the basement that I found the first victims of Paltori's lusts. The lights were off, but I could see well enough. Cages lined every wall, their bars grimy and stained. The cages were just big enough for the Purebloods to stand, but not so big as to let them move around freely. Water dishes were on the floor, and a bed of hay lined each cage.

I took a deep breath and let it out slowly between my teeth. These weren't vampire loyalists. These were people who were forced to feed the vampires—both in blood and lust. They weren't a threat to me.

The Purebloods were all staring at me with frightened eyes. They were all nude and sported multiple scars from repeated feedings. Very few had any modesty left. Those who did covered themselves as best they could with their hands. Most of them simply turned and offered themselves up to me.

It was all I could do to keep from being sick.

There was a table by the stairs and a set of keys rested on top of it. I snatched them up and began the process of unlocking all the cage doors. The Purebloods cowered in their corners, afraid I was going to punish them for some unknown offense.

"Go," I said as I opened the last cage. "Get out of here."

The Purebloods stared up at me, none of them moving. They had been treated like animals for so long, they didn't know what to do.

"I said go!" I shouted, my teeth sprouting from my gums in a gush of blood. I let my inner monster show, let them see the danger they were in if they stayed.

Someone screamed and they bolted for the door like a pack of wild beasts. They scrambled over each other, trampling anyone who was too slow. More blood was spilled, this time blood untainted by the curse of the werewolf or vampire.

My hunger raged within me. I fought hard to keep it in check. These pathetic creatures weren't food. Not for me. I couldn't give in to my darker nature.

I trembled and turned away from the fleeing mass of humanity. I hungered, but I wasn't like Paltori. I could control my lusts. I had to.

Minutes later, I found myself alone in the basement. No sounds came from above. The blood was already drying on me.

I let out my pent-up breath and wiped my sword clean with a rag I found in the corner. I sheathed the blade and went about gathering the rest of my weapons. I checked each room once more to make sure no one was hiding or locked away in some chest somewhere, then made my way out into the cool night air.

Now that the killing was done, I was exhausted. Just because I was one of the creatures of the night didn't mean I was impervious to the rigors of my craft. I wore down just like everyone else, though I lasted a whole lot longer than someone without a blood taint.

I made my slow way to my hidden motorcycle, a modified Honda DN-01. It was left untouched behind a small copse of trees just off the road leading to the Paltori mansion. Everything about it was black, including the piping. It was damn near invisible in the shadows of night.

It started up with hardly a sound, thanks to special modifications done by the only person in the world who knew who I really was. He was the one person I trusted with my secret. Without him, I would have nothing.

The roads were mostly empty this hour. Only a few vampires roamed the streets. Most had already taken to their homes for the coming day. Many of them probably were already in bed with a choice Pureblood or two. Chances were, the Purebloods wouldn't survive until dawn.

I was the only one who seemed to be doing anything about it. The Pureblood police didn't meddle in vampire affairs. They left the supernaturals to police themselves.

Humans as a whole had pretty much rolled over during the Uprising. They gave the vampires the night, hoping they would be left alone during the day. It worked to a point. At least until a vampire or werewolf showed up in the dead of night and killed your daughter.

I put the city proper behind me as quickly as possible. Just because the day was coming didn't mean it was safe to be out and about. Werewolves weren't restricted by the sun like vampires, though they tended to do their hunting during the evening hours.

And, of course, I couldn't be out in the sun either, being a vampire and all.

Soon, the Purebloods would be out in force, living their lives like the Uprising hadn't happened. The night to them no longer existed. It was a time of danger, a time to be forgotten. As long as the monsters left them alone, nothing that happened during the night mattered to them anymore.

And that was where I came in. The vampire Houses were a plague. They killed and maimed thousands for the sheer pleasure of it. They fed on many, raped and starved the others. Purebloods were nothing but animals to them, things to be used and discarded.

I couldn't let that happen. I had seen the worst of the worst firsthand. Death wasn't just my trade.

It was my life.

2

The house sat at the end of a long, sloping driveway. It couldn't be seen from the road. Trees lined the property, obscuring the house no matter which way you came at it. Only the driveway gave any indication that anyone lived up there.

It was home.

The house had been built before the Uprising, but not so long ago to make it old. It looked like any other house on any other street, but there were subtle differences that a normal house wouldn't have.

For one, there were secret compartments near all the doors where the keys were kept. I refused to take keys with me wherever I went, knowing that if I were to be captured, someone might eventually find the lock in which the key fit. I couldn't let that happen. Not again.

Also, instead of the single basement most houses sported, my place had a second, soundproofed basement. It was the only room in the house to which I didn't have a key. It was Ethan's domain, his laboratory, if you will.

Ethan did everything down there. He modified my Glock, as well as my Honda. He crafted my sword, my knives. He pretty much made sure I had everything I could ever want when it came to vampire and werewolf hunting.

I pulled into the attached garage and shut off my motorcycle. The night fell instantly silent. The closest house was a good two miles away. I could scream all I wanted here and no one would hear me, which was just the way I liked it.

I was glad to be home. I was mentally exhausted, a common side effect from my work. I had been planning the takedown of House Paltori for a good three weeks before I actually was ready to go through with it. Even then, things had gone terribly wrong far too fast. I should have taken Paltori down first, but one of his lackey's had gotten in the way and the Count had been able to avoid me.

At least until the end.

But I made it out alive, killing Count Paltori and all his wolves and vamps in the process. That was all that mattered in the long run. They wouldn't hurt anybody ever again.

The door leading from the garage into the house was locked. I lifted the light switch, box and all, and inside was the key to the side door. I unlocked the door, replaced the key, and headed inside my sanctuary.

All the lights were off inside, which wasn't too surprising. Although I shared my home with Ethan, he tended to spend most of his time in his lab, working. He was the only friend I really had. I had saved him from becoming vampire food years ago and he just sort of stuck with me. I liked having him around, even if he was a Pureblood.

I didn't need light to see by, but I flipped on the kitchen light anyway. It was close to dawn and Ethan would soon be making his way upstairs for bed. He, like me, preferred the night to do his work. I'm not sure if it was a product of living with a night-walking vampire, or if he just preferred the stars over the sun. Either way, it was his cycle, and I kind of liked having someone around the house when I was up and prowling.

"I'm home," I hollered just in case Ethan had called it an early night. I wasn't sure what he did down in the lab when he wasn't working on my gear. There was only so much he could do, especially when I was between kill runs and he had nothing to work on.

I didn't press him, however. What he did on his own time was his business. I wouldn't want him to know everything I did in my private time, so I had to respect his.

I shrugged out of my coat and tossed it onto the back of a dining room chair. My gun and shoulder holster hit the table next. My back was sore and my hands were still stinging from the impact of Paltori's blade meeting mine. All I wanted was a good soak in the bath to wash both the blood and the exhaustion from my body.

I headed for the stairs, removing my belt as I went. With the weight of my coat and weapons removed, I felt much more like a normal person. I might not actually be one, considering I was one of the monsters, but it was as close as I could get.

Ethan wasn't upstairs yet. His bedroom door was hanging open. I peeked in his room and grimaced.

Clothes were strewn about the room like a tornado had come through. A plate with something that looked like it might have once been a lump of cheese sat on the bed.

I might have taken him in when he was only a teenager, his parents having been killed by Count Valentino's thugs, but that didn't mean he always had to live like a kid on college vacation. It felt odd having to remind a thirtysomething to clean his room.

My bedroom was in much better condition. While it wasn't much to look at, it held all the comforts I needed. I tossed my belt on a chair by the door and sat down on the bed to remove my boots. My feet ached, and the idea of a bath was now so overpowering I almost went straight into the bathroom and jumped into the tub with my clothes on.

I pulled off my boots and set them by the bathroom door. I would need to clean the blood off them sometime after my bath. The stuff would set in if I didn't and then would be nearly impossible to get it out.

I was about to strip off my shirt and leather pants when my eyes fell on my sword. "Damn it," I muttered. I went over and picked up the belt again. Ethan would want to know what kind of damage I had inflicted on the weapons. I needed to get them downstairs before he called it a night.

Leaving my room in my bare feet, I padded down the hall and back down the stairs. The house was eerily silent. Even though I was used to it, it was somehow unsettling this time. It just didn't feel right.

"Ethan?" I called, stopping at the top of the stairs that led down into the sitting room. There was no answer.

Sighing, I made my way down the stairs. I was probably just paranoid. I usually was pretty high-strung for a day or two after a kill run. There was something about all the adrenaline pumping through my altered body that kept me on my toes long after I finished the job. A bath and a few quiet days would be all I would need to get back to normal.

Or my version of normal anyway.

The sitting room was dark and quiet. The door to the laundry room was hanging wide open, which wasn't a surprise. It was the door to the basement that made the hairs on my neck stand on end. It was slightly ajar.

"Ethan?" I said, this time much quieter than before. It wasn't like him to leave the basement door open. "You there?"

I drew my sword from its sheath. I nudged the basement door the rest of the way open. Faint light from the desk lamp resting on the table where a majority of my weapons were kept seeped up the stairs. I scanned what I could see of the room from the top of the stairs, but nothing seemed out of place.

I started slowly down, my sword at the ready. I still had my belt in hand and knew it would get in my way if something was wrong.

But how could it be? No one knew where I lived. No one knew who I was. Ethan had probably started to come upstairs and then remembered he forgot something in his lab and went back down to get it. It wouldn't have been the first time. As smart as he was, he could be scatterbrained at times.

A faint scuffling noise came from below and I froze on a middle step. I listened for any other sign that someone was down there waiting for me.

At first, there was nothing. I eased down a step,

keeping my eyes trained on the room below. The step creaked faintly and there was a sharp intake of breath from someone unseen in the basement.

I tightened my grip on my sword. Someone was in my house. Just the thought sent surges of rage through my body. This was my home, my sanctuary. This was the only place I had that was free from the nightmares of my life.

And someone had infiltrated it.

A clunk and the sound of the heavy second basement door opening caused my eyes to widen. Ethan.

I bolted down the last handful of stairs, my sword poised to strike. I hit the floor and opened my mouth to shout out a warning. I was too late.

"Kat?" Ethan said as he stepped into the room. His Tom and Jerry T-shirt had black smudges on it where he had absently wiped his hands clean while working. His eyes were heavy and his brown hair was rumpled as if he had fallen asleep down there.

Before I could warn him of the danger, a shape darted from behind one of the shelves in the room, straight for Ethan.

As fast as I was, I wasn't fast enough. The man grabbed Ethan and spun him around, using him as a shield. Something glittered in his hand.

"Don't move," he said. His voice sounded strangled, scared. "I don't want to have to hurt him."

I froze where I was. I recognized the object in his hand. It was one of my knives. The silver wouldn't hurt Ethan much, since he was as Pureblooded as the next human, but if the guy were to cut his throat, Ethan would bleed out just the same.

The man licked his lips and scanned the room. His eyes were wide, wild. He looked a lot more scared than I would have expected out of someone who had broken into my house.

It was then that I really took in his features. He was completely bald. There was no hair on his face or arms, or anywhere I could see, for that matter. His hands were trembling where they gripped the knife.

And in the center of his forehead was a crescent moon tattoo.

"Luna Cult," I said, nearly hissing the name.

The Cultist swallowed hard but didn't reply. He didn't have to. I would know that tattoo anywhere. Although I never actually dealt with the Cult personally, I knew them by reputation.

The Luna Cult was the scum of the Pureblood population. They worshipped werewolves, pressured others into joining their ranks like they were some sort of religion. They viewed vampires as the enemy, creatures who held down the beasts the Cult worshipped. It was the only thing about them I liked.

"Lady Death?" the Cultist said, his eyes finally resting on me. He was breathing fast and hard.

I tensed at the name but made no move toward him. I just stared at him, willed him to make a mistake. If I had had my gun, I could have put a bullet between his eyes before he knew what hit him.

My eyes flickered over to the wall where another five modified Glocks hung. Their clips were in the drawer of the table beneath them. It would take far too long to load one and fire. By then, Ethan would probably be dead.

"What do you want?" I asked, turning my gaze back to the Cultist. I lowered my sword in the hopes I would appear a little less threatening.

The Cultist swallowed again. He looked as if he

were trying to swallow a hunk of barbed wire. "I have a message for you."

"What message?"

Ethan squeaked as the Cultist shifted positions. A thin trickle of blood ran from his throat where the Cultist had accidently cut him.

"I was told to deliver this to you." He reached into his pocket and removed a balled-up piece of paper. He tossed it toward me. It fell to the ground a good foot from where I stood.

"What is it?" I glanced at the piece of paper but didn't move to pick it up. I wasn't about to put myself in any sort of vulnerable position, even if I did have a feeling this guy was scared out of his mind and was as likely to attack me as he was to stick his head into a meat grinder.

"An address. To our Den."

I blinked at him. Was he serious? "Why?"

The Cultist eyed my sword. "Would you mind putting that away? I didn't mean for you to find me in here. I just wanted to look around. I don't want to hurt anyone."

I tossed the sword onto the table to my right without hesitating. I still had my belt in hand. My knives were hidden in sheaths worked into the leather so that they were nearly invisible. There was a good chance he wouldn't know they were there until it was too late.

He visibly eased and the knife lifted from Ethan's throat. He still held him tight, however, keeping the weapon close just in case I made a move.

"Okay," I said. I shifted my grip on the belt so that my hand covered the hilt of a knife. If he were to ease up just a little more, I would have him. "Why are you giving me the address to your Den?"

"Because I was told to," the Cultist said. He spoke much easier now that I wasn't holding the sword. He must not have realized how dangerous I really was. "I was told to invite you to our Den. I wasn't given the details as to why."

I stared at the Cultist long and hard. This didn't sound like the Luna Cult. Their Den was hidden somewhere in the city. No one outside the Cult knew where it was.

And I was a vampire. Why would they tell me of all people where it was located? It didn't make sense.

"I've delivered my message," the Cultist said. "Now, I just want to go."

"Why'd you have to break into my house to deliver your message?"

"Oh hell." The Cultist wiped his brow with his free hand. "It was a mistake," he said. "No one answered the door and I just thought I might take a look inside, see how you lived. Shit. I didn't mean to get caught. I just want to leave."

"Let him go," I said. "Then we'll see about that."

The Cultist instantly let Ethan go and raised both hands. He still had hold of the knife, but it was no longer threatening anyone.

"Bad move," Ethan whispered, taking a quick step to the side.

As soon as he was clear, my knife was out of its sheath and was buried in the Cultist's thigh. He went down fast and hard, crying out in pain. I had the other knife in hand before he could think to react.

He looked at me through pain-filled eyes and dropped the knife to the floor. It clattered loudly on the concrete. "Fuck," he said. "I didn't mean to hurt him." He squeezed his eyes shut as he pulled the knife from his leg. He let it drop to the floor next to the other.

"It doesn't matter," I said. I wasn't thrilled about what I was about to do. It was this sort of thing that made my life almost unbearable. "You know where I live. You know what I look like. I can't let you leave here."

The Cultist fell back into a sitting position. He looked at me with an almost blank stare, as if he had already accepted his fate.

"That's why," he said. "I didn't understand until now."

I stared at him, at a loss as to what he was referring to. It could have been anything really. There were all kinds of rumors about me, most so far off base it was laughable.

But whatever it was, it didn't really matter. I couldn't let him leave here alive.

"I'll be, uh, in the other room," Ethan said. He wiped his fingers across his throat where the knife had cut him. He winced and frowned at the blood on his fingers, then hurried up the stairs and out of the basement.

I knelt in front of the Cultist, nudging both knives out of the way with my foot as I did. "I'll make it fast," I whispered.

The Cultist's eyes filled with tears and he nodded.

I rested my hand on his shoulder and squeezed. It was the least I could do.

Before he could resist, I gave his neck a sharp twist. His eyes widened for an instant before going dull.

His lifeless body slumped to the floor. I rose, dropping my knife beside him. The blood stopped oozing from his leg, which was good. I could feel my hunger wanting to take control. His blood would still be good for a little while longer.

I turned away, refusing to give in. He might have been a Cultist, but he hadn't deserved to die. Not really. Disgust fought with hunger for control of my stomach. I felt sick. I did what I had to do.

That didn't mean I had to like it.

3

Red-tinged water cascaded down my back and neck. The blood swirled down the drain, leaving a trace of red taint behind. My eyes were closed, hair dripping onto my face, concealing the pain hidden there. No one was there to see me, but I couldn't bear the thought of exposing my weakness. I was stronger than that.

Of regrets, I have little. Taking the life of a man like the Luna Cultist wasn't what was bothering me. It was the ease in which I did it that made my insides feel like they were twisting into knots. It was becoming far too easy to take someone's life. It should never be easy, even if they *are* something of a threat.

Okay, maybe I wasn't being honest with myself. Having to kill the Cultist *was* indeed bothering me. What had he really done, other than break into my house to deliver a message? He wasn't going to hurt Ethan. He had been scared, terrified really. Could I really blame him for that?

But he knew where I lived. No matter how much I might have wanted to let him live, I just couldn't do it. It was too dangerous allowing him to walk free. Sure, he had been sent to me by someone else who presumably knew where to find me. What did killing the Luna Cultist really solve?

I hated killing for no better reason than to protect my secrecy. No one should ever have to live like that. The Purebloods have their trained killers, men and women who could kill without a second thought. They could shoot a man at a distance, skewer him on the tip of a blade, and not blink an eye.

I didn't want to become like them. Killing vamps and wolves wasn't the same thing. They were tainted, their blood cursed. If left to their own devices, death and pain would follow in their wake. If nothing else, I was a perfect example of that.

I squeezed my eyes tight and tried to push the image of the Cultist's face from my mind. Even though I hadn't fed from him, I could still taste his blood in my mouth. He had bled little, yet I smelled it everywhere. It overpowered the werewolf and vampire blood that had covered me from head to foot.

The water pummeled my eyelids, beat at them so hard it stung. I took a large mouthful of water, swished it around, and spat it back out. I knew I could never rid myself of the taste. It was always there, waiting for the moment when I was at my weakest. It was a constant reminder of what I had become.

Blindly, I reached for the shampoo. The shower was almost like a ritual. I would wash my hair, my body, my spirit, in slow, measured movements. It would purge me of any guilt I felt. Normally, I would rid myself of the memories of the dead I couldn't save, those whose lives were forever ruined by the vampires I killed.

Tonight, there was something else to purge, something I never wanted to feel again.

Ethan knew why I did what I did. He would understand. The body would be removed without me having to see it again. It had been a long time since he had to dispose of a body at the house. I never wanted it to happen again.

I rubbed the shampoo into my scalp, digging my fingernails into the flesh. Not hard enough to draw blood, but hard enough to make sure any trace of blood—werewolf, vampire, or Pureblood—was cleansed completely free. I wasn't afraid of the blood mixing and tainting me. I hadn't sustained even the slightest of scratches in my fight with Paltori, and it would take far more werewolf blood than what was on me to contaminate me any worse than I already was.

The Den. My mind drifted from the Cultist to the reason he had been here in the first place. Why would the Denmaster want to talk with me? It had to be a trick.

But if they wanted me dead, why hadn't they attacked me here? They could have set a trap, used Ethan as a bargaining chip for my surrender. They could have even killed him and waited for me, killed me before I knew anything was wrong.

It didn't make any sense.

I washed out the shampoo and then turned my face back under the water. I grabbed the soap and began scrubbing at my body, starting from my face and working my way slowly down to my toes. I made sure to clean every crease of skin, every pore. No blood would remain.

The address had been scrawled on the small slip of paper just like the Cultist said it would be. There was no explanation, no information other than where I was to go. I had no idea why the Cult wanted to see me.

It wasn't much of a surprise to learn the Den was located on the grounds of the old university. Most Cultists tended to come from the college ranks. Disillusioned youths, tired of dealing with the horrors of modern society often turned down dark paths to satiate their own inner demons.

The water started to turn cold and I hurriedly washed the soap from my skin. I turned off the shower and dried myself off, starting with one towel to catch any missed blood and then another to finish the job. I scrubbed at my hair until it was as dry as I could make it, then let it fall around my shoulders. Tossing the towels on the floor, I grabbed my hairbrush and ran it through my hair a few times, just enough to get out the worst of the tangles and make sure there were no clumps of blood remaining. My hair was so dark, it was hard to tell sometimes.

Once I was sure I was as clean as I could get, I opened the bathroom door and stepped into my bedroom.

"Oh, shit, sorry," Ethan said, hastily turning away.

"What?" I said. I walked casually to my dresser to get dressed.

"I forgot you did that," he said, waving a hand in my general direction. His face was bright red. "Don't you take clothes in there, so, you know, you could change before coming out like that?"

"This is my bedroom."

"Well, yeah, but, I don't know . . . The door was open and I thought you would be decent and . . ."

"It's fine, Ethan," I said, mildly exasperated. "I'm

sure you've seen a naked woman before." I slipped
on a T-shirt that was three sizes too big. It served well
enough for a nightgown.

Ethan's face blazed even hotter. He stared at the
wall, fingers tapping his thigh as he waited me out.

"You can turn around."

He glanced over his shoulder and sighed in relief
when he saw me clothed.

"I didn't mean to walk in on you," he said. "I just
want to make that clear." His eyes darted down to my
bare legs and then snapped back up to my face.

"What do you want?" I said, sitting on the bed. I had
to fight hard to conceal a smile. Maybe I had been
wrong. Maybe he *hadn't* seen a naked girl before.

"Oh, right," he said, running his fingers through
his hair. He took a few deep breaths and his face
went serious. "I was thinking about something before
I got interrupted earlier."

I stared at him, studied him. He was lanky, though
not any taller than me. His hair was still a mess, but
that was normal. He had also changed since I had
last seen him. He was wearing jeans, a Scooby-Doo
T-shirt, and sneakers. His Tom and Jerry one probably had blood on it now.

"What about?" I asked as casually as I could. From
the tone of his voice, I knew I wasn't going to like
what he had to say.

"Killing to feed," he said. "There has to be another
way. We can try something else. I was thinking that
when we tried it the last time, I made some sort of
mistake. Maybe I could come up with some formula,
like synthetic blood or something. It might eradicate
the need for you to feed."

I tried to suppress my rise of anger. "You know this

is a sore point with me," I said. "And this isn't exactly the best time to bring it up."

"I know, but I am sure I can find a way for you to feed without the need for blood, or at least real blood anyway. There has to be."

"And what do you expect me to do?" I shouted, rising from the bed. Ethan took an involuntary step backward. "We already tried the animal thing. It didn't work. It will never work."

Ethan licked his lips and tried to smile. His hands were shaking. "I know we tried, but maybe we did something wrong. Maybe if I was given more time to test some theor—"

"We didn't do anything wrong!" I took a step toward him, my anger bubbling over. Even knowing Ethan as I did, knowing he only meant what was best for me, I couldn't keep my rage bottled up when my less-than-normal diet became the topic of discussion.

Actually, anything could set me off. The vampire taint had accentuated my aggressions. Any little thing could cause my anger to boil over. I had to be careful all the time. One slipup and I could kill someone I didn't mean to.

My thoughts flashed to the Cultist and some of my anger dissipated. Who was I to judge anyone? Ethan was only trying to help.

Ethan's eyes were wide. I turned away from him. I knew a lot of my anger stemmed from what had happened earlier. That and the fact that I hadn't fed for days. The longer I waited between feedings, the worse I got.

"Feeding on animals is to me like a blood transfusion from a cat would be to you. It just doesn't work. Nothing you can do will ever make it work."

"I know," Ethan said. "But I want to try. Let me at least try to figure something out. If it works, then great. If not, then I will come up with something else. There is no reason not to try." He gave a nervous laugh. "I just hate the thought of what will happen to you if you keep going down the path you are now."

"And what do you think is going to happen to me?" I asked, though I already knew. I feared it, too.

"You know the consequences," he said. "You see them every time you leave this house, every time you take on a vampire Count. Before long, if you keep killing, you'll lose something you can never get back."

I sat down heavily on my bed. I stared at the wall for a long time, trying hard not to think.

It didn't work.

"I've already lost everything," I said at a near whisper. All the anger fled from me in a gush of expelled air.

I knew I had been yelling at him for no reason. He only wanted to help, and for some reason, I was taking old frustrations out on him. It wasn't fair. I knew that. I just didn't know what else to do.

Ethan stared at me, stunned at my sudden shift. "I know," he whispered. I could tell he was suffering memories of his own.

We had met under some pretty dire situations. Both of us had been captured by a vampire Count, Count Valentino. Back then, we were both Purebloods, as was my brother, Thomas. Ethan's entire family had been killed by Valentino. He was the only one who had survived, though being locked up in a vampire's cell wasn't exactly surviving.

Thomas and I had been on a hunt. We were caught by Valentino's wolves and tossed in a cage to be tortured later. We managed to kill a few vampires and wolves before getting captured at least. In the end, it was probably the worst thing that could have happened.

I had been stupid and brought along my keys and identification. Valentino took them, gave them to a few of his lackeys, and sent them to find my family.

They killed everyone—my mother, my father, my friends and neighbors. Everyone I cared about was lost to me on that day, including Thomas.

And my humanity.

"What does it really matter?" I said, trying to push the memories as deep as I could. "I'm already damned as it is. I kill on a regular basis. Nothing can change that. I'm a monster, and that is just something we are both going to have to live with."

"You're not a monster," Ethan said. "Not yet. You don't kill for the pleasure of it. You do it because you have to." He chewed on his lower lip. "But having to kill all the time, it has to have an effect on you. I am scared the lust for blood will eventually take over. If we can somehow control the hunger, then we can conquer this thing."

I sighed and ran my fingers through the last remaining tangles in my hair. "I'm not going to let it control me," I said without conviction.

Ethan was silent for a long time. He worried at his hands, head bowed. I knew he was worried about me. I was worried about him as well. I had taken him in after I broke free of Valentino's grasp. He was all I had left. We both had suffered greatly at Valentino's hands. It was only fitting we stuck together.

"I think you should consider what he said," he said suddenly. He looked up and stared me straight in the eyes.

"Who? The Cultist?"

Ethan nodded.

"And what? Accept the offer to go walking into their Den? I doubt they want to make friends. It's more than likely some sort of trap."

"He may have been crazy, but he was honest," Ethan said. "The Cult wants something from you, and I think it might serve us well if you were to at least check it out."

"More than likely, the only thing they want is to see me dead."

"Are you so sure?" Ethan shook his head. "I'm not. If they had wanted you dead, they could have come in force, taken us both out before we knew what hit us. They could have waited until daylight, opened all the windows, and let the sun do their dirty work for them."

I glanced at the heavily draped windows of my room. The drapes were taped to the wall, sewed closed so that not a sliver of light could penetrate them during the day. I refused to lock myself away in some basement somewhere, afraid to enjoy the comforts of a life long lost.

"They worship werewolves," I said, turning back to Ethan. I didn't trust the Cult, didn't trust myself. What would I do if this whole thing was legit? Could I actually walk into the Den of a bunch of werewolf worshippers?

"There is something wrong with people who would want to run around with monsters like that. I don't think I could ever trust them."

He raised his eyebrows and gave me a coy smile. "I'm living with a monster, remember."

"That's different." I wasn't so sure how. Just because I didn't give in to my darker nature as willingly and as easily as the next vamp didn't make me any less a monster. What happened in the basement was more than proof enough for that.

"Is it?" Ethan shrugged. "I honestly think you should see what the Cult wants. I figure if it's some sort of trap, you could easily overcome a few Pure-blood humans. Just don't go in unprepared. Take your gear, be ready for a fight."

"I never leave my weapons behind."

"I know," Ethan said. He stifled a yawn. "Think about what I said. I'm going to get to work on your stuff, make sure it's ready in case you decide to take them up on their offer."

I nodded. "Okay," I said. "But get some sleep soon. You look tired."

"I will." He stretched and headed for the door. His shoulders were sagging and I knew he wouldn't be able to work much longer. He was pushing himself too hard.

I remained sitting on my bed for a good hour before finally getting up and closing my bedroom door. The sun was up. I could feel it through the walls. I double-checked the layers of drapes over the window, and satisfied, returned to my bed.

I curled up on the covers and stared at the ceiling. I was confused, unsure what path I should take. Deciding whether to kill a vampire enslaving and killing Purebloods by the dozens doesn't take much thought. Deciding whether I should go in and have a sit-down with a bunch of crazies who would rather be one of the monsters than stay human was taking it a bit far.

I closed my eyes, wishing I could fall asleep and let everything drift away. If I was lucky, things would sort themselves out while I was oblivious.

But that wouldn't happen. The Purebloods had closed their eyes to what was happening around them, and look where it has gotten them. They live in fear of the night, afraid to so much as leave their houses unless the sun is shining full in their faces.

Of course, it isn't just the vampires they have to worry about. There are any number of Purebloods who are just as dangerous as the vampires and werewolves and other supernatural beings that slither through the night's shadows.

A vampire isn't inherently evil. A werewolf isn't either. The capacity for evil is within everyone, whether they are a literal monster or not. Some just try harder to follow the right path than others.

I was beginning to wonder which path I was actually on.

4

I was up and dressed at dusk. I paused at Ethan's bedroom door and listened. He was snoring lightly on the other side. I waited there, my hand resting against the closed door. He had stayed up far too long, I was sure of it. He was normally up at first dark.

"Stay safe," I whispered, and hurried down the stairs.

I threw my leather coat on over my jeans and T-shirt, and headed down into the basement. I wasn't planning on working tonight, but I wanted to be prepared. Like most nights, it was always better to be ready for a fight than to go out unprepared.

I grabbed my sword, sheathed it, and took down a belt lit with a pair of silver knives from the wall. The gun I had used the previous night was down there now, cleaned, and fresh clips lay beside it. I holstered the gun, strapped on the belt, and pocketed a pair of silver-dust packets.

I might have looked like I was going out to war. I was simply going out for drinks.

I paused upstairs in the kitchen, hand on the side

door. I was leaving Ethan alone, leaving him while he was defenseless and asleep. A Cultist had gotten in the night before. What was to stop them from coming back to see what had happened to their friend?

I considered staying, at least until Ethan was awake, but changed my mind. Staying would be admitting it wasn't safe, that this sanctuary I had built for myself wasn't strong.

Ethan could take care of himself. He was strong, resourceful. If the Luna Cult really wanted something from me, I doubted they would send anyone else. If they really wanted to meet with me, I was sure they would know not to press.

I stepped out into the garage, putting my fears behind me. Within moments, I had the Honda started and was shooting down the road.

The landscape shot by, a blur just on the edge of my vision. I had driven the route so long, I knew where every pothole was, every turn in the road.

I tore through a small shopping district that was closed up tight. Not even the gas station stayed open this late. It was Pureblood country, one of the few places where vampires and werewolves had no place. The Purebloods were all tucked safely away in their homes, praying they would see the morning come, and life could go on like normal.

I put the closed shops, the darkened windows behind me, longing for that kind of life. I never had the chance to live a life like that. I was born to the dark, and in the dark I would stay.

It took a good thirty minutes to reach my destination and by then, I was ready for that drink.

The Bloody Stake was located in a part of the city only the insane dared to walk. Dim streetlights illuminated the sidewalk where prowlers were often seen drifting in and out of the darkness. Werewolves and vampires both came to hunt here, but they were far from the only predators. Purebloods made their own kills in the darkened streets and side alleys. They struck out at the monsters just as often as the monsters struck out at them.

The bar looked pretty much like any other dive from the outside, which helped it fit in nicely with the rest of the neighborhood. Cheap neon signs flickered on and off, advertising beer as cheap as the signs themselves. The stained curtains were nearly always drawn. They were covered in so many bodily fluids, they probably qualified as a crime scene. The shingles on the roof looked as though they had needed replacing ten years ago.

All of that was for show. It might look as though The Bloody Stake was going to fall in at any time, but for those who were brave enough to step through the doors, it served as a safe haven where Purebloods and monsters alike could coexist without fear of the hunt.

Inside, the place was well maintained and well-lit. The bar was always polished to a shine. Peanuts awaited customers who sat on the soft-cushioned stools. The tables were sturdy, bolted to the floor, and the chairs around them were surprisingly comfortable.

Not only that, but the food was good, the beer top-notch, and if you could stomach the less-than-human patrons, the atmosphere was surprisingly pleasant.

Bart Miller ran The Bloody Stake with an iron fist. He was tough as leather and looked the part of a street brawler. The bar had simply been named Bart's at one time, but when the vampires and wolves rose, he changed the name to The Bloody Stake as a kind of big "fuck you" to the vamps who had taken control of the streets. The name might be outdated now that knowledge of vampires was more well-known, but it still got the point across.

It took time, but a lot of the myths surrounding supernaturals had long been disproved. Garlic is just as tasty on a vampire's pizza as it is on a Pureblood's. Running water, holy water, or any sort of water outside of sewer water doesn't bother a vamp in the slightest. There are more than a few Christian vampires as well. They wear their crosses on their necks, carry their Bibles, and pray just like everyone else—even if they do so with blood on their lips more often than not.

Then there is the whole coffin thing. Vampires sleep on beds just like anyone else. Well, maybe not exactly sleep. Vampires don't need to sleep, but they do need to rest their bodies. Vampires aren't the undead of legend. They don't rise from their graves or any such nonsense. They are living beings just like the next human, though their blood is tainted.

In fact, vampires are just another kind of shapeshifter, like werewolves. They live longer, their lives extended by something in their blood, and the change isn't as complete as with a werewolf, but they are a shifter just the same. Some vampires have mastered the ability to change into another animal entirely, but they are few and far between.

Werewolves have their own set of myths to contend with. The biggest is, of course, the whole full moon thing. A werewolf can shift whenever it chooses. It doesn't matter if the moon is full, at half, or new. That's not to say they aren't weakened during the new moon. They are. Just like vampires gain strength at the apex of the night, werewolves become stronger closer to the full moon, their blood lust more powerful.

But that lust comes with a cost. Just like the tides react to the moon, so do people and animals. Purebloods tend to get a little kooky during the full moon. Murders, burglaries, and violence rise. Vampires have a harder time controlling their hunger and oftentimes find themselves feeding without knowing who they are feeding on.

Werewolves, on the other hand, go utterly mad.

It is called the Full Moon Madness. That is as technical a term as anyone has ever given it. Anyone who savors their skin stays inside during the full moon. Doors and windows are bolted. Lights are left off, and any sort of movement that might be seen or heard from the outside ceases.

The Madness wipes away any reservations about killing a werewolf might have. Wolves who had never hunted before would kill their mothers in a fit of rage. Wives turn on husbands, friend on neighbor, brother on sister.

It was a bloodbath waiting to happen and it was only a few nights away.

I parked my Honda in the small parking lot at the side of The Bloody Stake. The sign over the bar showed a scantily clad woman kneeling over a vampire dressed like Bela Lugosi in all those old Dracula movies. She had an oversized stake in her hand, and she swung it slowly up and down, repeatedly staking the silly-looking vamp in a flash of red neon blood.

I made my way to the entrance, smiling at the sign. Somehow, it always made me smile, despite the ridiculousness of it. Something about the threat it implied gave me a warm fuzzy feeling, even though a good number of the patrons would give anything to stake me the moment they found out I was a card-carrying vamp.

Bart was behind the bar like always. A scar ran down the right side of his face, a product of a fight that had ended with a couple of vaporized vamps and the corpse of the girl who had been playing one against the other. He nodded to me and went to fetch me a beer without waiting for me to ask.

I paused just inside the door and scanned the room, checking to make sure there was no trouble waiting for me. I didn't exactly have a lot of friends with the way I lived my life. The Bloody Stake was usually safe for everyone, but like what had happened to give Bart his scar, things did happen.

Mikael Engelbrecht, a Swedish man who had moved to the States for no better reason than to experience the women, sat in a corner with three girls draped all over him. None of the girls could be older than eighteen, and I had a feeling a couple of them were well under. They fawned over him, touching and caressing him like he was some sort of soft, cuddly animal.

Mikael gave me the slightest of nods, his slicked-back hair shining in bar lights. One of the girls glanced over at me, frowned, and then kissed him square on the lips. The other two quickly followed suit.

My eyes skimmed over them as I checked the rest of the bar. As far as I could tell, Mikael was the most dangerous person in the place, myself excluded. Thankfully, I counted him amongst my friends in an odd, "don't talk, don't tell" sort of way.

Mikael is a snitch. There is no glossing over it, and he would be offended if you tried. I got all my information on the vampire Houses from him. While he might look and act like scum, he was pretty loyal to his paying customers. He would never give me away, even if he really knew who I was.

I returned his nod, though he was too engrossed with the three girls' tongues to notice. I gave him a disgusted look and then headed to the bar where my beer was waiting.

I usually sat at one of the booths in the darkest corner of the room, but The Bloody Stake was crowded tonight. A pair of young couples were sitting at my usual table, laughing and rubbing up against each other like they were somewhere a lot more private. One guy was working his hand up his girl's skirt and she was doing nothing to stop him.

"I can move 'em," Bart said, leaning on the bar. "They've been here long enough, distracting anyone with a pair of eyes."

"It's okay," I said. "I just want to sit back and relax for a little bit. It's been a rough couple of nights."

Bart grunted and moved off to wait on someone at the far end of the bar. He favored his right leg as he moved—the result of yet another encounter with a less than friendly vamp. It was a wonder he could walk at all with as many fights as he has broken up over the years.

I turned in my seat so I could get a better look around the room. There was a mix of vamps, wolves, and Purebloods, though I couldn't pick the supes out just by looks. It was usually pretty hard to tell unless someone was going hairy or teeth were sprouting.

There *was* an old guy sitting at a table against the

wall who had a certain look about him that screamed supernatural. He was trying to hide the hunger burning in his eyes, but he was having a hard time of it. From the awkward way he moved and the way he couldn't hide his desire to feed, I guessed he either was pretty damn hungry or was new. He had probably been a bum some young vamp or wolf had turned on accident.

I watched him a moment, wondering if he would give in to his hunger, before finally turning away. If he did, he wouldn't be the first to do so, though it would be in the world's worst place.

While The Bloody Stake catered to everyone, regardless of blood, there was one big no-no that everyone had to follow: There was to be no fighting within the bar or within sight of Bart's property. I had seen more than one vampire lose his head when he couldn't control his hunger.

And that went for the Purebloods as much as it did for the vamps and wolves. Bart had no qualms about putting someone down who threatened the peace of his establishment. If you came here, you had to be prepared to behave, or else you would be leaving in pieces.

It was part of the charm of the place, really. It was somewhere I could go without having to constantly look over my shoulder. Sure, fights did happen, but Bart usually ended them before anyone got hurt. It might not make much of a difference if someone was to plunge a silver knife through my heart or blow my brains out through my eye sockets, but at least whoever did it would end up with their blood splattered on the opposite wall a second or two later.

Besides, most of the people knew each other by

sight here. Rarely were names exchanged; but if someone new were to come in, they were watched by the regulars well enough so that the risks were relatively low. No one here knew my name, knew what I did by night. Not even Bart or Mikael knew anything about me, aside from the fact I was a vampire. They were the only two in the place who knew that for sure.

I finished my beer and set it down, tapping it twice on the bar to let Bart know I was ready for another.

One of the girls at my old booth rose, her voice rising in anger. She slapped a hand from her hip and started for the door, ignoring the whine of the boy she had rejected. Her other two companions were still hanging on to each other like they were glued together. The boy's hand was so far up the girl's skirt now, I knew her sudden jerks and giggles weren't caused by a sudden chill.

A middle-aged woman sitting close to the door grabbed the fleeing young girl by the arm and yanked her into the chair next to her. She leaned forward and said something to the girl that sounded harsh and demanding. The girl paled, looked around the room at all the eager faces, and then stood, thanked the woman, and sulked back toward the booth. She sat down next to the oblivious couple, well away from the boy she had been sitting with originally.

Just because it was safe inside the bar and within sight of it didn't mean someone wouldn't follow you home when you left. It was one of the dangers of the place. A Pureblood wanting to risk coming to The Bloody Stake was best served to do it near first light or plan on a long stay. Leaving too early meant you were willing to risk getting attacked the moment you were out of sight of Bart's watchful eye.

I picked up my fresh beer and drained the bottle in one long pull. It was surprising how refreshing just coming here and people-watching could be. I was still worried about Ethan, of course. He might be resourceful and inventive, but he was still a Pureblood. He wouldn't stand a chance if the rumors of late were true and an actual werewolf was a part of the Luna Cult.

"Well, hello there." The young man whose date had left him sat down next to me. He had long, dark hair that cascaded around his shoulders and framed his youthful face. His eyes twinkled from the lights above the bar. They were stunningly blue.

He smiled and gave me one of those looks that said he was now available and looking. His eyes raked me from head to toe, lingering on my chest, before settling in somewhere below my chin. "Someone as pretty as you shouldn't be drinking alone," he said. "I could make sure you go home happy tonight."

"Piss off," I said, slamming my empty beer bottle down on the bar twice to get Bart's attention. He raised a hand and frowned at me as he filled someone else's order.

"Feisty," the young man said. He was little more than a boy, his features still soft, unmarred by time. "I like that in my women." His hand snaked across my waist.

Without thinking, I caught his wrist and leaped to my feet. I twisted the arm to the breaking point and with my free hand, caught him by his lustrous hair. I slammed his face down hard on the bar, pushing his already tortured arm up even farther. He let out a little squeak and stood on his tiptoes to keep as much pressure off his joints as he could.

"I said piss off," I growled into his ear. I pushed hard against his head, slamming his face into the polished wood once more, before letting him go.

The man's eyes were just about popping from his head as he backed away. He rubbed at his sore wrist and stared at me like I had just tried to kill him. His nose was bleeding, but it didn't look as though it was broken.

The girl who had so recently rejected him was on her feet as soon as he got back to the booth. She started touching him, making sure he wasn't hurt too badly. They both glanced at me repeatedly, as if they expected me to come over and finish him off.

I turned back to the bar to see Bart standing across from me, his shotgun in his hands. "I think you might want to call it a night," he said, his voice cold and hard.

I glanced around the room. The place had fallen deathly silent. Only the music blaring over the speakers marred the near-complete silence.

Everyone was staring at me, waiting for the moment when Bart would level the gun and blow me into next week. Some even looked excited by the prospect. Why else would so many Purebloods frequent a place that catered to vamps and wolves if not for the chance of violence?

"I guess you're right," I said with a sigh. I pushed away from the bar and tossed a fifty down next to my empty bottle. "A little extra for the trouble I caused."

Bart took the money and tucked it away in his apron. He grunted something under his breath and nodded toward the door, but at least the shotgun wasn't pointed my way. I had seen others killed for less.

Eyes followed me as I moved to leave. I could feel

them watching me, and it did nothing to help my mood. I had come to The Bloody Stake to ease my mind, to put things in perspective. Instead, I was in an even fouler mood than before.

The night had grown chill during my brief stay. The door swung closed behind me, cutting off the sound of music and rising voices. A couple was leaning against the wall of the bar next to the payphone, making out. They didn't seem to notice me as I swept past them on my way to my Honda.

The sound of the door opening and closing behind me caused me to tense. I slowed my pace and turned to look up and down the road as if trying to judge the traffic before crossing. I caught a glimpse of a hooded figure out of the corner of my eye. The figure was making its way toward me, acting as if it were simply out on a leisurely stroll.

I could tell by the stiffness of the hooded figure's shoulders that it was out for something else. Namely, me.

I squinted up at the sky and took a deep breath. It was clear the figure was coming after me, and it pissed me off to no end that I would have to do something about it. This was definitely not how I had envisioned my night out.

5

I turned and started walking down the sidewalk, away from The Bloody Stake, leaving my motorcycle in the parking lot. I walked slowly, listening for the sound of my follower's footsteps. Sure enough, my stalker altered their course to follow me.

I had no idea if my tail was after me because I seemed an easy mark or if they knew who I was. The Luna Cult came to mind, of course. I wouldn't put it past them to send someone to watch me, to make sure I didn't do anything rash while I considered their invitation. Hell, if they had sent someone to follow me, they could just as likely have me killed. I mean, I *had* killed their first messenger. I'm sure they knew that by now.

Then again, I didn't recall seeing anyone with a shaved head in the bar. Nor did anyone have the Luna Cult tattoo cut into their forehead. It's always possible they could have been in the bathroom or hiding when I came in.

Still, it just didn't make any sense. If the Cult had sent someone to follow me, they would have entered the bar after me, not before. There was no way they would have known I would have come here tonight.

Right?

No matter who my tail was, I wasn't about to let them catch up to me in the parking lot of The Bloody Stake. I had already caused enough of a ruckus there for one night. Any more and I wouldn't be going home.

I quickened my pace and my pursuer did likewise. I was pretty sure by the sound of his steps and the squareness of his shoulders that the tail was male. His boots hit the sidewalk hard enough to echo off the sparse trees lining the walk.

I turned down a deserted side street. I took a few steps before quickly ducking into an alley between two abandoned buildings. The shadows didn't hide me completely, but I didn't need them to. I only needed my little friend to blindly walk around the corner and into my waiting arms.

The footfalls neared the corner and I tensed. There was a moment's hesitation before my tail turned down the street, as if he wasn't quite sure he should follow.

He cursed under his breath and his steps faltered again. He was just out of sight. I could hear him breathing but a handful of steps away. If he took those last few steps, I would have him.

For a moment, I thought he had given up. I could imagine him standing there, scanning the empty street ahead, wondering where I went.

A second passed, then two, and finally, he started walking again.

He stepped into view, huddled in a leather jacket, a hood concealing his face. Before he could so much as think about looking down the alley, I reached out and caught him by the front of the jacket. He cried out in surprise as I yanked him toward me. With a practice twist of my wrist and a sudden shift of my weight, I sent my pursuer tumbling head over heels to the sidewalk. He hit hard.

I was on him before he regained sense enough to roll away. I slammed the back of his head down hard on the pavement once for emphasis before tearing off his hood.

Yellow eyes stared up at me and a low growl came from the throat of the man under me. The stubble of his cheeks thickened as I watched, and I could hear the sound of his jaws cracking as he began to shift.

I drew my knife and let the moonlight shine on the silver blade. The wolf's eyes immediately reverted to normal, turning from animal yellow to pale blue in an instant.

"Don't hurt me," he said. His jaw resettled and the hair retracted. "Please. I was just curious. I wasn't going to hurt you. I promise."

Now that he wasn't in the middle of a shift, I could tell the man under me wasn't much more than a kid. He was actually quite handsome, for what it was worth. Not that his looks mattered much to me. He was tainted.

"Curious about what?"

He swallowed and looked from side to side as if hoping some sort of rescue would walk into view. He must have been new to the area because only a fool would expect help here. Anyone in their right mind wouldn't help a dying man in the street, even if they knew him. Too many dark things lurked in the shadows to risk one's neck for a friend, let alone a stranger.

It didn't matter anyway. The buildings on the street

we were on were mostly abandoned. No one actually walked down the empty roads. Not unless they were looking for a fight. Or a quick death.

The young wolf looked back to me and tried to smile, though it was severely wanting in warmth. "I saw how you handled that kid in there. I just wanted to see how tough you really were, get to know you better, you know?"

"Satisfied?"

He nodded as best he could. "Yeah. Can you let me up now?"

"No."

His smile faded, and I could see the animal wanting to spring forth again. While he managed to control his inner beast pretty well, I was betting he was new to the werewolf lifestyle. An older wolf would have been fighting me by now.

"I didn't want to hurt you," he said, shifting his position under me. I tightened my legs, causing him to wince and fall still.

"I don't care if I hurt you or not." I waved the knife in front of his face. "Silver. I take it you know what a silver knife could do to you if I chose to use it?"

He ground his teeth and said nothing.

"So, now tell me, why were you following me? Did the Cult send you?"

He scrunched up his face in confusion. "I told you. I just wanted to check you out. I thought you looked pretty good and figured maybe we could have some fun together. I don't know anything about any Cult."

I doubted that. Everyone knew who the Luna Cult was. "Were you planning on feeding on me?"

He blushed and looked away. That was all the answer I needed.

"You would have found my blood to be unsatisfying," I said. I bared my teeth at him, showing him a hint of fang. My gums were oozing blood.

His eyes widened. "You're a . . ." He trailed off and swallowed hard.

"Now you understand." I tightened my hand on the hilt of the knife. "Who sent you?"

"No one," he said, more frightened than ever. All hints of his inner beast had faded. He was just a kid now, a terrified kid of no more than eighteen or nineteen.

"Then why were you following me? I doubt it was by pure chance you picked me out from the crowd. There were far easier targets if you had food on your mind. Are you sure there was no other reason why you chose me?"

He nodded. His head rapped against the pavement as he did. "I swear," he said. "This was my first night out. I wanted to see what it was like but didn't want to go all easy like others might have. I wanted a challenge. I saw what you did in there and figured you might provide that challenge. I'm sorry."

I bared my teeth again and let them push through the gums a bit farther. Blood dripped from the fresh wounds and ran down my lengthening fangs. The werewolf squirmed under me, and by the look on his face, he knew what could happen if he got too much of my blood in him.

I licked the blood from my lip before it could fall free and pressed the silver knife against his throat. There was a slight hiss as the silver burned his flesh, but he did well in not flinching away, or else I would have cut his throat right then and there. He stopped breathing and looked at me with wide, pleading eyes.

"I'm so sorry," he whispered. "I never should have followed you. It was stupid. I'm an idiot. Please, don't kill me."

"What's your name?" I asked, ignoring his gibbering. I eased off the blade so that it no longer burned him.

He took a shaky breath and a tear rolled down the side of his face. Christ, is there anything more pathetic than a sobbing monster?

"Jeremy. Jeremy Lincoln."

"Well, Jeremy Lincoln, I have something to tell you. Would you like to listen? It might save your life."

He licked his lips and more tears ran from his eyes. What kind of monster did it take to make another monster cry?

I took his silence as affirmation.

"You say this is your first hunt. Is that correct?"

He nodded.

"That means you haven't made your first kill, yes?"

"Yeah." Jeremy spoke so quietly a normal person wouldn't have heard it.

"I suggest you give up the hunt," I said. "You might enjoy it the first few times, but after a while, it will change you. There is nothing you can do to keep the hunger from creeping up on you, but you can at least do your best to fight it. Don't give in to it. Fight for as long as you can. You will never beat it completely. It will always be there, but fight it nonetheless. If you give in to the hunger, you won't survive the year. I'll make sure of that."

Jeremy bit his lower lip and tried hard not to cry any harder than he already was. His lower jaw quivered with the effort, but at least the tears had stopped flowing. I had to give him kudos for that.

"Do you belong to one of the Houses?" I asked.

His forehead crinkled as if I had insulted him and he shook his head.

"Then you are rogue, correct?"

He nodded again.

"Stay that way. If you fall under the power of a vampire House, then you are nothing more than a slave, a pawn they will use in their games. Do you want to be a slave, Jeremy?"

"No," he said, his voice somewhat stronger than it had been a moment before.

"I'm giving you this one chance to make amends for tonight. The last few nights have royally sucked for me, and one more body isn't going to make a damn bit of difference in the long run. I don't want to kill you, however. And I'm pretty sure you don't want to end up a corpse, now do you?"

Jeremy stared at me and didn't respond. His jaw had quit quivering, but his body still shook beneath me. I realized I was probably hurting him with how tight I had my legs clamped around him. I didn't ease up. The pain and fear might do him some good. If it could keep him from making the same mistake twice, then every ounce of pain would be worth it.

"I'm going to get up and let you walk away," I said. "I don't do this often. Never, actually. If I ever find out you went ahead and hunted someone else tonight, I will find you. If you hunt anywhere within the city, I will find you. It won't be hard. You gave me your name. I can find you wherever you are. Do you believe that?"

Jeremy paled and nodded.

"This is your last chance to keep your humanity. Don't waste it." I took a deep breath and closed my eyes. Jeremy tensed beneath me but didn't try anything. I opened my eyes and stared at him as if I could bore a hole straight through his head. "I can't save myself, but I can at least try to save you."

I let my fangs push all the way through my gums and blood spurted free. It splattered on Jeremy's face. Some got in his mouth. He cried out and began to thrash under me, spitting and gagging.

"It won't taint you," I said, rising. He promptly reached up and wiped the blood away with his sleeve. "There isn't enough there to taint you even if you were to swallow it all. Just take it as a warning. There are worse things than death, and if you continue on the path you are going, someone less inclined to set you free will show you all the nightmarish things that can be inflicted on someone like you."

I turned and walked away, leaving Jeremy to scrub at his face and hands. He could scrub as hard as he wanted, but the real taint, the taint inside him, would never go away.

6

I don't remember a good portion of the night. I just drove around and tried not to think about the mess my life had become. There was so much I hated about what I did, and yet, I couldn't quit. Quitting would be too much like giving in, and I was definitely not someone who gave in easily, if at all.

And the thing was, I wasn't even sure what was bothering me exactly. I should have been happy I might have set someone down the right path, even if it was only for a day or two. Jeremy Lincoln might never be normal—he was a werewolf now, which pretty much excluded normalcy—but there was a chance he might not end up following some Count's orders, killing innocents just for the fun of it.

Of course, there was the Luna Cult. Just thinking about them made me sick to my stomach. They wanted something from me, and there was only one way I could find out what it might be. Did I really want to go walking into the Den? I might have been invited, but that didn't mean I was going to be welcome.

Eventually, I headed home. Driving around, thinking about what I might or might not do, wasn't going to help anything. I needed to act.

The house looked empty from the outside. I approached warily on my motorcycle, knowing if anyone other than Ethan was inside, they probably already knew I was coming. Even with Ethan's modifications, the Honda was still relatively loud compared with the silence in which our house usually sat.

I pulled into the garage and coasted to a stop. I sat there, listening to the sound of the night wind whistling through the eaves. It had gotten colder during the night. I felt chilled from both the dropping temperature and my fear of what I would find when I went inside. I never should have left.

I knew my fears were irrational. If the Luna Cult really wanted to meet with me, they wouldn't risk sending someone else. Of course, they could always decide I wasn't worth the trouble and attempt to eliminate me.

Or I was just being paranoid. It wouldn't be the first time.

I slipped off the bike and drew my gun. Dawn was fast approaching. Though I couldn't see the sun quite yet, I could feel its creeping rays working their way toward the horizon. Soon, the telltale orange glow of the coming dawn would weaken me.

I crept toward the side door, each step slow and measured. I listened at the door, hoping to hear Ethan moving around in the kitchen, or hear the television blaring, though neither of us ever watched the thing.

There was nothing.

Of course, I really hadn't expected there to be.

Ethan would most likely be downstairs in his lab. And if another Cultist *had* decided to break in, there was a good chance he was hiding like the last.

I pressed myself against the wall as I removed the key. The wind gusted outside as I slid the key into the lock and turned it. The door fell slowly open. It squeaked open louder than I would have liked.

I waited. The garage had no windows, so I couldn't see out. Someone could have been watching me from the trees as I pulled up and could be working their way to the house that very moment. I hadn't even thought to pause to check behind me when I came up the drive. Anyone could have followed me.

My paranoia leaped to new heights. I had half a mind to open the garage door and peek outside before heading into the house, just to be sure no one was out there.

But that would take time. If someone was indeed inside, I couldn't waste any more time than I already had. I needed to get this over with before I drove myself mad.

I took a deep breath and glanced around the corner, spied the empty kitchen, and worked my way slowly around the corner until I was inside.

A solitary bowl sat in the sink and the lights were off. It reminded me too much of what had happened the night before and my grip tightened on the gun. What would I do if someone else was in the house? What if they had already gotten to Ethan?

I couldn't think like that. I could feel my anger boiling under the surface. My gums were tender from earlier and I could feel my teeth wanting to push through yet again.

I pushed my paranoia as far back as I could and tried to focus on the task at hand. Just a quick sweep through the house to make sure no one was lurking; then I could be done with this.

I sidestepped, gun pointed toward the dining room. The large curtains over the glass back door were pulled open. A glance outside showed me no one and I continued on into the living room.

Nothing moved. A small half-wall separated the living room from the front foyer, and a closed closet was just inside the front door. My eyes swept over the living room before checking the stairwells leading both upstairs and downstairs. All the lights were off, and my enhanced vision was unable to pick anything up as I moved toward the closet.

No one was in the foyer, which wasn't a surprise. The half-wall might have hidden them from view, but it would have been an awfully bad place to hide. I opened the sliding closet door, poking my gun in before I could see what was inside. A handful of coats and jackets, mostly Ethan's, hung from the heavy wooden hangers inside. Three pairs of work boots rested on the floor, and a fire-resistant chest sat in the dark corner.

Otherwise, the closet was empty.

I left the closet door open as I made my way from the foyer back into the living room. From there I had to choose which way to go. The upstairs contained three bedrooms and two bathrooms. It was unlikely Ethan would be up there. It was still too early.

No, if anyone was in the house, they would be downstairs. If it was only Ethan, he would be hard at work repairing my weapons. Besides, there wasn't much upstairs that would be of interest to anyone but me.

I took the stairs heading down into the sitting room sideways, making myself as small a target as I could. I reached the landing without confrontation and scanned the room slowly, making sure I verified that every shadowy corner was empty.

A fireplace stood against the wall, its embers cool since winter. Three comfortable chairs were arranged around the fire, an end table separating each of them. It was a cozy room, one I often sat in for long hours just recharging. I wanted nothing more than to sink into one of the chairs and watch the flames flicker over the dry logs in the fireplace with a cup of hot chocolate in my hand.

But now was not the time. I could worry about relaxing once I took care of my other problems.

No one was in the room as far as I could tell. I moved across the room to the laundry room door. It was open and it took only a quick glance inside to verify that it, too, was empty. From there, I went to the basement door. I stopped to listen for any sounds that might give an intruder away. Of course, if they were in the second basement with the door closed, I wouldn't hear a thing.

I listened for a good minute and a half before opening the basement door. It swung open on well-oiled hinges, hardly making a sound. The light was on downstairs, but not a single shadow moved at the base of the stairs. I went down carefully, my gun pointed straight ahead, ready to fire the moment I saw someone who didn't belong.

As I stepped onto the hard concrete floor, I breathed a sigh of relief. No one was there and everything was still in its place. I still had the entire upstairs and Ethan's lab to contend with, but seeing the basement empty lifted a heavy weight from my shoulders. It was unlikely someone would be hiding anywhere else in the house.

My tension eased and I dropped the gun to point at the floor, irritated at myself for being so paranoid. No one had ever broken into my house before last night. It had clearly affected me more than I realized.

I moved to the lab door and pressed my ear against the reinforced door. I knew I wouldn't be able to hear anything but did it anyway. Ethan had done a good job of soundproofing his workshop.

There was an intercom by the door. I hesitated on using it, knowing that if Ethan was at work, he wouldn't like being interrupted.

Still, I needed to know. It was the only way I could talk to him and make sure he was okay. Of all the doors in the house, Ethan's lab was the only one to which I didn't have a key. I couldn't even knock it in. It was built to resist even the strongest monster from getting inside. A bomb could go off and the damn thing would probably keep standing.

I pressed the Call button and waited for Ethan's response. I wasn't sure what he heard when I pressed the button, having never been down there since its installation.

"What?" he said. His voice shook ever so slightly. He sounded almost nervous.

I pressed the Talk button. "Are you okay?"

There was a pause. "Of course," he said. "I was just busy and you startled me. Is there something you need?"

"No, I'm good." I smiled and eased my gun back into its holster. "I just wanted to let you know I was home." I would still need to check the upstairs bed-rooms before doing anything else, but I was pretty sure my tension-filled stalk through the house had been entirely unnecessary. I felt pretty silly.

"K," he said, sounding somewhat relieved. "I'll be down here a little bit longer."

"See you later, then."

He mumbled something else I couldn't quite make out and the intercom fell silent. I stood there a long moment, contemplating pressing the button again to make sure he really was okay. He hadn't sounded it.

Instead, I turned and headed back upstairs to finish the rest of my search. While I was sure no one else was in the house, I wanted to check just to be sure. You couldn't be too careful these days.

It took me only five minutes to finish my search. The only disturbing thing I found was the way Ethan's room seemed even more tousled than before. One quick look in the bedroom closet assured me that it was Ethan's usual clutter. It never ceased to amaze me how much of a slob he was in his personal life. It was a stark contrast with his work, which was neat and orderly.

As soon as I finished checking the upstairs, I went down to the dining room table to clean my gun. I hadn't used it, but it made me feel safer just knowing the thing had been cleaned. If the modified weapon jammed, or God forbid, exploded in my hand, it might be the last thing I ever did.

There were better places in the house to clean the weapon, especially so close to dawn, but I liked it there. It was relaxing in its own way. I stared out into the backyard, wishing the light illuminating the patio was more than just the moonlight. I wished I could stand at that door, look out over the sunlit trees, and bask in the warm sunny glow.

But that was only a pipe dream, one I could never realize. My life revolved around the moon and stars now. In its own way, it had a poetic beauty about it. No one could deny the beauty of the night. But sometimes, it would be nice to trade the darkness for a glimpse of the light.

Of course, I had never been much of a day person, even before becoming a vampire. Both my parents had known life by the day, having lived before the Uprising. They could walk down the street at night without worrying that something might be lurking in the dark recesses of the night, hungry for their blood. Back then, wolves and vamps were just legends, tales told to children to scare them into their beds at night.

My brother, Thomas, had been born before me and had a few years of a normal life, though he wouldn't have remembered it. His first few years of life had been like any other child's before him.

But before he was three, the world changed: The vampires rose and took control of the night. Nothing would be the same ever again.

I was born the following year. Born to the dark, some would say. My parents hadn't wanted me, which I found out one evening by accident. I never blamed them. Who would want to bring a child into a world of nightmares and demons?

But they had me anyway. Maybe they hoped I would have a normal life somehow. Maybe they thought they could protect me from the night. After the initial shock of the Uprising, people moved on with their lives, lived their days as if nothing had happened.

Only during the night did they allow the reality of monsters walking the streets next to them affect them.

They had no choice. To forget the nightmares lurking outside was to invite those nightmares into your life. Those who tried to pretend vampires didn't exist, that werewolves lived only in fairy tales, ended up dead pretty damn quick.

The basement door opened and closed, bringing me out of my thoughts. A moment later, Ethan stepped into the dining room, his face weary.

"I made a few more dust packets," he said, wiping his forehead with the back of his hand. I could see traces of silver beneath his fingernails. "You should have told me you were getting low."

"It slipped my mind," I said, setting down my gun. "It tends to happen when I come home to find someone stalking through my house."

Ethan smiled. "I guess it might." He sighed and rubbed at the back of his neck, wincing. "Well, the knives are done, but the sword will need some more work." He yawned. "I can finish that tomorrow night. It seems your last run was pretty productive."

"You could say that," I said, clenching my fists. The thought of those Purebloods locked in cages brought a surge of anger with it. The worst part of my job was the memories.

Ethan yawned again and leaned against the wall. It looked like he wanted to say something, but he looked far too tired to think straight.

"You should get some sleep," I said. "I have more than enough weapons to last. You don't have to kill yourself fixing them. Slow down a bit, relax."

He smiled and shrugged. "I know. I just like making sure things are done in a timely manner."

I returned his smile. "Still, I don't like seeing you so tired. Someday, I might need you at your best. You don't have to sleep during the day. You aren't restricted to the night like I am."

"Yeah, but when would we have these little chats?" He laughed. "I like the night just fine. There are fewer distractions when it's dark."

I wasn't so sure about that but nodded anyway. There was something in his eye that said that wasn't the entire story. He definitely wasn't telling me something.

He sighed and rubbed at his eyes. "You should get some sleep, too," he said. "It's been a busy couple of nights."

"I don't need to sleep."

He gave me a look that said, "I already knew that," as clearly as if he had spoken it. "You know what I mean," he said. "You've got to give your head a rest or you're going to drive yourself crazy thinking about what you could have done differently, what you should have done, what might have happened. I can almost hear those wheels turning in your head."

I looked down at my gun. I knew he was right, but it was hard. As long as I kept working on something, even if it was as mundane as cleaning my gun, it helped ease my mind, but it only went so far.

"You're probably right," I said, sighing. I pushed away from the table and holstered the gun. "I need to go upstairs anyway. It'll be light soon."

"Really?" Ethan said. His eyes drifted toward the door where the night was quickly giving way to day. "I thought we still had a few hours yet until first light." He yawned. "Maybe that's why I feel like hell."

I smiled but didn't say anything. There was no

sense in chastising him about working too hard. It was really all he had left in his life. I definitely knew the feeling.

He started up the stairs but paused halfway up. "What are you going to do about the Cult?" he asked, turning to look back at me. I saw genuine concern on his face.

"I'm going to see what they want," I said. If nothing else, my night had ensured I had no choice. I couldn't go on like this, searching the house like a paranoid psychopath every time I came home. "If it's a trap, I'll be ready."

"Don't let them take your weapons."

"I won't."

"Good," Ethan said. "I'm going to bed." He turned and resumed his trek upstairs.

I watched him go with a frown on my face. I was worried about him. It wasn't just a fear that someone would come and kill him while I was out working. That was always a risk, one we both accepted.

No, it wasn't that. I was afraid he was pushing himself too hard to make me happy. When I took him in, I did so because we shared the same miseries, the same past. I never asked him to work for me like he did. It was his choice, always had been.

Then why did I feel so terrible about it?

I followed him up a moment later, taking all my weapons with me. I was feeling far too vulnerable to leave them anywhere but my bedside.

I passed outside Ethan's closed bedroom door and just stood there, listening to him move around on the other side. He was humming softly to himself. It was out of tune, barely recognizable, and yet it held a sort of contentment I couldn't quite understand.

I patted the door, quietly as not to let him know I had been listening, and headed to my bedroom to escape the rest of the day, wondering how he managed to be content when I was screwed up inside. I would give anything to know that feeling.

Somehow, I knew I was asking for the impossible.

7

The day passed slowly and I did the only thing I could do.

I thought.

Outside, the world was going on like it always had. Men and women went to work, spent time together, and more often than not, completely forgot about the horrors of the night. It was a peace I could never know.

And it wasn't just the Purebloods who experienced this. There were quite a few werewolves who hid what they really were and went about the day like normal people. They didn't hunt until the sun was down, choosing prey that wouldn't get them into trouble.

But that was something I could never do. Vampires couldn't abide the sun. How two creatures so similar had such a drastic difference in their makeup was beyond me. I sometimes wished if I had been turned into anything, it would have been a werewolf. Then I could enjoy the day, even for just a little bit. I still would be forced to hunt at night, but that would be a small price to pay for being able to stand under the sun.

Not for the first time, I wished something would happen, some change that would make all of this seem worth it. While I knew what I did was helpful, it didn't really affect me personally in any real way. I was putting my life at risk for others. Nothing I did would change what I was, who I had become.

And that was the thing. Why did I do what I do? I always looked down on those Purebloods who risked the night, putting their own lives at risk, for what? A fun night out with danger lurking around every corner? A chance to play supe without actually becoming one? Or was it more, a deep-rooted wish that a monster would strike out and end some unnamed torment?

Was it really so different from what I was doing? I was risking my life every time I went out. If someone were to ask me, I would say I didn't want to die. But was that really the truth?

I wasn't sure. You didn't go walking into a vampire House alone if you didn't have a desire to die, even a small one.

I rolled over in my bed and stared at the wall. None of this was helping. I was mentally torturing myself for no better reason than to forget the real problem I was facing.

The Luna Cult.

I knew I was crazy to even consider walking into their Den, weapons or no weapons, without knowing exactly what they wanted from me. There were rumors that they had one or more werewolves in their midst, rogues who had managed to escape the grasp of vampire Houses. If that was true, I was in for some serious trouble. No wolf would ever want to deal with a vampire like me.

I had been doing this for a long time, killing vampires and werewolves, never once considering that one of them might not be as bad as they seemed. I could see no way in which the Cult would ever want to befriend me. It was more likely they wanted me dead.

And there was only one way I was going to find out.

By the time the sun was down, I was dressed in my work attire, pacing. I felt constricted in my black leather; but when hiding in the dark, black was the obvious choice. Sometimes I wished I could just wear jeans and a T-shirt when on the job. It would be far more comfortable that way, but the thought of trying to get bloodstains out of blue jeans was enough to keep me from really considering it.

Besides, it was a fashion statement. I had to look good when I was killing someone. It was only polite.

I checked to make sure the clip of my gun was full before slamming it into place and holstering the Glock. I had both of my knives hidden in their sheaths at my belt, and my sword was hanging at my side.

Everything seemed in order, yet I still felt overwhelmingly underequipped. I was taking a risk going to the Den. I felt as though I should be taking far more firepower with me to balance out what would inevitably be a severe numbers disadvantage.

I slipped three extra packets of silver dust into an inner coat pocket on a whim. The stuff bothered me just as much as it would another vamp or wolf, but at least I would know to close my eyes and look away when the packet was broken.

I headed downstairs, looking like death in leather. Ethan was waiting in the dining room for me.

Worry lined his every feature, and he was absently playing at the collar of his shirt as he drank a cup of black coffee.

"I'll be fine," I said before he could say anything. "You know I'm used to this sort of thing. I have walked into rooms full of vamps and wolves and come out of it unscathed. This should be cake."

"I know," he said. "But the vampires and werewolves never know you're coming. The Cult will be ready for you."

"You're the one who suggested I listen to their messenger."

He smiled. "I know that, too, but still . . ."

I patted him on the shoulder. "Don't worry about me. It's just a bunch of Purebloods. They might be crazy, but they're still Purebloods. I can handle them."

"I wish I could believe that," he said, his face turning troubled. "It was just too easy for them to find us, to get inside. Could crazy Purebloods pull that off so easily? I checked the locks. None of them was busted or turned. All the windows were latched."

I glanced at the door and frowned. I hadn't thought about how the Cultist had gotten in. We didn't have a security system installed. Neither of us wanted the cops coming to the house if something were to happen. There would be too many questions, especially if the perpetrator turned up dead.

But even without the security system, the locks were the top of the line. There was no way anyone would have been able to pick them, and I sure as hell didn't forget to lock up before leaving. I'm far too paranoid for that.

My gaze traveled to the windows, but they were no help either. Bulletproof glass with heavy-duty locks on the inside made those puppies as hard to penetrate as the doors.

"Did he find the key?" I asked thoughtfully. It stood to reason that if the Cultist had indeed followed me home at some point, he could have seen one of us remove one of the keys. I never used the front door, but that didn't mean Ethan didn't.

"Could have," Ethan said, taking a sip of coffee. "I plan on changing the locks anyway. We can't let this happen again."

"I'll collect the keys and bring them in before I leave. You'll have to let me in when I get home."

"That could work . . ." Ethan said. "For a little while." He peered into his mostly empty cup. "Of course, they might have copied the key, so it wouldn't matter if you brought them all in or not."

I frowned at that. One copy could become two, could become three. There was no telling how many keys were floating around if they had copied one. Hell, they could have taken the key to the back door and I never would have known. I used the back door less often than the front.

My eyes traveled from the glass door to the trees beyond. The land sloped away, and all I could see were the trees surrounding the property. Anyone could be out there, watching. Waiting.

I shivered. I had always thought of the trees as protection. Now, they were a potential hiding place for someone to watch the house unobserved.

I pulled the blinds closed, cutting off the view. "Let me get the keys."

Ethan remained seated as I went out to gather the three keys hidden around the house. They all were in their places, but that meant little if the Cultist had brought a stolen one back. The front-door key was under the outside light, which swiveled up to reveal the small compartment. The back-door key was hidden just the same. I even brought in the key from the garage, even though I doubted anyone could get in that way.

I entered through the back door and tossed the keys on the table where Ethan still sat. His coffee mug was empty and he was sitting back, lost in thought.

"I will definitely need to change the locks," he said without looking my way. I wasn't even sure he was talking to me. He had that faraway look in his eye I had become accustomed to. He was thinking pretty hard. "I think I know of a way to do it without keys."

I didn't ask how. He had his ways. He had fixed up the Honda, my gun, and had figured out a way to make silver swords that would cut right through a vampire's spine. I wasn't about to question him on anything. The guy was a genius as far as I was concerned.

I reached into my coat pocket and removed the note the Cultist had left me. It was crumpled from the constant fingering I had done during the day. The scrawl on the page was hard to read, but there was no doubt as to where I was going. I had the address committed to memory since the first time I saw it.

"You better get going," Ethan said, rising. He took his empty mug to the sink and set it facedown inside. "I'll probably be working all night again and want to get started right away."

"Okay," I said. I rested a hand on his arm as I worked my way past him to the garage door. He

smiled at me, but it faded before I could look away.
He was troubled, scared for me.

I didn't blame him. I was scared for me, too.

The garage was as I had left it, the Honda the only
vehicle in the place. Even though I had just been in
there to retrieve the key, I felt watched, as if someone
was hiding in the deepest, darkest corner. I knew it
was my imagination, knew I was alone, but I walked
around the garage anyway, checking to make sure no
one was there.

A partly full gas can was sitting on the workbench
amidst a smattering of tools that I had never touched.
A light layer of dust covered most of the things in the
garage. Only the bike was clean of dust. Ethan rarely
came to the garage, even when he needed to work
on the Honda. Most of the time, we worked the heavy
motorcycle down into the basement and he would take
it the rest of the way down to his workshop on his own.

I got down on my knees and checked under the
bench, then went ahead and checked every pipe on
the motorcycle to make sure nothing was stuffed
inside or hidden under the seat. I scoured it, certain
I would find a bomb or some sort of tracking device.

There was nothing.

I shook my head, angry at myself for being so
paranoid. Again. Just because one guy got in didn't
mean the entire world was out to get me.

Of course, the moment I let my guard down would
be the moment someone planted something under
my seat.

I slipped on the bike and started it up. It sounded
loud in the closed garage. I pressed the button for
the garage door and it opened slowly, revealing the
night-shaded driveway inch by inch.

I walked the bike out, still feeling as though there was something I was missing somewhere, some important piece of the puzzle that would make everything clear. I had no idea what it would be. I wasn't even sure there was anything to worry about.

A blast of cold air swept over me, causing me to shiver. Just great. It was going to be a cold night. Just what I needed.

My gaze swept over the yard, down to the trees that hid the road from view. I fully expected to see someone moving, some glint of glass from binoculars, anything that would let me know someone was out there. As far as I could tell, the night was empty.

I hated feeling this way. I had no idea what I was walking into, which was something I wasn't used to. I liked everything to be planned out ahead of time. Walking into the Luna Cult Den without an inkling as to what they wanted from me was a far cry from a precise plan.

There was nothing I could do about it. The Cult knew where I lived. I had to do this or else they might never leave me alone. The thought alone was enough to cause my blood to boil.

I lifted my feet and gave the Honda gas. Gravel spewed from beneath my tires as I shot down the driveway.

Yeah, I was angry. I just hoped the Luna Cult was prepared to deal with the monster they invited to their home.

Then again, maybe not. It might make me feel better to knock a few heads around.

8

I sat idling across the street from a series of buildings on the Ohio State campus. What was left of it anyway. Some of the buildings were now being used for storage rather than classrooms. A few others were completely boarded over. Only the homeless and the desperate lived there now.

An air of desolation hung around this isolated part of the campus. My fear that this whole thing was a trap beat at the back of my head relentlessly. I could almost hear the alarm bells going off. No one could really have a base here, could they? Not even the Luna Cult could be that desperate.

Of course, it made perfect sense in a way. A place like this would be an ideal hiding spot. They couldn't very well keep their Den in a populated part of the city without attracting notice. It was perfect for their purposes.

The college had been hit hard during the Uprising. When the vampires and werewolves looked to increase their ranks, college kids were obvious targets. Too many people were crammed in too tight of spaces with far too many bars and parties keeping the young populace in a drowned state of befuddlement. Mistakes were made, regrets were high. The depression levels had to have been through the roof.

So when a vampire House needed to recruit, finding just the right kid whose life was in the dumps was easy enough. The same went for the wolves, though their numbers were mostly regulated by the vampire Houses. It was obvious why most vamps and wolves I had come across were in their early twenties when they were changed.

Now, the college—like nearly every other college across the country—was operating at only quarter capacity, if that. I had never been around when they had functioned at full capacity but I'd heard the stories. It was hard for me to imagine so many young people crammed into such a small space.

Looking around, I wondered how things could have fallen so far. You would have thought people would have banded together in places like this, formed a strong front against the monsters who threatened them. Then again, weren't teens always looking for a way to rebel? What better way to give the middle finger to society than to be turned into one of the monsters?

At least colleges were still running. That was something, I supposed. They could have just given up educating the youth or gone to full-fledged home-schooling. The far side of the campus was still packed, though in far smaller numbers than it used to be. Classes were still being held, parties still rocked the night, though they weren't as rambunctious as they had once been.

I scanned the empty buildings, looking for some

sign that any of them were in use. Windows were busted in most, the brick walls chipped and pitted. Graffiti covered almost everything. I could see a few crescent moons hidden in the mess. Someone from the Luna Cult had definitely been here.

Litter blew along the yellowed grass. Scattered papers and other unmentionables were caught in the tree branches. Someone's clothes were lying next to a building. They looked to have been torn off, though from where I sat, I couldn't detect any blood.

But despite the desolate look to the place, it didn't feel empty. A flicker of a shadow here, the sound of something scraping along a brick there, told me I wasn't alone. An owl hooted in one of the trees and then took off after some unseen prey. An animal screamed, its howl echoing down the long, empty alleyways.

A creeping feeling worked its way up my spine. I looked around but couldn't see anything.

I was being watched. There was no doubt about it. Somewhere, in one of the deep, dark shadows, someone or something was keeping a close eye on my movements.

I continued down the road, keeping my pace slow and easy. If I was going to do this, trap or not, then sitting around taking in the atmosphere wasn't going to get it done. Potholes made the going even slower than I would have liked, but at least they allowed me to keep a close eye on every shadow. If I went too fast, I could miss something vital.

I rounded a corner and the road became almost impossible to travel. The branches of a tree that had fallen ages ago were scattered across the road. A car lay overturned where the tree didn't cover, making the road impassible.

I was within easy walking distance of the Luna Cult Den, if that was where the address the Cultist had given me truly led. I hated leaving the Honda behind, especially in the middle of this hellhole. Who knew what kind of creature would mess with it in my absence.

But I had little choice. It was either find a place to park or turn around and go home. I wasn't going to be able to ride any farther.

I walked the bike backward until I found an alley that looked desolate enough to hide the motorcycle. I pulled into the alley formed by two buildings that were damn near leaning against each other and shut off the engine. A trash bin stood about halfway down the alley, blocking off the other side. It smelled heavily of decomposition and death. Either a dozen animals had crawled in there and died, or someone was using the bin as a dumping place for bodies.

I wasn't interested in finding out which.

I walked the Honda as close to the trash bin as I dared. It was well concealed in the shadows. As long as someone didn't walk into the alley, they wouldn't see it sitting there.

Crickets chirruped, another owl hooted, but otherwise nothing seemed to move. There was a rattle above as the wind blew through a broken shutter hanging from a boarded-over window. Other than the usual sounds of the night, it was pretty quiet.

I walked slowly out of the alley, keeping my eyes peeled for a glimpse of my unseen watcher. I could still feel their eyes on me, but no matter which way I looked, I could see no hint that anyone was there. It was unsettling.

There wasn't much else I could do now but go on. I would need to go deeper into the ruined portion of the campus to get to the Den. It wasn't a thrilling prospect, but it could be far worse. If the streets had been crowded, it would have been far harder to spot a threat. Here, where no one else roamed the sidewalks, any movement at all could be deemed dangerous.

I strode down the cracked sidewalk, my footfalls echoing eerily off the empty-seeming buildings. I kept my head held high as if I had every right in being there. To show weakness was to invite attack. Any wolves that might be lurking in the dark would go for easy prey first. I could only hope they took my confident stride, the glimmer of my weapons against leather, as a sign of someone not to be fucked with.

Although there were numerous flickering shadows that all but screamed watchers, no one leaped out at me. I was actually pretty surprised. In a place like this, a lone woman would have been mauled to death before taking a handful of steps. Either I was extremely lucky or the Luna Cult had a tighter hold here than I would have thought possible. I doubted my swagger would really stop a band of wolves from trying to eat me.

The ruined buildings eventually gave way to an empty green. At the far end of the green stood what was supposedly the Luna Cult Den. The grounds were in just as bad shape as the rest of the campus. But without all the decrepit buildings shedding their stone all over the place, it didn't look nearly as menacing. Through a copse of trees to my left I could see a small lake, its water shimmering in the moonlight. It must have been a beautiful place at one time.

I made my way down the empty expanse. I felt horribly exposed, but there was nothing I could do about it. The walkway branched off in a few places, but I kept to the path that led straight to the large building at the end.

If I knew my history right, the place had once been a library. It looked huge from the outside, a crumbling stone and brick monument of a time long passed. It might have been white once, but now it was more of a parchment yellow. Large windows dominated the front of the building, and the feeling of being watched increased a hundredfold.

My pace slowed as I neared. If this was indeed the Den, then I should have seen someone by now. A guard should have come out to stop me. They knew I would be coming at some point. Someone should have been there to lead the way.

Hell, I should have at least spotted a few signs that people had been here at all; but as far as I could tell, I was alone. There were no signs of life in any of the windows, no flutter of a ratty curtain, nothing. The building looked utterly abandoned.

Warily, I took the large marble stairs, my hands itching to draw my weapons. There was a feeling to the place that set the hairs on the back of my neck to prickling. And those damn eyes were still on me, watching.

I stopped at the double doors and considered what to do. I could simply knock on the smudged glass and wait, or I could just walk right in and see what happened. Neither scenario was very appealing. I was a sitting duck standing there, so I had to make up my mind fast.

I couldn't see anything through the glass doors. It wasn't that they were too dirty to see. It wasn't even that it was too dark in the building. Somehow, a combination of both managed to conceal any hint of what lay inside.

I wiped away some of the dirt and tried to squint through the grime that remained. Still nothing. My night vision as a vampire was pretty damn good. The fact that I couldn't see even the slightest outline of a chair or an old bookshelf through the glass bothered me more than the watchful eyes I felt on my back.

I didn't like this at all. Someone should have met me by now. Or at least attacked me. If this was indeed the Den, I should never have been able to walk up to the front door unmolested.

And where were the lights? The Cult was made up of Purebloods. They couldn't see in the dark. Unless they turned off all the lights for my benefit, I supposed. Something was definitely wrong here.

I reached out and pulled open the doors. What else was I going to do? I wasn't about to turn around and head back home after coming all this way.

The doors swung open soundlessly. The darkness from the inside seemed to ooze out from the gaping opening. I hesitated. This was definitely not right, not right at all.

I took a deep breath and held it. I was here for a reason. I could do this.

Taking one last glance over my shoulder, I stepped into the darkness, knowing deep down that it was the wrong thing to do.

9

Sudden light blinded me.

My hands immediately went to my weapons and I drew my sword. I couldn't see and that made me vulnerable.

I hated feeling vulnerable.

I blinked rapidly to clear my vision. The whole Den was aglow with the soft light from the overhead chandelier. Sconces lined the walls, and simulated flames lit up every shadow in the room. The floor beneath my feet was polished to the point it reflected every flicker of light.

And I wasn't alone.

It took a moment for my eyes to fully adjust. When they did, my tension level rose through the roof.

Tattooed faces stared at me from all about the room. Cultists watched me from the floor, as well as the second floor balcony. Everyone was shaven bald, including the women. There had to be two to three dozen people there, all of them wearing light brown robes tied at the waist by a cord. It was like I had walked into a monastery full of monks rather than the Den full of werewolf worshippers.

The urge to draw my gun and start firing was almost overpowering. They might look clean and ordered, but I had seen the Cult at their worst. More than one victim had lain beaten in the streets from a Cultist attack. They may clean up nicely, but they were still just a bunch of thugs.

But I held back. They had asked me to come here. This could still be a trap, but somehow it didn't feel like one. Not any longer. The Cultists could have jumped me the moment I was through the door. I had been blinded, stunned by the light. I had been vulnerable, and yet none of them took advantage of my moment of weakness.

I sheathed my sword and eased my hands away from my weapons, keeping my face serene. Many of the Cultists watched me with wary eyes, others with curiosity. But none of them made a move toward me. They just stood there, watching.

I glanced over my shoulder to the doors behind me. They had already swung shut. I hadn't even heard them close. I could see outside just fine, even through the grime. The green looked just like it had while I was out there. Only the door and the inside of the Den seemed to have changed.

What the hell?

"Impressive." I said, turning back to the Cultists. My voice seemed loud in the strangely quiet library. "You do know how to make a girl feel welcome, don't you?"

Not a face twitched. No one approached to guide me to their leader. No one even offered to tell me why I had been asked to come. It was as if they were waiting for me to make the first move.

I had no idea what to do. I hadn't been given a name. I didn't even get the name of the Cultist who had delivered the message. The only thing I knew for sure was that the Denmaster had supposedly asked for me. That wasn't a lot to go on.

"I received the message," I said loudly, so that everyone could hear me. "I need to speak to the Denmaster, if anyone would be so kind as to show me the way."

A Cultist came rushing down the stairs and headed right for me. I moved instinctively, drawing my sword and leveling it at him before he could draw within striking distance. He stopped, eyes wide, as the tip of my silver blade pressed into his throat.

The room fell still, not that many people were moving around before. It was as if my sudden movements had frozen everyone to the spot. I wasn't sure if anyone blinked.

I looked up and down at the Cultist who had charged me. He didn't seem to have a weapon on him. His hands were empty, and he was wearing the same robe tied at the waste by a thick cord that everyone else was wearing. If he was hiding a knife on him somewhere, I couldn't see it.

He swallowed and trembled where he stood, but he didn't back away. His mouth worked silently as if he was too frightened to speak. I didn't blame him. I didn't know what to say either.

A large Mexican Cultist strode out from the crowd. His face was a mask of poorly concealed rage. I tensed, ready to draw my gun with my free hand if he made an aggressive move. I didn't want to have to fight, despite having drawn my sword. They might be Cultists, people sworn to the wolf, but they were still Purebloods. I didn't want their blood on my hands. At least not tonight.

"Stand down," the Mexican said. He stopped about a foot from where I had his friend at sword point. He glowered down at me, using his size to try to intimidate me. On someone else, it might have worked. "I don't know who you think you are, but you will not come in here armed."

I stood my ground. This guy was just as big as a pro wrestler, but he was still a Pureblood. I had nothing to fear from him. He might be able to bench-press me twenty times over, but that would do him little good with my sword jammed down his throat.

"I was invited," I said. "If you didn't want me here, then someone shouldn't have been sent to fetch me."

"Where is Joshua?" the big man demanded. "He hasn't returned." His fists clenched at his side. "Did you kill him?" His eyes traveled to my weapons. "You are no better than the vampires."

"Let her through," someone called from the second floor. The voice was faint. The speaker sounded scared. I wasn't sure if he was afraid of me or the big Cultist blocking my way.

The big Cultist tensed and glanced over his shoulder toward the source of the voice. He ground his teeth and then turned back to me. He thrust out a hand, palm open and upturned. "Weapons."

"I don't think so." I still had the other Cultist at sword point, but my Mexican friend seemed to have forgotten him.

He sucked in an angry breath. "Give me your weapons."

"Are you deaf?" I said, ignoring his outstretched hand. I had already had enough of this guy. "I said no."

"You cannot come in here armed. Turn over your weapons or I will take them from you."

I laughed. "I'd like to see you try."

The Cultist bared his teeth at me. They were the normal, everyday teeth that any human would have. It was far from frightening.

"Pablo!" a voice rang out over the assemblage. "Let her in."

Pablo stiffened but didn't move. His eyes bore into me as if he thought he could force me to do what he wanted with his gaze alone. I could almost see the steam poring from his ears.

I had to admit, I was mildly impressed. The guy stood no chance against me, and yet he stood there defiant, as if he was the one who held the advantage. He might be big, but I was the one with the weapons.

"Pablo," the speaker's voice lowered to a near growl, "get out of her way."

Pablo glared at me a moment longer before stepping aside. He took his eyes off me long enough to glance at the tall, cloaked figure coming down the stairs, before turning his hateful glare back to me.

I dropped my sword and the smaller Cultist scurried back among the crowd. He felt at his throat and looked relieved that I hadn't drawn blood.

The other Cultists bowed their heads as the figure descended. I couldn't see the man's face. A hood concealed his features from me, but by the way everyone bowed to him, I guessed I was looking at the Denmaster.

"She has weapons," Pablo said, though his voice had lost its edge. "She went for them the moment she stepped in here. She's dangerous."

The cloaked man stopped on the stairs and stared at the Mexican. The entire room was silent. I couldn't even hear the other Cultists breathing.

Pablo gulped and bowed his head like everyone else. He seemed to diminish in size with every passing second.

"Welcome," the cloaked man said once Pablo was sufficiently cowed. He continued down the stairs. "I was hoping to be here to greet you the moment you arrived, but something came up that required my immediate attention. I hope you will forgive us for our inhospitable welcome."

"I'll live," I said. "What do you want?"

"Right to the point, I see," he said. I detected a smile in his voice, though I couldn't see it beneath the hood. "If you would follow me, I will take us to a more private part of the Den where we can talk without interruption." He bowed his head to me before walking across the room.

I glanced around the room. Every eye in the place was now on me. Privacy would be good. I didn't want there to be any accidents like with the last guy.

But did I really trust this guy? He may have gotten Pablo to stand down, but that didn't mean he was my friend. As far as I knew, he was leading me into a room full of nasty surprises. Everyone seemed to be on the up-and-up, but it didn't mean that was the case. This *was* the Luna Cult, after all.

I ground my teeth as my eyes passed over Pablo and over to the cloaked man. I really had no choice.

I came here for a reason and I would see it through regardless of how I felt.

The man was waiting for me at the far end of the room. He held a door open and was standing to the side. "After you," he said with a slight bow.

I started across the room, back stiff, hands ready. Pablo murmured something under his breath I was sure I wouldn't have liked if I had heard it.

I kept walking. No matter how much I didn't like him or like the situation I had put myself in, I couldn't bring myself to walk away. If I didn't find out what the Cult wanted, it would bother me until it drove me crazy.

I paused just outside the room. From the door, there was little to see in the room ahead. I glanced at my host and he gave me another faint nod.

Without another word, I stepped across the threshold.

10

I wasn't sure what I expected when I entered the room. Some part of me thought the room would be in shambles, even after seeing how clean it had been in the front room. That was how I had always viewed the Luna Cult. They were a bunch of thugs running the streets who spent more time inflicting pain and terror than doing things like bathing or changing clothes.

But instead, I was met yet again with a rather pleasant room, furnished as if it were well used and well loved. This was definitely not how I pictured the Luna Cult Den.

Old plaques hung on the walls around the room. I wasn't sure if the plaques were remnants from when the place was a library or if they were important to someone in the Cult. I didn't get close enough to look.

A desk with a leather office chair behind it sat by a large window overlooking the green. The far end of the lake could just be seen over the trees. A couch sat along the wall to my right and two matching recliners to my left, all facing the desk. The place was tidy, clean, and had an air of practicality I wouldn't have expected from the Luna Cult. It was stunning how different they were at home than when spotted in tattered clothes on the streets.

Two men rose from the couch as I entered. One was short and scruffy and welcomed me with a wide smile. He looked as though he hadn't combed his hair in a good three months, if not longer. His cheeks were covered in a patchy sort of stubble that ran all the way up his cheekbones to just under his eyes. His eyebrows were bushy, hanging above his eyes like giant caterpillars. He folded his hands behind his back, ruffling his already wrinkled suit. He gave off an air of friendliness that was hard to ignore.

The other man wasn't nearly as friendly looking. His hair was soft brown, mingled with flecks of gray. It was clipped short in a buzz cut that exposed a flaking scalp. His jaw was square, just like everything else about him. His shoulders fell perfectly in line with the floor, his posture perfectly straight. His shoes were polished, his coat buttoned at the navel, which just served to add to his rigid manner.

Neither man had a crescent moon tattoo.

Buzz Cut frowned at me as I walked in. His eyes flickered to my guide before settling on me. Disapproval was clear in his gaze, but he kept his mouth shut. That was a plus. It was clear he wanted to say something, and if he did, I might just have to punch him in the mouth. I knew whatever this man said wouldn't be pleasant.

"Lady Death," my shrouded guide said, closing the door. He moved to stand beside the desk, keeping his back to me. He gently tapped his fingers on the polished wood. "Also known as Kat Redding. Is it short for something?"

I wanted to keep my eye on Buzz Cut because, quite frankly, I didn't trust him, but the mention of my given name startled me. Only Ethan knew my real name. Ethan and the dead.

The mysterious man shifted and I noticed for the first time how his hood seemed to slope funny to one side. It wasn't anything I could put my finger on, but the whole thing seemed off, as if my eyes just weren't seeing him right.

"Don't call me that," I said.

"What? Lady Death? Mrs. Redding?"

"Either."

"Then what should I call you?"

I brushed a stray lock of hair out of my eyes. The movement caused my coat to fall open just enough to expose the hilt of my sword. Buzz Cut's eyes widened, but he didn't make a move toward me or say anything.

"Kat, if you like," I said. I hated him knowing so much about me, but if he had to call me something, my first name would be less damning if others were to hear. "But I would prefer if you forget all those names. I don't exactly like having who I am spread about. In fact, I would like to know how you know me, how you knew where to find me."

"In time, Kat, in time." The cloaked man shook his oddly shaped head. "Is your first name short for something?"

"Why does it matter?"

"It doesn't." He sighed and moved around his desk, then took a seat. The leather chair creaked as he settled his weight. "I just want to know."

"It's not."

He turned his face up to me ever so slightly. I still couldn't see a damn thing in the hood, and it was starting to piss me off. By now, I should have caught a glimpse of something in there. I mean, even a sliver of light finds its way into the darkest corners now and again, but this guy's face seemed to be made of darkness.

Now that was an unsettling thought.

"Not what?" he asked. I heard the smile in his voice.

"Not short for anything."

"So Kat is your given name? Interesting. I would have thought it might have been short for Katherine or Kathy, maybe even Katelyn."

"Why the fuck does this matter?"

There was a stretch of silence. Buzz Cut was still staring at me, refusing to show even a hint of amusement at the inane conversation. The short guy was rocking back and forth as if he couldn't stand still and would bolt from the room at the word go. His hands beat a staccato on his hips.

I waited the men out. I don't know if he was trying to soothe me or irritate me. If the plan was to do the latter, then he was doing a damn fine job of it.

"I am Jonathan Alucard, in case you are wondering," the cloaked man said. "Frankly, I am surprised you haven't already asked a hundred questions. I know I would have if I had been in your situation."

I rolled the name through my memory banks. It didn't ring any bells. "I figured you would get to the point soon enough."

"Fair enough." Jonathan bowed his head. "These are my associates." He motioned to the short, jittery man. "Gregory Hillis."

"Pleasure," Gregory said. He bowed and beamed at me as if the brief introduction was the greatest thing to happen to him in his entire life.

"And Nathan LaFoe."

Buzz Cut grunted and his frown deepened. He didn't seem to be as excited to make my acquaintance as his companion.

Jonathan leaned back in his chair. I still couldn't see under the damn hood even though he was looking directly at me. Or at least, I thought he was. As far as I knew, he could have his eyes closed.

"I suppose you are wondering why I asked you here, why I would send someone to deliver my message for me?"

"It crossed my mind."

"I have a favor to ask of you." Jonathan leaned forward, crossing his hands in front of him on the desk. Aside from the hood and cloak, he looked like any other businessman ready to talk. It was pretty disconcerting considering this *was* the Den of a wolf worshipping cult.

"Many have questioned my decision to come to you, though I did keep it quiet as to who you really are. Only a select few know your true nature." His gaze flickered to Nathan and then back to me. "But I believe this course of action is best. No," he corrected. "It's the only course of action left open to us."

He paused and spun his chair around so he could look out the window. Nothing moved out there but the faint blinking light of a plane in the distance.

"So what's with this place?" I asked. "That was a pretty interesting show with the lights back there. You do that for everyone or just for me so I would feel special?"

Jonathan laughed. "You *are* special, no doubt; but no, anyone who comes through those doors gets the same show."

"How'd you do it?"

"Pardon?"

"How'd you make the lights come on like that? I couldn't see a thing through the doors."

"Ah," he said. "It's a glamour. We like our privacy here. To let others see the lights would be like a beacon to our location. We really don't want people knocking on our doors uninvited."

"A sorcerer," I said, my voice hitching on the word. "Someone here is a sorcerer."

Jonathan cocked his head to the side and I was pretty sure he was staring at me. It made me feel all kinds of uncomfortable not knowing what he was thinking. I could usually discern someone's thoughts by their eyes, but with Jonathan, I had nothing to go on.

"I can do only minor glamours," he said at last. "It isn't much, but it helps keep us hidden from unwanted notice. Anyone looking through the front door or one of the windows will only see a dark, abandoned building." He paused. "It isn't perfect, but it serves its purpose." He took a deep breath and let it out in a sigh. "Of course, not many people reach the doors uninvited. We just like to take the extra precautions in case someone gets through our security."

A sorcerer leading the Luna Cult? Great. As if having to deal with a bunch of werewolf lovers wasn't bad enough.

Jonathan stood and walked around his desk. He stopped all of five feet away from me and I still couldn't see his face. "I should probably explain something to you first," he said. "The more you know going in, the more likely you are to understand why I came to you. There are certain things you should know, things best shown to you rather than told."

"Sounds like a plan," I said. Something about Jonathan's tone had me on edge, but I managed to keep my cool. So far, aside from Pablo's attitude and Nathan's angry demeanor, no one had really shown me much in the way of hostility.

Jonathan glanced over to his two associates and nodded ever so slightly. Both Nathan and Gregory sat down, though Nathan did so much slower, as if he wasn't sure it was the right thing to do. The tension level in the room rose tenfold, and I desperately wanted to know what was going on before I accidently shot someone.

"Would you care to take a seat?" Jonathan asked, motioning toward one of the recliners. It was black leather and looked really comfortable.

"No thanks," I said. "I'm fine just where I am."

Jonathan bowed his head in acquiescence before speaking. "I thought you might say that. I take it some of the rumors about you are true. It's probably why I haven't seen Joshua since he was sent to deliver my message." His tone hardened. "I assume he is dead."

My hand slowly fell to my waist. I didn't draw, but I wanted to be ready. I didn't like where the conversation was heading.

Nathan started to rise, but Jonathan waved him back down. The big man hesitated, his frown deepening, before settling back down on the couch.

"He broke in to my house."

Jonathan leaned back against his desk and sighed. "I should have expected it, really. Joshua is an impulsive man. He was to deliver the note and leave before anyone knew he was there. I should have realized he would want to see you himself."

I glanced at Nathan before answering. The big man was glowering, but he didn't seem like he was getting ready to fight. Yet.

"I didn't want to do it," I said. "But I don't like people knowing where I live, which brings me back to my question. How did you know where to find me?"

"It wasn't easy, honestly. Even though I knew who you were, you had moved to a new location before I could act on my knowledge. It made tracking you down that much more difficult."

I clenched my fist. How long had this guy known about me? "How?" It was all I could think to say.

"You made a mistake," Jonathan said. "It happened a long time ago, back before you were as well equipped as you are now. Back before you had made a name for yourself."

I stared at him, unsure what to make of the statement. What kind of mistake had I made, other than getting myself captured once? I was always careful, even back when I was young and stupid.

Jonathan stood silent for a long moment before speaking again. "*I* was your mistake," he said. His hands slowly rose to the hood concealing his face and slid it slowly back from his head. There was a shimmer, as if the air around his head was disturbed by some unfelt wave of heat; then his features came into focus.

One side of his head was normal. His eye was blue, his hair a curly brown. Laugh marks creased the corner of his mouth, and wrinkles, probably caused by natural good humor, webbed outward from his eyes.

The other side of his face, however, was a nightmare.

His right eye was bloodshot. The blue iris was speckled with so much red it was almost blackish purple. His cheek was all scar tissue, and his mouth curved ever downward as if the nerves had been damaged so badly they were useless. There was no hair on that side of his head. In fact, there was no head there at all.

Instead of a rounded skull, the right side of Jonathan's head was flattened at a downward sloping angle. It looked as though someone had neatly sliced that part of his head off, missing his brain by scant millimeters. Skin that looked to have come from elsewhere on his body was stretched over the horrific wound. It was pink and wrinkled, as if it had been badly burned.

I wanted him to raise his hood, to hide the disaster of his face, but Jonathan let the hood fall back, leaving me no choice but to stare at him.

"Do you remember House Valentino?" he asked. His words were now slightly slurred. The glamour that had disguised his features within the hood must have also adjusted his voice to hide the speech impediment caused by his damaged face.

I nodded, slowly, too stunned to even think. Valentino's wolves killed my family. There was no way I could forget him. "Count Valentino," I said, my voice surprisingly strong. "He's dead."

"I know. In fact, his real name was David Smith." He laughed, though it had a bitter edge to it. "It's a little-known fact that most vampires change their names when they begin to rise through the ranks. House Smith doesn't quite have the same ring to it as House Valentino, no?" Jonathan took a deep breath and let it out slowly, as if preparing for his next words. "I belonged to that House at one time."

I stiffened and drew my sword. I had killed everyone connected to House Valentino. Or so I thought. If Jonathan had somehow survived, then there was only one thing he could want from me. Revenge was a pretty big motivator.

I started to move forward, intent on finishing the job I started. Valentino and his wolves ruined my life. His House may have been destroyed, but the damage he caused was so massive, I had yet to recover.

I probably never would.

"I didn't ask you here to harm you," Jonathan said without moving. Nathan had moved to the edge of his seat, ready to spring the moment I made another move toward his master, no doubt.

"Then why am I here?" I stopped, though I kept hold of my sword. I knew the anger was showing on my face. I was so upset I could hardly think. That wasn't good for anyone.

Jonathan stood and turned his back to me. He walked slowly to the other side of his desk as if I wasn't holding a weapon that could cleave the rest of his head from his shoulders. There was a lot more trust in that simple act than I would have expected.

"Don't get the wrong impression," Jonathan said, easing into his chair. "While I was bitter at first, I came to realize that you, unwittingly, had set me free from my bonds. No longer was I bound to the rules of a vampire House. I was free to act on my own."

I studied Jonathan, trying to figure out what he was getting at. It took a few moments, but finally something clicked. A regular Pureblood never could have survived his wounds. And if he were a vampire, he wouldn't have been set free, as he put it, at the death of Count Valentino. That meant . . .

"A werewolf."

Jonathan nodded. "Very astute of you."

"I killed everyone," I said. "I'm sure of it. I counted the bodies."

"Almost everyone," Jonathan said, nodding. "When you broke free, you inadvertently set my new life into motion. You almost killed me, should have even. I was bleeding from the wound you inflicted on me." He smiled. At least, half his face did. "But I didn't die. I learned the error of my ways in that sword strike, learned I didn't need to be subservient to the vampires. I could find my own path, forge my own life."

"But how?"

Jonathan shrugged. "I don't know. Call it fate, if you will. The bleeding eventually stopped and I was able to crawl out of the wreckage of the House. Some Luna Cult members found me and brought me in. They took care of me, nursed me back to health when I surely would have died otherwise."

I closed my eyes for a second to compose myself. This was definitely not what I had expected when I came here. Having old memories brought back to the fore was a torment that went far beyond pain.

I opened my eyes and stared at him hard. "Did you kill my family?"

"No," Jonathan said, his voice firm. "I know what happened, and I am sorry. When Count Valentino ordered your family's death, I stayed behind. I had nothing to do with the slaughter."

He seemed so genuine I couldn't help but believe him. I'm not sure what I would have done if he would have admitted to killing my parents, my friends.

Would I have risked being overwhelmed just to kill him?

"You changed my life," Jonathan went on. "I survived and realized that living my life a slave to the vampires was not a life at all. I could have found another House and risen in the ranks there, but chose instead to stay with the Cult, to work with the Denmaster to form our own vampire-free House."

"Wait," I said, shaking my head. "You aren't leader here? Then who is?"

"Simon is our Denmaster, not that you would know him. He doesn't know who you are."

I frowned. "I don't understand."

"Simon is the reason I have asked you to come."

I was about to ask him about Simon, but it was then that something else he had said hit me. "A vampire-free House?" I said. "Are you serious?"

"Just because we aren't vampires doesn't mean we can't have our own House. We stand against the vampire Houses, refuse to bow down to them. The Luna Cult has given us more power than we ever dreamed possible, and we do not wish to relinquish that power and return to our subservient ways."

I tried to come up with something to say, but words failed me. This was insane. Werewolves didn't have their own Houses. They were the pawns of the vampires, supposedly the weaker of the two shifters. They protected the vamps, were their daytime guardians. They didn't form their own organizations. There was no werewolf union. It just didn't happen.

"Come," Jonathan said, rising. "I want to show you something."

I looked from Jonathan to the two men sitting on the couch. This whole thing made no sense. If they were indeed werewolves who had rebelled against the vampires who enslaved them, then why would they have come to me, a vampire? If he had been a part of House Valentino like he claimed, Jonathan would know what I was. He would have seen my fangs, seen my rage. Hell, he might have been responsible for what I had become.

Nathan and Gregory both rose. They had no weapons on them. At least none that I could see. They moved to stand beside Jonathan as he reached a hand beneath his desk. I tensed, expecting him to pull a gun; but instead, I heard a click and the wall to my left slid open. He gestured me toward the yawning darkness.

"Please," he said. "We need your help."

The sincerity in his voice left me speechless. I could easily kill all three of them, I was sure. I probably should have.

Then again, they could have had me killed already if that was what they had planned. There had been more than enough opportunities for that. I couldn't bring myself to kill them, not until I knew what they wanted. After that, we'd see what happened.

I bowed my head slightly and sheathed my sword. I took a step back, clearing the way to the new opening. "After you," I said.

Jonathan gave me his half smile and then a quick nod. He ushered Nathan and Gregory ahead of them. They passed by me and headed down into the darkness.

"Thank you," Jonathan said as he came up next to me.

"Don't thank me yet," I said. "I haven't agreed to

anything. I'm still trying to decide if I should kill you or not."

He nodded as if he wouldn't have expected anything less, then followed his two associates into the gloom.

I stared after him a moment, wondering if I was doing the right thing. This wolf might have been responsible for my change, for the loss of my family. He had been there when I killed Count Valentino and his followers. He had to be guilty of something.

I took a deep breath, swallowed my anger, my fear, and followed the werewolves down into the darkness below.

11

"This part of the Den was here before we took over," Jonathan said as we made our way down the stone stairs. Moisture seeped in through the walls, staining the stone a muddy brown. It smelled of mold and dampness that could only mean we had traveled well belowground.

"I don't think the people who owned the place back when it was a library used it for much of anything," he continued. "When we found it, there were hardly any signs that anyone had ever been down here at all. I think it might have originally been planned to be used as a bomb shelter of some sort." Jonathan shrugged. "We made some changes so we could use it for something else."

We reached the bottom of the stairs and entered a large room that looked to be twice the size of the Den above us. The whole place was made of stone. Pillars dotted the room and held the roof above our heads. A stainless-steel table sat at the room's center, and a variety of surgical instruments lay on a tray next to it.

Cells were built into the walls. They surrounded the entire room. There had to be at least twenty of them, if not more. Their bars were made of what looked to be heavy iron, and they were mounted into the stone from ceiling to floor. There were no windows anywhere down there, which further solidified the idea that we were well underground.

The place reminded me forcibly of a vampire dungeon. When he had said it might have been an old bomb shelter, my mind had immediately gone to Ethan and his private second basement. Even though I had never seen his workspace for myself, I knew it looked nothing like this.

Now I could think of nothing else but the cages in which the vampires usually kept Purebloods. It made me sick to even think about it.

But unlike the vampire dungeons where there could be dozens, if not hundreds of caged Purebloods, only one of the cells was occupied here. From where I stood, it was hard to make out the hunched form lying on the stone floor. Growls and whines came from the thing, and it shuddered uncontrollably as if it had a permanent case of the shivers.

I stopped at the bottom of the stairs, refusing to go any farther. Whatever the place was, it wasn't somewhere I wanted to be. I had been trapped in a cell like these before. It wasn't an experience I ever wanted to repeat.

"Don't worry," Jonathan said, striding across the room. "We aren't going to harm you. Like I said before, we need you."

Nathan and Gregory took up positions on either side of the occupied cell. They stood well back from the cage, as if they didn't quite trust what was inside.

Gregory's smile wilted as he stood there, eyes flickering back and forth from Jonathan to the thing within the metal bars.

"I want you to see this," Jonathan said, turning to me. "You of all people will understand what we are going through. You will know the pain we are suffering."

"What's going on here?" I asked, gesturing toward the creature trapped within the cage. I didn't like this at all.

"I know how it looks," Jonathan said. "But no one has ever been kept here against their will. Come. Look in the cage. You will understand once you see."

I hesitated before finally crossing the room. I kept telling myself I was being stupid for ever trusting the wolves. Werewolves were the enemy. I killed them just as readily as I killed vampires. Not to mention the fact that one had once belonged to a House that killed everyone I knew. These three should have been dead long ago.

But somehow, someway, they trusted me. Okay, maybe that wasn't entirely true. Nathan looked as though he trusted me about as much as I trusted him, which was not at all. Jonathan was the one who seemed to trust me for some reason, and it appeared that was all that mattered in the end. I owed it to them to at least take a look at what they had.

I stopped two feet from the cage. Nathan and Gregory both took a step back to give me more room. Jonathan flipped a switch and an overhead light dimly lit the creature within the cell. It was just barely bright enough for me to get a good look at it without having to use my vampire-enhanced vision.

The creature lay on its stomach, its neck bent so

that I could see only the nape of its hairy neck. It was nude, clearly humanoid, and covered in a light coating of fur. The snarls and whimpers shook the creature, as if making any sort of sound caused it pain.

"What is it?" I asked, my uneasiness going through the roof. I was sure I had seen something similar to this before but refused to believe it.

"Look closer," Jonathan said. "I think you know."

My throat went dry as I took a step forward, putting myself far too close to the cage. Seeing this once had been bad enough, but I felt compelled to take a closer look just to be sure.

The creature's head snapped up at my approach. Its ears were human, and the long dirty blond hair on its head looked normal. It rose to all fours and turned to face me. I took an involuntary step back.

Its face was partially shifted to wolf. The nose was elongated, but it still looked like a human nose. The eyes were yellow, yet still held the shape of the human eye. The beast's lower jaw was partially extended, showing vampiric fangs thrust out from ruptured gums that dripped blood in a constant plink. Its chest was coated with dried blood, and the floor in which it had lain was sticky with it.

The creature roared and leaped at the bars. Its human hands ended in claws that raked at the metal. Its belly was void of hair, as if the transformation had started taking place at its back but hadn't worked all the way around to its front. It was quite clearly male.

"Thomas." The name slipped through my lips before I could stop it. I knew that what I was looking at wasn't my brother. It just reminded me of him, what had happened to him.

"No," Jonathan said, coming to stand next to me. I

didn't even react to his nearness, though my instincts told me I should have. If he had wanted to, he could have driven a blade straight through my heart and I wouldn't have been able to stop him. "It's not your brother."

I swallowed a few times before I could speak. "I know. But . . . who would do this? Valentino is dead. Was it an accident?"

"No, House Tremaine did this." Jonathan spat the name. "They are a Minor House looking to increase their power base by bringing the Luna Cult into their ranks."

I turned a shocked expression toward him. A vampire House wanted to assimilate the Luna Cult?

"They found out there were werewolves in the Cult, and they somehow managed to capture our Denmaster." Jonathan lowered his head. Fear was evident in his voice. "This was Simon's second. They sent him to us as a warning, as a reminder of what they can and will do if we do not cooperate."

I turned back to the creature in the cage. I knew what had caused the mutations within the beast. I just couldn't believe anyone—vampire or werewolf or Pureblood—could ever do that to another person. A few drops of blood didn't do this. This definitely didn't happen by accident.

Vampire and werewolf blood have similar qualities. It's like the difference between what makes a house cat different from a tiger. They are similar beasts, but different in obvious ways. The vampire gets to keep much of its human form, whereas the werewolf undergoes radical changes.

But they both still have the same hunger. They both need the blood to survive. They hunger for it.

The wolf often craves the meat of their victims as well, whereas the vampire tends to only want the blood; but in essence, it's only a minor difference to the same monster.

Despite the similarities, however, the blood doesn't mix. I could never feed on a werewolf, and a werewolf could never feed on me. To do so would create a monster like what lay behind the heavy iron bars.

The creature roared and threw itself against the far wall. Blood sprayed from its mouth. It dug at the stone wall with its claws as if it could claw its way out. The look in its eye was one of pure madness, of pure hunger.

"I know what happened to your brother," Jonathan said, his tone low and sympathetic. "I was there, but I did not take part. I never condoned turning another human being, cursing them to this sort of fate."

Hearing Jonathan talk about Thomas brought a sharp pain to my chest. I didn't want to listen anymore, didn't want to have anything to do with the Cult or the pathetic creature trapped within the cage. It hurt far too much.

"I also know that while your brother's blood has become mixed, he at least escaped with his life. He helped you escape before the Madness took him. He might still be out there."

"Stop," I said. Anger surged through my body, and it took all my self-control not to draw my weapons and kill him where he stood. The urge was so strong I was shaking with it.

I backed away from the cell, fighting myself with every step. The creature in the cage howled and thrashed, clawing at the wall, at the bars, at anything it could get its hands on. I doubted there was anything left of the person the werewolf once was. It was a mindless beast now, its only urge was to kill.

"Help us," Jonathan said, moving between me and the beast. "They have Simon, our Denmaster. I can only stand in his place for so long before some will begin to question me." He glanced toward his two associates. "If we don't bow down to House Tremaine by the midnight before the first night of the full moon, they will infect Simon with vampire blood. He will be driven crazy, turned into a mindless monster. You cannot let them do that to him."

"Why not?" I said, turning a steely gaze on him. I didn't like being reminded of my past failures. "Why would you come to me? You know I care nothing about werewolves and the Luna Cult. Why would I help you?"

"Because you are the only one I know who knows what it is like to live with this kind of weight on your shoulders." Jonathan met my stare without flinching. "And you are the type of person who would do something about it."

I glanced past him to the two men by the cage. Nathan was glaring at me, eyes full of all the hatred he could muster. Gregory stared back at me, his face void of any expression.

"Please," Jonathan said. "I have kept your secret for years now. I could have turned your name over any number of times to any number of people, but I didn't. I believe in what you do . . ." He paused and frowned. "To a point, anyway. Do you realize what would happen if House Tremaine took over the Luna Cult?"

I thought about it. If this Minor House were to assimilate the Luna Cult, taking on their Purebloods, as well as their werewolves, they could easily jump quite a few rungs in the power struggle that defined vampire society. Sure, as far as I knew there were only a few wolves in the Cult, but there were so many Purebloods they could turn, they might even leap to the top of the ladder. If they did that and someone who knew my name joined them . . .

Jonathan must have seen the understanding dawn in my face. He nodded and spoke slowly, keeping his tone light, unthreatening. "And since we know who you are, where you live, things would become quite difficult for you. House Tremaine would eventually get this information from someone in the Cult that is privy to what I know. They would come after you."

"Is that a threat?"

"No." Jonathan shook his head. "I am just stating a fact. Only I know for sure where you live. Nathan and Gregory are the only other two who even know who and what you really are. With Joshua dead, no one else knows."

He was showing a lot of trust in telling me that. Still, just the thought of anyone knowing who I was didn't sit well with me.

"Then what is to stop me from killing you three now and taking care of all my problems at once."

Nathan took a step forward, his hands balled into fists, but Jonathan motioned him back with a wave of his hand.

"Nothing," Jonathan said. "I hope you would consider what it would mean to allow someone like Count Tremaine to gain so much power. If he could do this"—he waved his hand toward the beast in the cell—"then what's to stop him from doing it to someone else? There could be an epidemic."

I frowned. I hated to admit it, but he had a point. The Luna Cult was far-reaching. There were hundreds of members in Columbus alone, and if they were to fall under the power of a single vampire entity, there was no telling what kind of havoc they would cause. How long before Tremaine's influence spread throughout Cult Dens across the globe?

"Think of it as a chance to take down a Minor House. We want to work with you. We don't have to hate one another. We have the same goals."

I glanced back at the cell, at the beast it contained. I looked from the good-humored Gregory to the surly Nathan. The cold stone walls seemed to close in on me, forced me to realize how fragile this situation really was. All it would take is blood, just enough to contaminate any one of us, and we would end up like that creature bashing its brains out in the cell. Tremaine would do it. What was stopping him from doing it to everyone who stood in his way?

"Okay," I said, taking a deep, cleansing breath. I knew I was crazy for even considering it, but honestly, could I really let Tremaine do this to anyone else?

The answer was no. I would rather go down fighting than to let this happen to others, even if they were werewolves. No one deserved that fate.

I let out the pent-up breath and looked Jonathan straight in the eye. "What do you have in mind?"

12

We went back upstairs, Jonathan in the lead, Nathan and Gregory at my back. I wasn't too thrilled about having the two wolves behind me, but what could I do? If I would have objected, I was sure Nathan would have made something of it. The big guy was just itching for a reason to start a fight.

Besides, I wasn't in the mood for a confrontation right then. My mind was whirling with what I had seen, what I had learned. I couldn't let what happened to that creature in the basement happen to anyone else, even if it was a werewolf.

We settled back in our original places in the office. I was going to stand, but after Jonathan took his seat behind the desk and Nathan and Gregory resumed their places on the couch, I decided it might be prudent to go ahead and have a seat. I sat down on the edge of one of the leather chairs, back straight, shifting to try to make room for my sword. It's pretty hard to sit comfortably when carrying so many weapons.

"The full moon begins in four night's time," Jonathan said once everyone was settled. "We are to

meet with Count Tremaine three nights from now. I
am allowed to bring up to ten Cultists with me, werewolves included, but no other weapons."

I listened, though I could hardly believe I was
doing it. Jonathan was a werewolf, after all. And since
he had been part of a vampire House, I was sure he
was guilty of hundreds of atrocities, even if he claimed
he hadn't taken part in destroying my life.

What was wrong with me? I should have killed him
as soon as he revealed himself to me.

Maybe I was just getting soft. I never used to take
it easy on anyone. Pablo would have been missing his
head the moment he stood up to me. Nathan's hateful glares might have earned him a gun in the face.

Then again, I knew what Jonathan's reasons for
taking me down into the basement had been. He was
manipulating me. I knew it. He used my past, my
love for my brother, to force my hand, to make me
side with him. He knew I couldn't let that sort of
thing happen again.

Still, I might not be as broken as he might think. I
knew what he was doing. Because of that, I knew I
couldn't trust him as much as he would like me to.
Just knowing what I did gave me the advantage over
him, even if he didn't realize it.

"Tremaine is demanding our unconditional loyalty to their cause," Jonathan went on. "They want us
to turn over all the wolves and have them take the
Oath. They want us to be the day watchers for the
vampires of the House, to be their enforcers. In
return, we get to keep our Den and work indepen-
dently whenever we aren't needed."

"It doesn't sound like that bad of a deal," I said. "You
get to keep your Den while gaining the protection

of a Minor House. Some wolves would kill for that. Many have."

I spoke without really thinking about what I was saying. I sure as hell didn't want the Cult joining with House Tremaine. It just seemed odd that they wouldn't take the deal, especially since it would give them a sort of protection. As it was, the Cult was in danger. Being taken in by a Minor House really wasn't all that bad when the alternative was a slow, painful death.

Minor Houses were usually outside my reach. If Tremaine were to take in the Luna Cult, there was no way I could deal with them. If I had the Cult at my side, then perhaps something *could* be done about House Tremaine. It might just give me the edge I needed to combat their numbers.

What was I thinking? The Luna Cult at my side? Maybe I wasn't just getting soft, maybe I was losing my mind.

"They have our Denmaster," Jonathan said, shaking his head. "They tainted Byron. Why would we want to submit to slavery when we have a chance to wipe out the vampires who threaten us? We would be saving werewolf lives, possibly even bringing them to our side. We could free our people."

"So you plan on recruiting from House Tremaine?" That made a lot more sense than just wanting to remain free. Freedom these days often meant a shorter life span.

"Of course." Jonathan folded his hands on top of his desk. His half-face looked me up and down as if weighing my reaction. I did my best to keep my face blank. "What else would we do? The wolves of House Tremaine are only there because they know of no other life. If we can show them they can have their freedom, that they don't have to be subservient to the vampires, perhaps even more will follow in our footsteps. We can end the rule of the vampire Houses. Without the werewolves doing their dirty work, they will have no powerbase left to stand on."

"A rebellion."

Jonathan smiled and sat back in his chair. "I wouldn't go that far. Rebellion is such a harsh word. Perhaps we should call it an emancipation. We are just trying to free those of us who are being held as slaves, nothing more."

A flurry of activity outside the door caught my attention. I could see shadows moving from beneath the door, but no one knocked or called out for help. Other than the scuffling of feet, there was little to the excitement. At least there wasn't screaming. Whatever was going on out there was obviously being handled.

"It's nothing," Jonathan said. "Someone stumbled into our territory. They are being dealt with."

I looked away from the door to study Jonathan's face. He kept it carefully blank. "How do you know? Are you a telepath, as well as a sorcerer?"

He laughed. "Hardly." He motioned for me to join him at his desk.

I rose and moved to stand opposite him. He pointed to the top of his desk. A small screen was embedded in the wood. I hadn't noticed it before because of all the stuff on the desk. The screen was protected by a layer of glass that was scratched from all the work that had been done on top of it.

I leaned forward so I could get a better look at what was on the screen. I could see the campus green from what looked to be the perspective of the Den. A shaggy-looking man was being hauled away by Pablo and one of the other Cultists I had seen inside. The man was screaming soundlessly, shaking his head back and forth as if he knew what was going to happen to him.

It wasn't hard to figure out. Even I knew werewolves had to eat sometime.

The thought made my stomach clench. It wasn't in hunger, but in disgust. All the man had done was walk onto the green, probably just wandered there accidently, and now was likely to become wolf food.

"You didn't think we didn't have security precautions in place, now did you?" Jonathan said, almost solemnly.

I shrugged and returned to my chair. "Not so hi-tech, no. What will happen to him?"

"What would you do in our situation?" He stared at me with a knowing look. "We cannot let others know we are here. He saw someone come in. He had to be dealt with."

I couldn't help but think back on the Cultist who had delivered Jonathan's message. He hadn't really deserved to die, but I couldn't take the chance he might tell someone else where to find me. Jonathan was only doing what he thought was best for the Cult.

That didn't mean I had to like it.

"The monitor outside the Den isn't the only one we have," Jonathan went on. "There are a few more feeds from around the campus so we can keep an eye on what's happening close to our territory. We do not use it for the hunt, if that is what you are thinking."

"It crossed my mind."

"We only want to protect ourselves."

It did make sense, more sense than I would have

liked. I wondered how far-reaching their security system really was. Did they plant a camera out by my house? I might have to walk the grounds some night to find out.

"So what exactly do you want with me? I just finished a run and I typically don't get involved in anything until I've had time to recuperate."

Jonathan glanced at his two associates. Gregory's smile had returned. Nathan was as tense as ever, and I saw him shake his head with the slightest of motions when Jonathan's gaze swept over him. If I hadn't been looking right at him, I would have missed it.

"We want you to come with us," Jonathan said, turning back to me. "We will get you in the mansion and once inside, we want your help to take it down. We want you to kill Count Tremaine and the other vampires."

"Tall order."

"With four of us, it's possible." Jonathan ran a hand through his hair. What was left of it anyway. "Our main priority is getting Simon out of there alive and untainted. We would like to get out without having to kill any of the other werewolves, though I realize that won't be possible. I will do what I can to convince some of them to join our cause."

"How do you even know Simon is still alive? Have you talked to him since his capture? I wouldn't put it past a vampire Count to kill an enemy and lie about it until he gets what he wants."

Jonathan took a deep breath. The thought obviously troubled him. "We have only Tremaine's word at the moment. But as long as there is a chance, I can't turn my back on Simon. I will demand to see him as soon as we are inside, of course. Once I see that the Denmaster is safe, we can make our move."

He made it sound almost easy. I had to admit, it was intriguing. Even if the plan failed, I should be able to go in and kill a few vamps and wolves before slipping away. With any luck, the Cult and House Tremaine would kill each other off and I could just mop up whatever remained later.

"So how do you plan on doing this without weapons?" I asked. "Taking down an entire House like that won't be easy with them. It's damn near impossible without some sort of firepower."

Jonathan glanced at his associates and frowned. "We were hoping you could help us with that part," he admitted. "I am pretty sure they will check us over at the door. You don't exactly look like a Cultist, nor do you smell like a wolf. Your scent is . . . different. Their sniffers would pick you out immediately."

"I'll take that as a compliment."

"There may be another way in, but we don't know the layout of the mansion well enough to be sure. If we can get you past their sniffers, then perhaps there will be a way to get you armed."

I rubbed my temples. Why was I here again? "I won't go in without my weapons."

"Then we must come up with a way to get them inside with you."

"No."

I was so surprised by the strange, deep voice, I actually jumped. Nathan rose to his feet. He turned on Jonathan with his hands balled into fists.

"Sit down," Jonathan said, his voice tight.

"We can't trust her," Nathan said, jabbing his thumb at me. "She's too dangerous. We can't let her have her weapons while the rest of us go unarmed. She could turn on us at any moment. She *is* one of them."

"She has her weapons now," Jonathan pointed out. "She could have used them at any point during our talks and we couldn't have stopped her."

Nathan glared at me. His eyes were tinged yellow.

"He has a point," I said, smiling. "I could have killed you ten times over if I had wanted."

Nathan's upper lip lifted in a sneer, but his eyes betrayed him. They had bled back to full human. He had regained at least some control of his emotions. "You could try it."

I almost laughed. I had to give him credit, he was pretty confident despite the odds. I *was* the one with the weapons.

"Sit down," Jonathan repeated, his voice hard. He stood and leaned on his desk, his fists bunched. His face was red with anger, and I was afraid the side of his head might split open from the stress of controlling all that rage.

"If someone goes furry, they are losing their heads," I said, looking from one wolf to the next.

Nathan's jaw tightened so much I heard it pop. He sat back down on the couch so hard it bounced Gregory about an inch into the air. The big wolf sat stiff and refused to look anywhere but directly in front of him.

Jonathan glared at him a moment longer before easing back onto his chair. There was a beep from in front of him and he glanced down at the monitor built into his desk. The tension seemed to ooze out of him and his smile returned.

"Tell you what," I said. I wanted to get out of there before someone's control broke and I had to start killing people. "I'll look the place over tomorrow night. I know where Tremaine's mansion is. If I remember right, there is a hill covered by some trees behind it. I can scout from there."

Jonathan nodded slowly. "If you can get in with your gear, we can find a way to have you meet up with the rest of us once we are all inside. We will need to make sure you are dressed for the occasion. You won't be able to go in dressed like that."

I didn't like the idea of wearing anything else but my work attire. But right then, I wasn't going to argue. I refused to go into a hostile situation without my weapons. It might mean House Tremaine will become the most powerful House in all the state, maybe even the country, but at least I knew who to kill to keep my secrets from getting out if it came to that.

"We could dress you as a new member, give you the tattoo . . ." Jonathan was speaking more to himself than to me, but I wasn't about to let that last comment slide.

"No way," I said. "I'm not getting inked for this."

"Relax," he said, smiling. "It would be one of our fakes. We give them to initiates who want to test the waters before leaping head first into the Cult. If they don't like what we have to offer, then they are free to go and can wash off our mark. It allows them to meld back into society without having a constant reminder of their former allegiances stamped across their face."

"You let them go?" I doubted it.

"They are never allowed to come to the Den as initiates, or even know where it is located. We have places within the city where they stay. Most of the Cultists you see out on the streets are from these ancillary groups. The ones who are too violent, too attracted to death, but do not wish to leave the Cult itself, often remain in these groups. They are not allowed into the true Luna Cult."

I nodded. It made sense to a point. I had always thought the Luna Cult was a life sentence. It stood to reason that the sort of life the Cultists led was not for everyone. How often does a teenager change their mind about what they want to do with their lives?

"Scout the mansion," Jonathan said, rising. "I will eagerly await your results."

"How am I supposed to get hold of you?" I asked, standing.

"You frequent The Bloody Stake, correct?" I nodded. "I will have Gregory stay close to the area. If you have anything to pass on to us, just go to the Stake and he will find you."

Jonathan reached a hand across the desk. I stared at it like it was a snake for a long moment before finally crossing the short distance between us. I took his hand in my own. It was actually warm and comforting. We shook.

"I hope you can find a way inside. I'm not sure how else we are going to get you in with your weapons. We can't do this without you."

I dropped his hand and resisted the urge to wipe it on my pants. As comforting as his touch might have been, it still felt like I had just shaken hands with the devil. Maybe I had.

"I will find a way in," I said. I started for the door.

"Oh, and Kat?"

I stopped and glanced back. I was surprised at the warmth in his smile, as if I had made his day just being in the same room with him.

"Thank you."

I nodded and left the room. No one bothered me as I crossed the Den and headed for the front door. The Cultists watched me go without trying to stop me.

I paused at the door leading to the empty green. I had half a mind to turn around and tell Jonathan to forget everything. Did I really want to get involved in what amounted to a war between vampires and werewolves?

I smiled. Maybe it wouldn't be so bad, after all. There was a good chance they would all kill each other. It would make my job a whole hell of a lot easier if they did.

I pushed open the doors and stepped out into the brisk chill of night, leaving the Luna Cult Den behind.

13

I had to fight the urge to draw my gun and stalk my property when I returned home. I believed Jonathan when he said no one else knew where I lived, but I just couldn't shake the feeling of being watched. He *was* a werewolf. Could I really trust him? And who was to say that someone hadn't followed Joshua, the Luna Cult messenger, to my home?

But I managed. It wasn't so much that I didn't want to go out and check the tree line. I did. I just didn't feel like making the effort. My heart was resting somewhere in the vicinity of my stomach after having old memories dredged back up. It was making me cranky.

I knocked on the side door after testing it to make sure it was locked. I stood in the garage, my head hanging as low as my heart, and waited for Ethan to let me in.

It took him a good three minutes to get there. I had to knock more than once, and with each hammering of my fist, my agitation grew. This whole thing was becoming a big mess, bigger than I had anticipated.

I pushed open the door as soon as Ethan disengaged the lock. I walked past him without a hello or a second glance. He was alive. That was good enough for me.

He stepped aside without a word. This wasn't the first time I had come home in a funk. He knew better than to say anything until I was settled in, back in "home mode" rather than "kill mode."

I went straight up the stairs and into my room, closing the door behind me. I shrugged out of my coat, removed my belt and shoulder holster, and tossed the entire bundle onto a chair. I peeled out of my clothes, exchanging leather for flannel pants and a too-large T-shirt that hung nearly to my knees.

I stood there a long moment, staring at my reflection in the mirror. There was no hint of the vampire I had become. If I were to go by looks alone, I probably could pass as a scared, if not a bit hardened, young woman. It was hard to believe there was a monster hiding somewhere within that soft-seeming exterior. Even my black hair didn't betray the darkness that lurked inside.

I hated looking at myself like that. I knew what I was, knew what I had done. No matter how I looked, I was a monster. Nothing could change that.

But that didn't stop me from wishing.

I closed my eyes and didn't open them again until I was turned away from the mirror. I went to my bureau and opened the bottom drawer. Slowly, almost reverently, I removed old clothing I hadn't worn for years and set them aside. Each piece was a memory

I didn't want, a memory I couldn't forget. They reminded me of a life I no longer had.

Right then, I needed to remember.

Buried beneath the old clothing was a small wooden box. My hand trembled over it, hesitating. I wasn't really sure I wanted to look at what was inside. It would only serve to open the wounds that were already beginning to fray. Looking at what was inside would be like poking at a wound to see if it would still bleed.

I snatched the box out of the drawer, angry at myself for even hesitating. I was stronger than that. This was something I needed to do. I needed to remind myself why I kept going, why I did what I did.

Hands trembling despite my self-reproach, I clutched the box to my chest. I kicked the drawer closed for good measure and made my way to my bed. I sat down on the floor, cross-legged, using the bed for a backrest. I ran my finger over the unadorned lid of the box, felt the grain of it, let it soothe me.

It almost worked. If it wasn't for the knowledge of what was inside, I might have sat there until morning just touching it. Memories were just that, memories. They could be forgotten, brought back whenever the need arose. Or they could work at you, eat at your core until nothing was left.

I wouldn't let that happen. My past was my past, I knew that. It wasn't like I would ever forget what had happened. I just needed a little reminding every now and again.

The key was already in the lock at the front of the box. I never had a reason ever to take it out. Ethan would never go through my things, and it was unlikely anyone would care about what was inside anyway. They wouldn't be valuable to anyone but me.

I turned the key and flipped open the lid. I gathered the contents in hands that were still shaking. No one else would have noticed their slight tremble, the way my fingers twitched almost involuntarily. Only someone of my enhanced senses would notice it. *I* noticed it.

There were four photos in all. The first was of Ethan and I, standing next to each other. My arms were crossed and an irritated look marred my face. Ethan looked overjoyed. He had wanted the picture, had set the timer on the camera himself.

I set the picture aside with hardly a glance. It was only in the box with the others just in case something happened to him. Or he got old and died on me. That was something I didn't want to think about. A vampire's life span isn't all it's cracked up to be. I had no desire to see anyone I care about grow old and die. But what could I do? I wasn't going to taint him.

The next photograph was of my mom and dad. It was taken before the Uprising, and they looked as happy as two people could be together. Children were just a distant dream to them then. They were young. Innocent.

It had taken me a long time to find that picture. It wasn't as if I could just go home to retrieve it after they had died. After Valentino's wolves killed everyone in the area, rogue wolves moved in, claiming the territory for their own. The place had been swarming with them, still was. Going there to retrieve this one memory had nearly cost me my life.

I ran my finger gently along each smiling face,

wishing I could touch them for real. It was my fault they were dead. I would never forgive myself for that.

I set the photograph reverently on top of the one of Ethan and I. The next picture was of my mom and dad with a baby Thomas. He had to have been no more than three months old at the time. There was a trail of drool running down his chin, and he was staring at something hovering just over the camera-man's head.

I stared long and hard at the photo, burning its image into my brain. I had almost forgotten that drool, that innocent look. I tried not to think too hard about it. There had been time yet for them to be happy. Monsters were just legends. They had happiness. They knew love and life, and all that went with it. What had it been like to enjoy a child without worrying about whether your precious baby would end up some monster's lunch?

Or worse, become one of them.

I closed my eyes and took a deep breath before setting the picture aside and looking at the next photograph.

The picture was of Thomas and I, standing arm in arm, dressed to kill. Literally. We thought we were invincible, that we could walk into any vampire House and kill anyone we chose. We had stuck to rogues mostly, since an actual House was a bit much for us at the time. We learned that the hard way.

It was also before the tainting of my blood. My skin was tanned back then, though I had little sun. I just tanned real easy. My hair was long and curled, dyed a deep crimson that had long ago faded. I didn't have my current stock of silver weapons, just a plain sword I had been given by someone who was much better at what I did than I was. I had a regular old gun, a couple of stakes that turned out to be hardly useful, and a bowie knife I used to saw off vampire heads when the sword just wouldn't do.

Thomas was dressed just the same. We both were wearing camo, which was silly in itself, considering we worked in the city. Every time I thought about those days, I had to wonder how we ever survived intact as long as we did.

Thomas's brown eyes stared out at me from the photograph. He had gotten our mother's eyes. They were deep, soulful eyes. People had often commented on how different we were, but so alike. Even our eyes were a different color, his brown to my blue. His cheekbones were higher, his brow wider.

But the similarities were there. Always had been. We had always stuck together, stayed by each other's side. He had always protected me.

I don't know how long I sat there staring at the picture of us together. Eventually, a soft knock at the door brought me out of my trance. I blinked and turned my head to the door, but didn't answer. I wasn't sure I had a voice to answer with.

The knock came again and the door opened slowly. Ethan poked his head in, looked at me, looked at what I held in my hands, and then made his slow way across the room. He sat down on the floor next to me.

"I owe a lot to the both of you, you know," he said, sucking in a heavy breath. "If it wasn't for both you and your brother, I wouldn't be here today."

I didn't say anything. I gathered all four pictures and returned them to their resting place within the box. I remained sitting, staring at the closed lid as if

I could see through it to the pictures inside. I was afraid to speak, afraid my resolve would break and I would bawl like a baby.

It had been nearly twenty years since I last cried. I didn't feel like starting again now.

"When they had me, I was certain I was going to die," Ethan went on. "They didn't care I was just a kid. They were going to use me like everyone else. Heck, I think they had bigger plans for me. I saw the way they looked at me."

I glanced up, pulled by Ethan's voice. There were tears there, just behind his eyes. His head was down and he was looking at his hands. The hair on the left side of his head was mussed as if he had been running fingers through it for hours.

"You saved me," he said. "You didn't have to. Not after what you had just experienced. You could have let me lie there in that cell and rot. I would have understood." His next words were spoken so low even I could barely hear them. "But you didn't."

I felt a pang of guilt. I might have saved Ethan from dying at the hands of House Valentino, but there were others I had failed to save. Purebloods had died. Lots of them. I hadn't been able to control my hunger. I killed at least two myself before I was able to control my newly acquired appetites.

And there was my family, of course.

"Thomas's sacrifice weighs on my mind daily. I didn't even know him, but I love him for what he did for me. And you . . . you suffered the most, sacrificed the most."

I winced. I wasn't sure if "sacrificed" was the right word. It had been all my fault. Sometimes I found myself jealous of Thomas, of what he had become.

He didn't have to live with the aftermath of our failed run. He had no mind left to think with.

No, I was the one who bore the weight of it all. It rested squarely on my shoulders, and I would carry it until I died. My friends, my family, they were all gone. I would avenge them, would make up for my mistake.

"Don't blame yourself, Kat," Ethan said as if he had heard my thoughts. "It wasn't your fault. House Valentino did this to you, did that to him. Without you, I would be dead. Others would have died. Many others."

"I know," I said, breaking my self-imposed silence.

"You can't save everyone. I know you would if you could, but you can't." Ethan rose. He started to reach for me, to rest his hand on my shoulder or to brush the hair out of my face. I'm not sure which. Before he could do either, he pulled his hand back. He looked as though he had something else to say, but swallowed his words before they could be uttered. He turned away without another word and hurried out of the room.

14

I don't remember the day passing. At some point, I got up and went into the bathroom to run a hot bath. The scent of lavender filled the room as I slipped into water that was just this side of scalding. It covered me like a soothing blanket, eased my mind to the point I might have drifted off if I was able.

Instead of sleep, I found myself floating on the edge of oblivion. I didn't want to think, didn't want to feel. I closed my eyes and forgot about everything.

Eventually, I made my way to my bed. I fell into it as if it might swallow me whole. I slipped under the blankets and laid there, my entire body weak from the sunlight just outside my window. I couldn't see it, but I could still feel it there. I had half a mind to open the blinds just to have one last glimpse of the sun before it killed me.

I don't know how long I lay there in the comforts of my own bed. All I know for sure is that when I opened my eyes again, the sun was down and I felt cleansed of the emotions that had threatened to overwhelm me. The pain was still there, deep within my gut, but it was overpowered by another pain, one I had become used to. One I loathed.

I rose from the bed and went to my window. I slid the heavy drapes aside, lifted the blinds, and opened the window. It was a crystal-clear night. While there was a brisk chill to the air, it felt good on my face, my bare skin. I breathed in the fresh air, sucked it in as if it might be my last clean breath.

I was shaking, but it wasn't from the cold. The pain ate at me, caused my hands to tremble on the windowsill. It burned like fire throughout my body.

I was hungry.

A shape fluttered by the open window. It was nothing more than a dark imperfection against the night sky, indistinct. The leaves of the trees rustled with the breeze, playing a quiet lullaby for those who slept. It was a welcome song to those of us who walked the night. Somewhere in the distance, a dog howled and barked twice before falling silent. A loon called out only to have its call go unanswered.

I closed the window and locked it. I wanted to be out there, hunting with the rest of the beasts. It was a primal urge that welled up deep from within my gut. It had a stranglehold on my mind, a thirst that wouldn't ease until I gave in to it. I wouldn't be able to think clearly.

I needed to hunt. The need was a part of me now. I couldn't turn it away.

My mind was made up before I knew for sure what I was going to do. I threw on my work attire. The leather felt good against my flesh, hugged me tight like a lover.

The urge to feed was so strong it nearly crippled me. I struggled to buckle on my belt, slip on my shoulder holster. My hands were shaking so badly I was afraid to even check the gun to make sure it was loaded. By the time I donned my coat and opened my bedroom door to head downstairs, I was damn near ravenous.

Ethan had already risen for the night. I could smell his lingering scent in the hall. He had gotten up early and had breakfast. I knew it long before I reached the dining room. There were breadcrumbs on the table and an empty glass sat at its edge. I could smell the orange juice, as well as Ethan's saliva on the glass.

I gritted my teeth and made my way to the door. I didn't want to stick around and have Ethan stumble in on me while I was in such a sorry state. I was pretty sure I could keep from attacking him, but I didn't want to chance it. I had never lost complete control around him before, at least not since the day we met in House Valentino's cages.

That wasn't to say he hadn't seen me fight off the hunger many times before. I didn't like to feed. I would put it off forever if I could. So when the hunger did finally fall upon me, it left me in a pretty bad way.

I left through the side door, locking it behind me. I figured Ethan would let me in when I got back. Once he realized I was gone, I was sure he would wait for me. He probably had seen the warning signs coming already and had gotten up early so he wouldn't risk facing my hunger-induced wrath.

The garage was dark and chilly. I quickly topped off the tank with spare gas we kept in cans in the garage. I wanted to get more than a quick meal in tonight. I wanted to scout House Tremaine after my hunger was sated. I didn't want to have to stop once I got started, and running out of gas on the way home was unacceptable.

The Honda started up right away and I pulled out of the garage without a backward glance. I had enough of my mind left to press the button on the garage door opener before I was too far down the road.

I had no idea where I was going at first. I didn't want to lurk around the Minor House until later, even if I wasn't in full-on vamp mode. The earliest part of the night tended to be the most active when it came to security on a lot of the Houses. I was sure they had guards posted throughout the day and night, and the trees I hoped to use for cover would definitely be watched.

But eventually security would fall lax and I could make my move. I just had to bide my time.

The road hummed under my wheels as I sped along. Houses whipped by, barely seen as I blurred past. I was going far too fast for the quality of the road, and I knew if I were to hit the city proper at those speeds, I would have to slow down or risk getting pulled over by one of the rare night cops who patrolled the city streets.

It wasn't as if I was afraid of them. The cops were all Purebloods, and silver was just as illegal for them to use as it was for me. The worst they could do was try to arrest me and lock me up. That didn't scare me. I knew I could get away if I had to.

What I was afraid of was hurting one of them. If someone were to get in my face tonight, I wasn't so sure what I would do. I was in no mood to deal with anyone, let alone someone who thought they could push me around just because I was a girl.

The wind whipped back my hair and sent my coat flapping behind me. It pulled at me, tried to rip me from my seat like it was some sort of leather parachute. Bugs flittered by, buzzing about my face, splattering on the windshield. A raccoon stared at me from the side of the road, its eyes reflecting yellow in my passing headlights.

I slowed down as soon as I realized where I was headed. There had been no conscious thought to my direction. It just sort of happened. It was the perfect place to give in to my darker side.

I pulled on to the main drag and merged with traffic. Cars rolled up and down the road at a leisurely pace, many of the drivers looking for their next mark. Women walked the streets in high heels, spandex, latex, and fishnet, all interwoven together, concealing so little they might as well have gone naked. Men in wide-brimmed hats and loud suits that clashed with colorful undershirts stood at the entrances of many doorways, watching the women pass, calling out to them in leering tones.

Just another day on High Street, the seediest part of the city.

I had no idea what the place had been like before the Uprising. I somehow doubted all the scum of Columbus just happened to show up after the vampires rose to power. The place reeked of degradation. It was just off the campus, might even have been a part of it at one time, but now it was a long line of pavement, neon signs, and hotels that catered only to the perverted.

It was never safe on High Street, not even for the monsters. More women and men ended up dead here than anywhere else. I think most of the women offering themselves up for the vamps and wolves actually liked it that way. You didn't come here unless you had a death wish.

The pimps were mostly Purebloods, though a few rogue werewolves and vamps were mingled in with the rest. It was impossible to pick them out just by sight. They kept a pretty low profile, not wanting to attract the attention of any of the vampire Houses, lest they be dealt with in quite an abrupt manner. Rogues didn't last long. They were either assimilated or killed.

I kept my head down as I drove toward the parking garage. Part of me wanted to have nothing to do with the place, knowing I was just as likely to get attacked as I was to be an attacker. The sensible part, however, insisted I needed to be here. Where else would I find someone I could feed on whose memory wouldn't weigh on my conscience later? This was the worst of the worst.

The garage was a mammoth of a building. It was far bigger than was necessary, though it had been built before the vampires had taken over, so it might have been full more often than not in the past. Most people who hung out on High Street lived within walking distance. Anyone who was visiting for the first time often took a cab or rode with friends. It was too easy to have your car come up missing, or worse, occupied by someone waiting for your inevitable return.

There was no on-street parking anywhere, nor were there parking lots that hadn't been converted into something else, so I had no choice but to park in the garage. I drove halfway up, choosing a level that was mostly uninhabited. I had seen only a handful of men in a tight group a level below me, but by the time I had parked and was walking toward the exit, they were gone.

My footfalls echoed loudly in the mostly empty garage. A car started up somewhere above me and then sped down the ramp, tires screeching as if they were running from something. They probably were.

I kept my eyes on the shadows, my hand near my weapons. I really didn't want to have to draw at all, considering every weapon on me was illegal and would bring half the city down on me if they found out I had them out in the open. Thankfully, I reached the bottom floor and was heading out without running into anyone.

A ticket booth stood at the entrance to the garage. The barriers that used to block off the entrance had been torn down and the booth trashed long ago. A mannequin sat in an old chair, surrounded by broken glass, condoms—used and unused alike—and a smattering of other pieces of discarded trash that was best not lingered upon. The mannequin, though faceless, seemed to watch me as I stepped out onto the bright lights of High Street.

I squinted into the sudden light. A neon sign blazed across the street so brightly I damn near needed sunglasses. A pair of streetwalkers sauntered by, paying me disgusted glances as if the healthy dose of leather concealing most of my body was an affront to them. Maybe it was. This *was* the place to go to shop for skin, after all.

I ignored them and fell in behind a group of teenagers out gallivanting in the streets. They stuck close together, laughing and pointing at anyone who struck their fancy. It was these kinds of Pureblood kids who didn't last long here. They would be corpses or worse by the end of the night if they kept it up.

I let them have their fun, however. Now was not the time to get involved. I had things to do.

I kept my eyes peeled for any likely marks. A man staggered out of a building ahead of me, bumped into a trash can, and fell over in a heap with his head mere inches from the road. A girl who looked to be no more than thirteen lifted up her shirt to some passersby, earning a few whistles and catcalls. A pair of lovers groped their way toward a hotel, barely making it through the door before the first article of clothing fell to the ground.

But none of them was a likely target. They might not be the most desirable of folk, but they weren't doing anything that deserved retribution. Eventually that girl might end up dead, mauled by some wolf who got a little too frisky, or the lovers murdered in their beds, but as it was, they weren't the kind of people I went after.

It wasn't until the group of teens I was following passed an old concert hall that had been turned into a nightwalker's rave joint that I spotted a potential mark.

He was following a young woman who was wearing a tight halter top and a skirt so short I could see the bottom of her ass swaying with her strides. The straps of her bright pink thong rode high on her scrawny hips, a beacon for the eye. She had on knee-high boots with heels so tall she was walking on her tiptoes. I had no idea how that could ever be comfortable.

I crossed the street, leaving the gawking teenagers to their fate, and fell in behind the man. His long trench coat was brown and faded. A baseball cap was pulled down to conceal his eyes, and he kept fingering something in his pocket. The entire time I followed him, he didn't take his eyes off the girl in front of him. I could smell his desire.

The girl turned off down a side alley and kept walking, oblivious to the stalker behind her. The man paused long enough to look both ways before taking off after her. He didn't bother looking behind him. Amateurs.

I didn't make the same mistake. I leaned against the wall and pretended to check my nails as I looked to make sure I hadn't gained a tail of my own. Once I was certain it was clear, I slipped into the alley as quickly and soundlessly as I could.

The air was dank and smelled heavily of urine and reefer. Puddles with condoms and well-smoked blunts floating in them lined the entire alleyway, and I had to step carefully to keep from stepping in someone else's bodily fluids.

The man and girl disappeared around the corner of the building ahead. A moment later, there was a quick intake of breath and the start of a scream that was quickly choked off. I kept my pace quick and light, not wanting to alert the man that I was coming.

I drew a knife from my belt and turned the corner all of fifteen seconds later, keeping the weapon concealed in the folds of my jacket.

The girl was pressed against the wall. Her stalker had a knife pressed against her throat, a dirty, rusty thing that probably wouldn't cut much more than butter. The girl's hands were free, her eyes were wide, and she was whimpering, yet she made no move to escape. With his free hand, her attacker reached up her too-short skirt and pulled her pink thong down around her knees.

I was on him before he knew I was there. My knife pricked his throat and he froze as it slid around to his jugular. A thin trickle of blood ran down his neck where I nicked him.

"Too cheap to pay?" I whispered in his ear.

"This is none of your business," the man said. He was still slightly bent over, hand still wrapped around the girl's panties. His knife had slipped down and was now resting tip-first in the hollow of the scared girl's throat. He sounded nervous, but not nearly as scared as he should have been.

I grabbed him by the arm and yanked the hand holding the knife away. The short blade fell to the ground with a clatter. I twisted his arm behind his back and he straightened, finally letting go of her thong.

"Go," I said, motioning with my head for the girl to leave. "Go home. Learn from this."

She pulled up her underwear, grabbed a bright pink purse from the ground, and ran down the alley without a word. She looked back once, eyes wide, before finally vanishing out of sight.

I spun the man around and slammed him up against the wall. His eyes were bloodshot and seeping but didn't have that terrified look I would have expected. The blood on his neck stood out starkly against his pale skin. I might have thought him a vampire, if not for his lack of reaction to the silver blade that had nicked him. He was definitely a Pureblood.

"Preying on women isn't exactly the wisest thing to do nowadays," I said, pressing the knife a little tighter against his throat. He made a strangled sound and his eyes widened a bit. I think he finally understood what kind of trouble he was in.

He tried to push me away, using the wall for leverage. He was much bulkier than I was, probably by a good seventy pounds or more, and he topped me by a good foot, yet he could hardly budge me. His eyes widened even further as realization set in.

"You . . , you're one of them," he said. He winced as the knife scraped his throat. "I have connections. I can get you whatever you want."

The hunger raged inside me, demanded to be quenched. This man was scum. He would have raped that girl and probably killed her afterward. I didn't care what kind of information or whatever he was offering might be. His connections meant nothing to me.

Blood spurted from my gums as I gave in to the hunger. The man tried to fight me off, push me away, but it was no use. He pleaded for his life, cutting his throat with every heavy gasp of air. He smelled of smoke and alcohol and sweat.

But most of all, he smelled of fear and blood.

I ignored his protests and pleading words. I wiped my knife on his shirt, cleaning off his speckles of blood. I didn't need it there to hold him. I had only needed it to make sure his blood was pure.

Leaning forward, I licked the blood trailing down his neck, tasted it as I might a fine wine. It was sweet on the tongue, even mingled with his rancid sweat. He gurgled something inarticulate, then opened his mouth to shriek.

All that sprang forth was blood.

15

The blood dried quickly. It was nearly invisible against my shirt and coat as I sped down the pavement. My hunger was sated, but I was not satisfied. In fact, I was sick to my stomach.

There was no doubt the man had been swine. His removal had made the streets the tiniest bit safer, though it would be a miracle if anyone noticed. There was no telling how many other women he had stalked like that, how far he had gone. Tonight could have been his first and last time out. Or it could have been one in a hundred.

In the end, it didn't matter. No matter how corrupted he might have been, he had still been a man, a Pureblood whose mind had been tainted, though his blood had not. I could have scared him, tossed him around a bit, cut him, and then let him go. A good scare might have set him straight. I mean, I had just cut a werewolf some slack just the other day, why couldn't I have done it for this guy?

I knew why, of course. I had to feed. It was what I had gone there to do in the first place.

Instead of scaring him off, I did what I needed to do. I tossed his corpse into a garbage bin, his body drained. Someone would find him eventually. Would anyone care?

The fact of the matter was, I was angry. Normally after feeding, I felt a bit disgusted with myself, worried about my soul and so on; but for some reason, this kill bothered me more than it should have. It weighed on my mind, made me question my reasons for going out like I had.

I knew I wasn't fully in my right mind. The moments after a feeding were oftentimes filled with ecstasy. There was a sort of high that went along with the blood. It cascaded through my body, burst through my brain, and sent shivers down my spine as I drank. It was a drug.

And like any other drug, there was always a downside to the high. Coming down was hard, sometimes crippling, and it happened far too fast. No more than fifteen minutes had passed before I started regretting my actions.

I licked my lips. I could still taste the stalker's blood on them. My gums were sore, but my teeth had retracted back to normal. I had washed the blood off my face as best I could before heading back to the Honda; then I used wet wipes I kept under the seat to clean the rest from my face and hands. A werewolf would still smell it on me if I got too close, but I didn't plan on getting close enough to anyone for it to matter.

I had been stupid. I should have gone to Tremaine's mansion first. I could have hunted afterward. And who knows, there was always a chance one of his

Pureblood servants would happen upon me. They I could kill without regret.

But it was too late now. I was full, my senses tingling with fresh blood. Now it was time to get to work.

A truck pulled up close behind me. Its headlights lit up the road. I glanced over my shoulder in irritation. The truck was coming up on me fast, so I swerved to the edge of the road to give the asshole room to pass. The driver was straddling the yellow center line, sticking straight on it like he was on tracks. No other cars were on the lonely stretch of road.

The truck pulled up next to me and kept pace with me as we raced down the road. We were both moving far too fast, and I had to swerve closer to him every few seconds to keep from hitting a pothole or a fallen branch or some other obstruction. No one bothered keeping up with these lesser traveled roads much anymore.

I growled under my breath and glanced into the cab of the truck, hoping to catch the driver's attention. I wanted him to either pass me or let me back onto the main part of the road before I crashed into something.

There were two men in the cab. The passenger had a short, spiky haircut dyed purple. Multiple piercings ran along his ears, nose, and lips. It looked like he had been trimmed in metal. He had a knot of scar tissue in the middle of his forehead like he had at one time had a close encounter with a werewolf. It looked like a large chunk of his flesh had been torn away and had healed. Badly. I couldn't make out the driver.

The passenger grinned at me and leaned partway

out of the rolled-down truck window to blow me a kiss. His skin was discolored and lumpy.

The driver growled something to his passenger, and a large, meaty hand reached out and yanked the pierced man back into his seat. After a few heated words, the pierced man flipped the driver off with both hands before turning his double bird to me. He spat at me and cackled.

Before I could return the favor, the truck finally picked up speed. I followed the spiky-haired passenger with my eyes, just barely resisting the urge to draw my gun and shoot him. It might be hard to hit a moving target, especially since I was trying to control my own vehicle, but I was a pretty damn good shot. If nothing else, I was sure it would scare the shit out of him.

A growl came from right beside me. I turned my head just as a large mass of fur, teeth, and claws leaped from the back of the pickup and hit me hard in the side. The force of the beast's body striking mine sent us both flying from my motorcycle, which promptly tipped over and went sliding down the pavement, throwing up sparks in its wake.

The wolf landed on top of me, just barely keeping a hold on my arms as we went tumbling over and over at the side of the road. We came to a stop twenty feet from where he had struck me, our crashing tumble hindered somewhat by the soft grass and brush that lined the road.

I bucked as we came to a stop, hoping to throw the wolf off me, but it managed to regain its balance just before I could throw it. It pinned me to the ground, gaping maw hovering mere inches from my face.

My coat was tangled around me, restricting my movements. My sword was digging into my side, and there was no way I could draw it, either of my knives, or my gun without disentangling myself first. I kept one arm pressed into the wolf's throat, pushing at it with all my might, keeping it from closing its teeth around my face or tearing out my throat.

The wolf howled, lifting its head for an instant before diving back toward me. My arm gave a little and its gnashing maw closed a hairsbreadth from my nose. It reared back once more and I quickly adjusted, jabbing three fingers into its throat as it started forward. Its howl turned into a strangled, hacking cough.

The moment I felt the wolf's hold on me weaken, I arched my back and used my legs to piston my hips off the ground. The stunned werewolf lost its grip on me and started to fall to the side. It just managed to get a claw down into the ground before falling completely over, halting its movement, but I had enough leverage to buck it off me the rest of the way before it could fully regain its balance.

The werewolf hit hard on its side but was back on its feet just as fast as I was. I came up in a flurry of black leather, my coat unwinding from around me. By the time I reached my feet, my gun was in my hand.

The wolf growled and charged me. I sighted it down, but it was too close. It hit me just as I pulled the trigger, and my gun went spinning from my hand as we fell into another deadly roll.

We came to a stop, me on top this time. The wolf swiped at my face and I was just barely able to jump back before the claws would have taken my eyes. It rolled over and I noticed for the first time that the thing wasn't a mere "it," it was definitely a "he."

The werewolf paused a second to size me up. I was sure he had a grin on that maw of his, though it was impossible to tell. He sure as hell seemed to be enjoying himself if the rest of his body was any indication.

He charged before I could reach for my sword. I dodged the attack, just barely missing getting disemboweled by his razor-sharp claws. Instead of my gut, his claws caught my coat and tore right through the tough leather.

"Goddamn it," I said, spinning around to face the wolf. I was more pissed at him for ripping my coat than attacking me. I was going to have to pay to get the damn thing fixed.

The wolf stood, slavering. I wasn't sure the thing knew what he was doing. He looked hopped up on something, eyes wild and fierce. His coat was mangy, ratted in places, and looked as though he hadn't washed in years, if ever.

It was then I saw the scar in the middle of his forehead. It matched the one I had seen on the passenger's face almost exactly. It was a bare spot, void of fur, and the scar tissue was knotted and pink.

I didn't have time to consider the implications. The wolf came at me hard and I quickly stepped to the side just as he dove for me. He caught nothing but air, and I was able to take the moment it took for the beast to get back to his feet to pull out both of my knives. I didn't wait for the werewolf to turn around. Each knife left my hand almost as soon as it entered it. They spun end over end and embedded themselves in the werewolf's back.

He hardly even noticed.

The wolf turned and howled at me, saliva dripping from his jaws.

"What the fuck?" I said, taking a step backward. The silver should have paralyzed him. Werewolves couldn't shake off silver like that. There was no way the damn thing should have been standing. It was impossible.

No matter how impossible it might have been, the wolf was doing more than just standing. He came at me again, his gait only minutely hindered by the knives in its back. Hell, I wasn't even sure he felt pain.

I drew my sword and fell back into a defensive retreat. What the hell was I going to do against the thing if silver didn't stop it? I was sure if I could manage to cut off his head or scramble his brains with a bullet, the wolf would die. Then again, who knew? Things weren't exactly happening like they should have been as it was.

As the wolf approached, I swung my sword in an upward arc, hoping to catch him off guard and disembowel him. He altered his course at the last moment as if anticipating the move; then he went tearing past and around me.

A mournful howl lit up the night, and it took me a moment to realize it was coming from my attacker. The wolf looked at me, half crazed, half lucid, and then charged again. He was panting, whimpering deep in his throat. Maybe he did feel pain, after all. That was something at least.

I sidestepped the newest charge and kicked something on the ground. It clattered away from me and came to a stop a foot away. I glanced down and saw my gun. Moonlight glimmered over its oiled surface.

I dodged the wolf's next attack, catching his claw with my sword. The wolf dropped back with a snarl, blood dripping from his wounded hand. The silver still didn't seem to be affecting him, but at least he could be hurt.

I snatched my gun from the ground as the wolf flexed his massive, clawed fingers. A drop of dark blood fell from the wound and splattered on the ground. He growled low in his throat and took an angry step toward me.

"Fuck you," I said, raising the gun. I didn't hesitate. I pulled the trigger.

The bullet took the wolf square in the scar on his forehead. He staggered back, and for a heart-stopping instant, I was sure he was going to come right back at me.

Instead, the wolf blinked once, took a step toward me, and then fell flat on his face. He was dead before he hit the ground.

I took a deep breath and lowered the gun. What the fuck had just happened? I glanced down the road, certain the truck would be idling just within sight, but as far as I could tell, it was gone.

But that didn't mean it would stay gone. The other two could be back at any minute to pick up what they would believe to be a well-fed wolf. All they would get would be a dead one. I wasn't about to be here when they returned.

I hurried over to the wolf and removed my knives from his back. I cleaned them on his mangy fur and sheathed them, along with my sword. I kept my gun in my hand and kicked him once for good measure. He was definitely dead.

I wished I could have seen who he had been when

he wasn't a wolf, but that would require him to change. Dead werewolves stayed in whatever form they died in, so this was all I was going to get.

I hurried over to my Honda. It was lying on its side, the engine having died when it hit the pavement. I righted it and winced when I saw the long scrape along the right side where it had hit the ground and skidded. I touched the scratch with my fingertips, baring my teeth at the gouge I felt there. I had half a mind to put another bullet or two into Mr. Furry for damaging my bike, but that would just waste bullets. He was as dead as he was going to get.

The motorcycle started up okay, at least. As far as I could tell, the damage was only superficial, but that didn't mean I wasn't pissed off about it. Someone was going to pay for this. Big time.

I pulled onto the road, paying my dead friend one last glance before tearing out into the night, more pissed off than I had been in quite a long time. I wanted nothing more than to seek out the truck and kill both the driver and passenger, but that would have to wait. I had more important things to do.

16

I parked my Honda behind the backstop of an old ballpark that hadn't been used in what looked to be ten years. Tall grass swayed with the night breeze, and the stench of a rotting animal nearby crinkled my nose. The place was isolated and dark, the perfect place to leave my motorcycle while I scouted House Tremaine.

I was anxious to get moving, but something kept nagging at the back of my mind. It had bothered me all the way to the ballpark, kept prickling just beyond my consciousness. I sat there, trying to figure out what it was.

A car drifted by, its headlights illuminating much of the baseball diamond, though I was well hidden behind the backstop. It would take someone actually shining a light directly on me for anyone to see me there. The night was still young. I had time to think.

It wasn't such a surprise I was attacked on the road. It happened quite often on back roads. Joy-riding wasn't something anyone ever did during the night anymore. It was just as bad as walking down a dark alley in the seediest part of town at midnight. You were just asking for someone to come try to tear your throat out.

No, it wasn't the fact I was attacked. It was the scar.

While I wasn't able to make out exactly what had caused the scars on both the passenger of the truck and the werewolf, I was sure I knew what they meant. Who else slapped marks on their foreheads to let others know whom they belonged to?

"Jonathan." I whispered his name as a curse. The Luna Cult had tattoos right where those scars were. If the wolf and his friends were members of the Cult sent out to kill me, then they might have tried to remove the tattoo in order to hide their identities in case they failed.

But those scars had been old. It was doubtful that they had removed them for this purpose only. So then why had they done it?

I tried to make a connection. I knew my attackers had something to do with the Luna Cult. It would be too big of a coincidence otherwise.

I just couldn't figure out why they would remove their tattoos like that. The tattoo was a mark of pride for the Cultists. For some, it was who they were. I seriously doubted a Cultist would remove his tattoo for any reason.

But then why?

Maybe when I was done with House Tremaine, I would have to pay Jonathan a little visit.

I turned away from my bike and started toward the road. My footfalls sounded far too loud in the eerie quiet of the abandoned ballpark. Not even a dog barked in the distance.

Tremaine's mansion was a few blocks away, nestled

in a quiet section of the rich district. I made my way there, sticking to the darkness provided by trees and gently rolling hills. I moved quick and silent, head on a swivel. Anyone could be out there watching me.

Many of the residential districts of Columbus had undergone severe changes in scenery after the Uprising. Families were booted from their homes so the vampires could take over, live at their leisure. The Major Houses built mansions on sprawling properties that might have at one time been entire neighborhoods. Most of the lesser Houses simply moved into large estates already in place.

House Tremaine was one of the latter. I passed it often enough when working my way deeper into the vampire residential districts. A hill dotted by pines and oaks served as its backdrop. A large pond decorated the front yard and oftentimes, revelers could be seen from the road, slipping in and out of the water before heading inside to feast on blood.

Tonight, however, the pond was as empty of revelers as the sky was of clouds. I could just see the front door where a man was talking with a woman in the spill of light cast by the front window. I couldn't tell if they were vampires, werewolves, or Pureblood servants from where I was, but I was pretty sure they were a part of the House, not some visitors.

The girl turned her face away and the man reached up and cupped her face in his hands. He leaned forward, kissed her, and then buried his teeth in her neck. She writhed against him but didn't fight back. After a few minutes, she slumped in his arms and he carried her back inside.

I felt sick to my stomach. I knew the girl wanted to be fed upon, knew she probably enjoyed it in some sick way. Vampire bites weren't like in all the old stories. There were no pheromones in the saliva or anesthetics or anything like that. The bites hurt. Badly. Only the sick and perverted could enjoy that kind of pain.

I used the trees to slip unnoticed onto the hill at the back of the property. I stayed well back from the House, not wanting to be spotted by the werewolf sniffers I knew would be lurking. There didn't seem to be anyone around, but that didn't mean anything. Anyone could be lurking somewhere in the dark. A vampire could be pretty damn still when they wanted to be.

I kept low to the ground, moving light and quick. Barely a leaf rustled as I passed on vampire-light feet. I did my best to keep a heavy number of trees between me and Tremaine's mansion, but there were still bare patches where walking exposed under the moonlight was inevitable.

Lights were on in nearly every room of the place. From where I crouched behind an old oak, I could just make out the black shape of the driveway that snaked down toward the road.

The mansion sat well back from the road, and a good portion of it was hidden behind large pines. From the road, only the pond and front entrance could be seen clearly. The pond itself was illuminated by soft lights. At the end of the drive, there was no gate, which had always surprised me. Even the Fledgling House I had taken down just a few days ago had had one. Tremaine was either extremely confident or extremely stupid.

Most vampires were like that, really. They thought they were invincible, and oftentimes wouldn't bother using security when something wasn't going on. Only when tensions were high did they use more than a few guards—mostly wolves stuck patrolling the grounds or watching front gates or doors. It made slipping in pretty easy sometimes.

It seemed as though Tremaine wasn't planning on any trouble. There was no one on the roof, and as far as I could tell, no one peeked out the windows to scan the grounds. Without a gate, there was no guardhouse at the base of the driveway, which left him pretty open for attack if someone were interested in taking him down.

Still, I wouldn't want to take a chance that I overlooked something and go charging in without planning ahead first. I scanned the mansion, searching for some way in that didn't look as though it was heavily used.

There was a window with a vent beside it on the side of the mansion in which I was looking. The window was open a crack and there were no lights on inside the room.

I watched the room for a good long while. It looked like it was the laundry room, if the vent was what I thought it was. I was pretty sure that traffic through the room would be light. If nothing else presented itself before long, the laundry room would probably be the best access point. Not too many vampires thought about guarding their soiled sheets.

I remained crouched behind the tree for a good hour more, simply watching. There was a back door, but I doubted going in through any door would be a good idea. Doors tended to be watched. I couldn't risk being seen the night of the assault until things were well under way. Getting caught because I used the wrong entrance would more than likely mean the fighting would start long before we were ready.

At one point, a petite woman who had to have been only half my size came through the back door and walked the perimeter of the yard. She didn't look like she was doing much more than going for an evening stroll, but I knew better. Her hand lingered at her side, fingers ready to draw a weapon that was hidden by a long coat.

It was pretty brilliant, really. Send out the smallest and weakest looking member of the House in the hopes that anyone lurking around the property might take that as a chance to attack. She probably had enough firepower under that coat to stop an army of wolves.

Of course, silver being illegal, it would only stop attacking vamps or wolves for a few moments before they would be on her. My guess was she was either a really powerful wolf or vamp, or she was completely expendable. No House would risk the wrath of the other vampire Houses by using silver.

A nearby rustle brought me to my feet. There was a deep-throated cough, followed by someone spitting somewhere to my right. I tried to see past low-hanging branches but couldn't make out much of anything from where I stood. The oak was a good place to see the mansion. It wasn't so good of a place to spot a watchman in the trees.

I slipped back up the hill, out of sight of the mansion, and waited. I could have probably fallen back all the way to my motorcycle and avoided a confrontation entirely. I might have if it wasn't for the fact I was there to scout the place. Finding out what kind of security they kept was part of scouting.

A few moments later, a stocky man with a pencil-thin mustache strode into view. His hair was parted to either side and greased down like he was some early era gangster. He even wore a tailored suit straight out of the early 1900s. He carried no weapon that I could see, but there was something about him that spoke of a man ready and willing to do some serious violence at the drop of a hat.

I held my breath as he passed. He paused almost directly in front of me, his neck craned to the side as he sniffed the air like a dog. His head swiveled from side to side, his beady eyes scanning the trees all around him.

I slowly slid my hand down to the hilt of one of my knives. If he made so much as a single step more in my direction, I would bury it to the hilt in his throat. I didn't want to do it, knowing that if I did, it would only make things harder in a few days. A dead body tended to draw attention and security would be through the roof.

The man licked his lips and stuck out his tongue like he was tasting the air. He smiled and turned to look down at the oak I had so recently vacated. He sauntered toward it, glancing from side to side, almost casually. He crouched down and touched the ground where I had stood, then looked either way as if trying to determine which way I had gone.

I moved my other hand to my gun. I was dealing with a werewolf for sure. No one else could sniff someone out like that. And even then, only the older, more powerful wolves could do it so easily.

Vampires were hard to scent out, considering they didn't sweat like a normal person.

It was then I remembered my earlier encounter. I would have wolf scent on me, as well as the lingering scent of blood from feeding. It was somewhat comforting to know that he probably wouldn't have smelled me otherwise, though it did little to alleviate my current situation. If he could smell the old blood, then it was only a matter of time before he sniffed me out.

I waited for him to make his move. If I was forced to kill him, I would have to drop him fast. If he warned anyone I was there, things could get ugly in a hurry. If I could kill him in one stroke, I might be able to drag him away and hide the body so that it wouldn't compromise the Luna Cult plan, though I was sure it would raise suspicions if one of Tremaine's wolves came up missing. There was really no way to do this and not cause problems later.

The wolf stood and scanned the trees once more. He withdrew a small case from his coat pocket. It looked to be made of silver, though I knew there was no way it could be. He removed a thin cigarette wrapped in brown paper and produced a match from his coat. The sweet scent of cloves filled the air as he lit and puffed on the cigarette.

He stood there a moment longer, smoking and scanning the area before sauntering back toward the mansion, humming to himself.

I watched him walk all the way back in disbelief. He had scented me out, I was sure of it, and yet he lit the cigarette, obscuring my scent, and walked away. Either he was really bad at what he did, or he was confident

I wasn't a threat. Maybe it was the Pureblood scent that did it.

Once he was out of sight, I headed back toward my Honda. I wasn't sure if the wolf would tell Count Tremaine of my presence or not, but I didn't want to risk it either way. I moved quickly, not bothering to keep as quiet as I should have, knowing I might only have minutes before more wolves would be on me.

Just as I broke cover from the trees, headlights appeared down the road, coming from the direction of House Tremaine. I dropped down into a ditch, pressing myself as close to the ground as I could. The vehicle rumbled past without slowing, and I was on my feet and moving again before the taillights were out of sight.

A few minutes later, I was on my motorcycle. My scouting was done, though I wasn't sure how safe my entry point would really be.

I had snuck into vampire Houses under worse circumstances, so it really wouldn't be any different than before. This actually seemed pretty easy compared with some of my other grand entrances. As long as no one was doing the laundry when I slipped in, I figured there was a chance I might get in unobserved.

Of course, there was one little thing I needed to take care of before settling on any course of action. If I wasn't satisfied with the result, then someone other than Count Tremaine would be feeling the biting edge of my sword.

And this time, I would make sure he didn't survive it.

17

No one tried to stop me as I marched down the sidewalk toward the renovated library that was the Luna Cult Den. The more I thought about my night, the angrier I became. I knew Jonathan had to know who my attackers were. The scar in the middle of my attacker's forehead was too much of a coincidence for there not to be some sort of connection.

I could feel eyes on me as I made my way to the Den. I knew more than one Cultist was probably watching me from the windows or other secure locations around the green. I didn't know how much Jonathan was able to hide within his glamour.

And, of course, Jonathan himself was probably watching me on his little monitor.

I pushed open the doors and strode inside, breaking through the darkness, into the light. Even though I knew the sudden light was coming, it still caused my step to falter, and I had to close my eyes tight against the glare. I doubted I would ever get used to the sudden change from dark to light. Not that I planned on coming to the Den often enough to get used to it.

There weren't nearly as many Cultists lurking around as there were the last time I was there. There were still enough to ensure my good behavior, or at least, whatever good behavior I was willing to impart. If I felt like shooting someone, I would. There was nothing they could do to stop me.

I forced a smile and asked the first person I saw to fetch Jonathan for me. The Cultist could have been no more than seventeen. He held a book in his hands, a finger marking his page. His scalp looked freshly shaved, and whoever had done it hadn't been too careful about it. Tiny nicks marred his head, the scabs still fresh and gooey.

The Cultist stared at me and didn't move. I don't think he knew what to think about my abrupt appearance. I didn't recognize him from the last time I was there.

I looked around the room, my forced smile fading. Faces peered out at me from the railing above, curiosity prevalent amongst them. No one looked like they had any intention of doing what I wanted. Why would they? As far as they knew, I was just some mercenary Jonathan had hired to help them out.

Pablo stepped into view a moment later. He glowered at me from the second floor, his anger displacing the curious faces. "What are you doing here?" he demanded. He started down the stairs, slowly, meaningfully. "You weren't invited this time. You have no business here."

I ground my teeth to keep from saying something rash. I was in their house, their home, and I would have to abide by their rules. For now. I wasn't sure

Jonathan or the Cult had anything to do with the attack. Until then, I needed to keep myself in check.

"I need to speak to Jonathan," I said. "Where is he?"

"Busy."

"Tell him I'm here. He will want to see me." I was pretty sure he already knew I was there. Even if he hadn't been watching his monitors, someone would have told him. People weren't just allowed to waltz on in uninvited like I had.

"He might, he might not," Pablo said, reaching the bottom of the stairs. He stopped with his arms crossed, head lowered so he was just about looking through his forehead to see me. I think he meant it to look menacing. "You aren't wanted here."

The young Cultist on the stairs closed his book and retreated somewhere above, out of sight. He could probably feel the tension in the room as much as hear it.

"Don't make me go in search of him," I said. "I've had a real pissy night, and I don't feel like dealing with your bullshit."

Pablo's expression tightened and he took a threatening step forward. I drew my gun and aimed it at him, using his tattoo as a target. Screw diplomacy. This was the way I preferred to do business anyway.

"I wouldn't come any closer if I were you," I said. The smile that reached my lips wasn't forced this time. It wasn't pleasant either.

"Enough." Jonathan's voice rang out from upstairs. He stepped into view a moment later, the young Cultist close behind. Jonathan's hood was up, concealing the ruin of his face. "How many times is this going to happen? I don't want someone getting killed over nothing."

Pablo glanced up the stairs and bowed his head, cowed. "She wasn't invited," he said. "She walked right in here as if she belonged with the rest of us. She disrespects us."

Jonathan sighed and came down the stairs. "Until further notice, she is to be treated as one of us. She can come and go as she pleases. As long as she abides by our rules and avoids violence, no one is to hurt her." His head turned my way. "Would you mind putting the gun away?"

I had half a mind just to shoot Pablo and get it over with. I didn't like being here as it was, and the rude bastard only made it worse. It was clear he didn't like the idea of treating me as a member of the Cult. Neither did I. I wasn't a werewolf or a werewolf worshipper. I killed them and Jonathan knew it, even if the others didn't.

I put away my gun and lowered my hands to my hips. If Pablo made a move for me, I could have a knife out and in his throat before he closed the distance. I still wasn't sure he hadn't been the one to order the attack on me, so I was itching for a reason.

"Would you follow me to the office?" Jonathan said. He turned without another word.

I followed him across the floor and into the office we had held our earlier meeting. I offered Pablo a quick, satisfied sneer before I went. I couldn't help myself. I could tell my being there was eating at him.

As soon as the door closed behind us, I had the gun back out and had it pointed straight at Jonathan's mangled face. He had removed the hood the moment he entered, so I could see his surprised expression. No one else was in the room.

"Who was it?" I demanded, taking a step away

from the closed door. I moved so I could keep an eye on it, as well as on Jonathan. I didn't know what kind of tricks he might have up his sleeve. I mean, he *was* a sorcerer. Glamours might not be the only thing he could do.

"Who was what?" Jonathan raised his hands, palms outward. His surprise faded and was replaced by a curious look. He didn't seem too concerned about the gun I was pointing at him, which served only to piss me off more. He eased himself down on the edge of his desk.

"The wolves that jumped me. No one but you and your goons knew I was going to House Tremaine tonight, and I find it hard to believe it was just some random attack. Did you send them? Did you think you could get rid of me that easily?"

Jonathan opened his mouth and then closed it without speaking. He went pale and his hands dropped to his sides. He looked utterly stunned.

"What?" I said, my will wavering. Something was clearly amiss.

Jonathan took a deep breath and looked up at me, a pleading look in his eye. "Please," he said. "Put the gun away and I will explain everything."

"Then you know who is responsible for the attack?" My grip tightened on the gun.

"I think so."

I bit my lip to keep from cursing. I had been such a fool to think I could trust the Luna Cult, even a little bit. What did I really expect from a bunch of werewolves and their worshippers?

"It isn't what you think," Jonathan said. "Let me explain, and if you think I intentionally deceived you, I won't stop you if you decide to shoot me."

My aim wavered and then finally dropped, though I didn't put the gun away. "Make it quick."

"First, can you tell me what he looked like?"

"The wolf?"

Jonathan nodded.

"He was hairy. They all look alike."

"Did you see him before he changed?"

"No." I paused. Why was I being difficult? I wanted answers. "The passenger of the truck wasn't shifted, if he was a wolf at all. He had a pretty nasty scar on his forehead. They both did. It was what made me think of you and the Cult." I left out the bit about my silver weapons not working on the wolf. I wasn't so sure I could trust Jonathan with that information.

"Because of our tattoo."

"Yeah, a little too coincidental, don't you think?"

"You would be right," Jonathan said with a sigh. "There was something I should have told you when you were here last. I didn't think it would come up. I see I was wrong."

"And that something is?"

Jonathan slowly stood and motioned toward the chair behind his desk. "May I sit?"

I waved the gun toward the couch. "Sit there," I said. I didn't want him behind the desk where there might be some sort of alarm or intercom.

Jonathan took a seat on the couch without complaint. He sat back and folded his hands in his lap. "There are those who do not agree with how the Cult is run. I believe those who attacked you belong to this group."

"Rebel wolves."

"Only one, originally," Jonathan admitted. "Adrian Davis. He was Simon's second at the time of his defection. He left before Simon was captured, taking quite a few Luna Cult Purebloods with him, most of them the more violent of our members." He scratched the flat part of his head. The sound of his nails on the scarred flesh made my skin crawl. "He believes we should turn all the Cultists, making them werewolves. In doing so, we would have much more power, would be able to take down the vampire Houses on our own if that was our desire."

"Why don't you?"

"Because that is not our way. While many in the Cult wish to be turned, not all of them do. It is one thing to want to be a werewolf and an entirely different thing to actually be one. The reality of the change doesn't really hit many until it is too late to go back. It would be like wanting to be immortal and then finding yourself bored with life. There is no going back."

I frowned. It made sense in a way.

"When Adrian realized we weren't going to change our minds, he left. The Cultists who went with him had been the most adamant about being turned. They tore away their tattoos with their newly gifted claws the moment they were turned. They turned their backs on everything the Cult stood for."

"Which is?"

Jonathan smiled and shook his head. "It is hard to explain. We only want freedom for the werewolves under control of vampire Houses and to provide a place for them to belong. We aren't the heathens many make us out to be."

I still wasn't so sure about that, but I held my tongue. "And if this Adrian defected, then how did he know where to find me? It doesn't make sense he would know if he is no longer a part of your inner circle."

"No, it doesn't." Jonathan looked me in the eye. "I, like you, doubt it was a random attack. This was done with the express intent of taking you out of the equation. Someone must have informed him."

I mulled over that for a moment. There were quite a few people I thought capable of doing such a thing, Jonathan included. I didn't know much about the Cult and its inner workings, but I had a feeling everything was on a need-to-know basis. No one but Jonathan, Nathan, and Gregory knew who I was. It had to have been one of them.

"I didn't think Adrian would become an issue," Jonathan went on. "He turned those Cultists who followed him, and they have pretty much kept to themselves since then. I haven't heard anything about them for at least three months now. I thought they might have left town, found a new place to set up their own version of the Cult."

"It seems you were wrong."

"Indeed."

A tense silence fell between us. I could almost taste it in the air. I really wanted to believe Jonathan, to accept what he told me and walk away, but it was hard. I wanted the chance to take down House Tremaine, wanted it with all my heart, yet I just couldn't force myself to trust him like I needed to. He was a werewolf. Even if we were working together, we were still enemies.

And why hadn't he told me about Adrian in the first place? I asked him as much.

Jonathan smiled bitterly and shook his head. "I had hoped to have heard the last of him, and that we would never have to have this conversation. His issues are with the Cult, not vampire politics. My best guess is he decided to come out of hiding just to mess up my plans out of pure spite. I doubt we will hear from him again."

I somehow doubted that.

Jonathan rose, keeping his hands in plain sight. "Please," he said. "I didn't mean for this to happen. Adrian is my problem, and I will see about taking care of it. I should have told you up front."

"You're damn right you should have," I said, but my heart wasn't in it. Damn. He had convinced me with pretty words that he wasn't involved. I still couldn't say the same for anyone else in the Cult, but I was pretty sure Jonathan had nothing to do with it. It looked like I wasn't going to get to shoot anyone just yet.

"I hope this doesn't affect your decision to help us?"

I thought about it. If someone was tipping this rogue werewolf off, then there was a chance they could tip Count Tremaine off as well. Was I ready to take that chance?

"No," I said, holstering my gun. I couldn't pass this opportunity up. "Not yet anyway."

"Good." Jonathan took a deep breath and let it out in a relieved sigh. "Did you get a chance to find out anything about House Tremaine tonight? Or did this little inconvenience derail your reconnaissance?"

I told him of what I saw, including the wolf who had almost sniffed me out. Jonathan listened as I spoke, nodding all the while. When I was done, he moved to sit behind his desk—after making sure it was all right with me, of course.

"I think we can work with that," he said. "If something happens and you are discovered, the rest of us will do what we can to make sure you can get out. You are there to help us. It is the least we can do."

"Thanks," I said, though I hoped I wouldn't need that kind of assistance.

"I will try to linger near any stairwells I see that might lead down to this room you found. You can try to slip in with the rest of us there. It is risky, and if nothing else, you can say you got lost. They might not believe it, but as long as you look innocent enough, they might just let it slide."

I wasn't so sure the plan would work out the way we hoped. Honestly, it was pretty weak, and any number of things could go wrong at any moment. The window might be down and locked. The door to the laundry room could be locked. Hell, I could make my grand appearance just as some Pureblood worker arrived to dump the latest load of laundry in the wash.

But I agreed to it anyway. While the slightest mistake could ruin everything, it was a chance I was willing to take. I took those kinds of chances nearly every day of my life. What's one more?

Besides, I wanted to take down this Minor House. The more I thought about it, the more I liked the idea, even if it was extremely dangerous. If we could take down House Tremaine, then perhaps I could learn something that would help me in the future. It would be nice to be able to do more than Fledgling Houses and rogues.

After a few more minutes of planning, Jonathan showed me to the front door. Pablo was nowhere to be seen. He was probably sulking somewhere, cutting the heads off dolls or something. I stepped out into the night and stood on the top step, breathing in the fresh air.

I almost turned around and went back inside. I hadn't told Jonathan about the werewolf's seeming resistance to silver. Information like that could be valuable to him, might change things.

Then again, what if he already knew? Maybe Jonathan himself was resistant to the stuff. It would explain why he never seemed too nervous around me and my silver weapons. While I could still cut his head off, the silver might not paralyze him.

Or maybe I was just exaggerating things. The wolf had looked pretty bad off. Maybe his blood had been so convoluted with drugs or a poison of some sort, it neutralized the silver. There were a ton of things I didn't know about the blood taint that could have affected it.

I sighed and allowed myself a smile. Even after my encounter with the werewolf and my near discovery at House Tremaine, I felt pretty damn good. I knew I shouldn't have, considering the danger I was putting myself in, but I couldn't help it. I had survived yet another night. Another werewolf was dead, and if things went according to plan, quite a few more wolves and vamps would be dead in just a couple of days.

I wrapped my coat around me and headed for my scratched Honda, hoping for once the good feeling would last for more than a couple of hours.

18

I got home just before dawn. I barely made it into my bedroom before the first faint rays of the sun touched the sky. I would have been okay with a minute or two in the sun, but more than that would be fatal.

I took a long soak in the tub to help ease the stress that had built up over the last few days. I was absolutely wired after my night. I scrubbed hard at my skin, trying to remove all traces of blood and wolf scent. Even though I couldn't smell it on me, just the thought had my nose twitching.

My leather coat had protected me from the worst of the scrapes during my fight with the werewolf. It was pretty roughed up, but it was still wearable. The tear in it pissed me off to no end. I would either have to get it fixed or break down and buy a new coat.

All I had were a few scrapes and a cut on my palm I hadn't even noticed until I was sitting in the tub. I felt bruised all over, but the pain would fade. It would all heal by morning.

Which was more than what I could say about my

Honda. The motorcycle was scratched up pretty bad; it would take Ethan days to fix it. He had mended worse. Still, it was just one more thing on top of a whole lot of crap I didn't want to deal with.

I had a long time to brood over it, too. The day crept by much slower than I would have liked. I still had to get through another full night and day before heading to House Tremaine with the Luna Cult. In that time, I planned on keeping myself busy. I wanted to learn as much about Tremaine as I could in my limited amount of time. I only wished I could go out and do it during the daytime. It would make the hours much more bearable.

Ethan was up and moving before nightfall, which was a surprise. He had hours yet in which he could sleep. I listened to him get into the shower and get dressed. A few minutes later, he was downstairs, and the sound of a power drill filled the once-silent house. By the time he was finished, night had fallen.

"Come here," Ethan said as soon as I stepped into the living room wearing my leather. I had stuff to do. "I want to show you something." He seemed giddy as he went to the back door and slid it open. I followed him outside.

A square box about the size of a matchbook was on the wall next to the door. The outside light that was usually there was resting on a small glass standing just outside the door. I reached out and flipped open the lid of the box, revealing a smooth black surface.

"A fingerprint reader," Ethan said. It looked like it took all his self-control to keep from jumping up and down and clapping. "I will need to program our prints in later, once I get the rest set up. I will need you for that. I still have to finish all the wiring, so if you have somewhere to be, that's fine."

"Yeah," I said, inspecting the reader. "I shouldn't be too late."

"I think I can have this thing up and running before morning. It should keep out any more unwanted visitors." He grinned. "Unless they cut a hole in the roof or blow us up or something."

Somehow, I didn't think he was joking. "I will let you know when I'm back."

Ethan closed the box and glanced over his shoulder, out toward the trees. He shuddered, and for a moment, I thought he might bolt inside like a scared rabbit.

I went back into the dining room and he followed me, breathing a sigh of relief once inside. He didn't much care for the outdoors. I kept walking, going straight to the basement to gather some fresh weapons.

"Be careful tonight," Ethan said, walking close behind. "I have a bad feeling."

"I will." I grabbed an extra clip of ammo, though I hoped I wouldn't need it. Gunfire tended to draw attention. Tonight, I just wanted to talk. I tossed the knives I had used on the wolf on the table, replacing them with two fresh ones. "I don't plan on getting into any fights tonight."

"You didn't plan on getting into one last night either." He picked up one of the knives and turned it over in his hands. There was a slight nick in it where I must have hit bone.

"I'll be more careful." I checked the clip already in my gun and holstered the weapon. I really wanted to clean it before having to use it, but it would have to wait. I could have grabbed another one, though I would have insisted on checking it as well before leaving anyway. I didn't want to waste any more time than I had to.

I left Ethan to his work and was on the road within minutes. I planned on being home well before morning. I was still uncomfortable about leaving him home alone. Predators could be anywhere, and anyone could break in at any time. And after my latest attack, I was feeling more paranoid than ever.

But Ethan would manage. He always did.

The air was crisp and filled my lungs with a chill that felt blissfully good as it spread through my body. The sky was clear, and the moon dominated the sparkling heavens. We were just a couple of nights away from the full moon and I could already feel it working its lunar magic on me. I felt more alive than I had in weeks.

The Bloody Stake parking lot was full. I was forced to park by the Dumpster, which served to depress me even further about the condition of my bike. It almost looked natural there now, with its horrendous scratch. I could smell stale beer and rotten food even before I shut off the engine, and I hoped it wouldn't permeate the motorcycle's metal. It was already damaged enough. I didn't need it to smell like shit, too.

Inside, all the tables were taken, as were most of the barstools. I scanned the room until my eyes fell on Mikael in his usual spot, girls intertwined amongst his limbs. I went straight to his table and sat down across from him.

"I need a minute with Mikael here," I said.

The girls pouted, but they left when Mikael nodded

to them. He gave one a painful-looking pinch on the ass before turning to me, grinning.

"What can I do for you?" he asked, leaning back. He spread his arms across the back of his booth, exposing a thick gold chain with a large pendant dangling from his neck. "It's been a while since you have employed my services. I was beginning to wonder if you'd forgotten me."

"I need information."

"What kind of information, my sweet?" His accent was thick, almost unintelligible. It probably was to anyone who hadn't spent time with him and learned to decipher his thick drawl.

"House Tremaine," I said, biting back a retort. I hated when he called me that. Anyone else would have been knocked flat on their ass the moment the words left their mouth. But it was Mikael, and I hadn't exactly given him my name. He had to call me something, and "my sweet" wasn't the worst I had ever been called. "What can you tell me about them?"

"What do you want to know?"

"Anything. I have some business with them and would like to know what I am getting into before I take the plunge."

Mikael's smile widened. He might not know I was the one the vampire Houses called Lady Death, but I had an idea he suspected. It was hard not to. Every time I came to him for information on a House, that House was usually in ruins within a few weeks.

"You should be more specific," he said. "I know quite a lot about Tremaine, more than I knew about that last House you asked about. What was it? Paltori?" He smiled and shook his head. "It's a shame what happened to him, yes?" He sighed. "I can give you some information on Tremaine, but I'm not at liberty to say everything I know."

I clenched my teeth. Damn. "He has you in his pay at the moment?"

He shrugged noncommittally. "I can tell you they are a Minor vampire House, though I am sure you already knew that. They are pretty low on the totem pole for being a Minor House, however, and recently, they have fallen even farther. They were bested by another House only a few months ago, so their numbers are much lower than they should be. It was a miracle the other House let them survive." Mikael drank something from a pale blue bottle. It smelled like cat piss. "Other than that, there is little I can tell you."

I wanted to press Mikael for more information but knew it would be useless. Someone from House Tremaine had paid him for information of some sort. He would never tell me who or why and would keep anything they requested from him a secret. Mikael was good that way, though I didn't like the idea of him working for a vampire House. It made my dealings with him seem that much more dangerous.

"Thanks anyway," I said, rising. "Enjoy your girls." I turned to walk away.

"Wait," he said, leaning forward and resting his forearms on the table. "I do have some information you might be interested in. It has nothing to do with House Tremaine, but I think you will find it valuable nonetheless."

I returned to the table, my interest piqued. "And what might that be?"

Mikael sat back and smiled. He glanced at the empty table in front of him and then back to me. I produced a pair of hundreds and slapped them down. When he didn't speak, I added another.

"Someone has been asking around about some-one called Lady Death," he said, his voice low. "Asking a bit too much for their own good, I think."

I tensed and eased down into the booth across from him. I tried to keep my face calm and my voice even calmer when I spoke. "Why do you think I would care?"

"Come on now, my sweet." Mikael chuckled. "I don't know if you are working for her or if you are the bitch herself, but I know you have something to do with her. It wasn't too hard for me to piece together."

I groaned inwardly. I knew Mikael might have suspected, but he was far more sure of himself than I liked. And here I thought I had done a pretty good job of keeping my identity a secret. I mean, Kat Redding was a name that hadn't passed many tongues in quite a long time.

But Lady Death . . . that was a name spoken of quite often amongst the vampires and werewolves. To be connected with that name was a damn near death sentence.

"Let's say I do know her," I said. "What was this person asking about?"

"Asking if anyone knew her true name, knew where he could find her. He was pretty adamant about it. He said he has a job opportunity for her or some such. He wouldn't get into specifics. I think he was . . . unsatisfied by my answers."

"And why are you telling me this?"

Mikael smiled. "Because I like to keep those I work for well informed. It keeps them coming back, yes?" His smile widened. "And with information, comes money, and with money, I have my livelihood. This man refused to pay, so he is no good to me."

A cold chill ran up and down my spine. What kind of information did Mikael have on me? My head would carry quite a hefty sum if someone decided to go through him to get to me.

Thankfully, I trusted him enough not to turn me over to anyone. Not while I was still paying him at least.

"Can you tell me who was asking?"

"He didn't give me a name."

"What did he look like, then?"

Mikael ran his fingers through his hair. They came away wet and sticky. "You do seem quite interested. Maybe I do have you pegged. Perhaps if I ever need any information on Lady Death for my own personal database, you might be willing to trade it for my knowledge. There are certain things I know that might come in handy if ever you choose to take me up on the offer." His eyes were glimmering.

"Maybe," I said, though I doubted I would ever take him up on it. I didn't want anyone to know any more about me than they already did. "If I do know this Lady Death the vamps are so afraid of, that is."

Mikael looked around the room and leaned forward. "You would be well served to take care of yourself," he said softly. "You aren't exactly Pureblooded yourself."

I clenched my fists under the table and counted slowly to ten. Mikael knew too much. Anyone else would be dead.

"What did this guy look like?" I spoke slowly and even managed to force a smile. "Just tell me so I can get out of here. I have some things that need taking care of tonight."

Mikael's smile faded. "I don't need to tell you." He spoke at a near whisper. "I can show you."

I quickly stood and looked around the room. No one was watching Mikael and I do business. Most of the tables had three or four occupants, drinking and laughing amongst themselves. There was a medley of faces at the bar itself, but if any one of them was the questioner, they didn't show it in any way.

It wasn't until my eyes fell on a table in the far corner and its lone occupant seated with his back to me that I knew. All I could make out from where I stood was his long brown hair and square shoulders. He wasn't drinking anything, wasn't eating anything. He was looking out the window as if he were waiting for someone.

"Exactly," Mikael said, following my gaze. "What are you going to do now?"

I stared at the man a moment longer before answering. Loud music blared out over the speakers nailed to the walls in all corners of the room, drowning out individual conversations. Bart stood at the bar, paying me only casual glances—most likely making sure I didn't start any more trouble. The patrons were all involved with their own drinks and friends, oblivious to anything but whatever was in front of them.

I smoothed down my coat and brushed back my hair. How did this guy know to find me here? I guess I would find out.

I glanced down at Mikael and gave him a smile that wiped the grin clear off his face. His eyes widened a little and he scooted farther back in his seat.

"I'm going to introduce myself," I said, my voice cold, calculated. "It would only be polite."

19

My coat swished around my ankles as I approached the man sitting alone by the window. I walked slowly, never taking my eyes from the back of his head. Eyes followed me as I passed. Soft snickers and whispered words barely registered on my conscience. I had a vague impression that Bart was watching me with a disapproving glare.

I wasn't exactly sure what I was going to do when I met the man. He was asking about me but didn't know what I looked like, what my real name was. He only knew me by my reputation, which meant he could be anyone. There was a chance I could get information out of him, pretend to be someone else and hope he let something slip. If he was working for someone, I wanted to know who.

If he was working alone, he would be easy enough to handle. He was just one man and I was a practiced killer. I wouldn't be able to do it here, of course. I could wait for him to leave The Bloody Stake and follow him back to whatever hole he crawled out of and finish him there. It would be quick and as painless as I could make it.

Then again, if Mr. Questions was working for someone, I would have to be a whole hell of a lot more careful. He might not be the only one watching for me. He might not truly be alone either. Any one of the patrons could be working with him. Hell, half the bar could be for all I knew.

I took a wide berth around the table and sat down across from him. He looked at me without blinking, as if my joining him was exactly what he had expected. His face was made up of harsh features, dominated mostly by a beak nose that jutted from his face like an ice pick. Eyebrows too narrow and too angled to be natural looked to be painted on above his eyes. His cheekbones formed shelves under those dark blue eyes, giving him a decidedly haunted look.

"I knew you couldn't resist," he said. His eyes drifted over my shoulder and back out the window. The curtains were slightly parted, giving only a partial view of the parking lot. "I knew if I waited here, you would eventually show up."

"And who in the hell do you think I am?"

He smiled, revealing a jagged collection of teeth. Shit. Those teeth could mean only one thing.

I was dealing with a werewolf. An old one.

"I had heard a certain lady of the night frequented The Bloody Stake. I learned there was also a high probability that she would be coming here quite soon." His gaze turned back to me. "I presume you are she."

It felt like a hundred spiders were crawling up and down my back. The man's gaze was so penetrating, I was sure he could read my every thought. I no longer cared why he was looking for me or whom he might be working for. This guy was a danger all his own.

I ran my hand over my mouth to gather myself before speaking. I wouldn't show fear. It had been a long time since anyone had been able to unsettle me so much with just a look. This guy was more powerful than I had given him credit for at first. Then again, I *had* been looking at the back of his head. It's hard to judge someone when you couldn't see their eyes.

"Okay," I said. There was no point in denying who I was. He would probably sniff out the lie. He probably had seen me with Mikael and put two and two together. "What do you want? Who are you? Who are you working for?"

"I am here because I have a proposal for you." His gaze shifted from my face to my hands, which were now precariously close to my weapons. He didn't seem too concerned. We *were* in a no fighting zone, after all. "As for who I am working for, that is my business, not yours. If you decide to take me up on my proposal, then we shall discuss the benefits of our cooperation and what it means to those who now lay claim over me."

The night had just begun and I had already had enough of it. I motioned for Bart to bring me a drink. He was already watching me, so I figured I might as well put him to work. I kept both my feet firmly planted on the floor as I shifted my chair around so I didn't leave my back exposed to the window, while at the same time keeping myself as far away from the wolf across from me as I could.

He had me in a precarious predicament. There was no way I could watch the window and the door and him all at the same time. He probably sat where he had for that reason alone.

"What kind of proposal are you offering, Mister . . . ?"

"Davis." He gave me such a sinister smile I just about drew on him then and there. This guy gave me a serious case of the heebie-jeebies. "My name is Adrian Davis. I'm sure you have heard of me by now."

If my blood hadn't run cold long ago, it sure as hell would have then. It was like ice tearing through my veins, and it took all my self-control to keep from lashing out at the first mention of his name. This was the bastard who had sent the wolf after me. He was a rebel Luna Cultist who had refused to play by the rules, making up his own rules instead.

And here I was sitting across from him in a crowded bar where violence was met with a shotgun blast to the head. My night was just getting better and better.

"I know who you are," I said, barely concealing my anger. I was damn near frothing at the mouth.

"Jonathan has probably already told you enough lies about me to set you on edge, to make you wary of me. I can smell your anger, your fear. You are a vampire, correct? I hadn't believed it possible at first. A vampire walking into the Luna Cult and coming out with her head intact? It almost defies belief."

Bart arrived with my drink and set it down in front of me. He glanced at Adrian before giving me a warning glance. He walked away slowly, mumbling to himself.

"I only know your name," I lied. "Jonathan didn't tell me much. What else do you know about me?"

Adrian smiled bitterly. "Not enough, obviously.

Let's just say my information has been limited as of late. I know only what I was able to gather from the streets and a few choice informants. Not good ones either."

"What do you want with me?" I took a drink from my bottle. It was cold and would have been refreshing if I could taste anything other than the bile in my mouth.

Adrian looked past me again to stare out the window. I wanted to turn around and see what he was looking at out there, but I didn't want to turn my attention away from him. He was dangerous. He might not abide by Bart's rules. He could have my head off before Bart could pull his gun, I was sure. This guy seemed the type.

"I know of what you have done to the vampire Houses during the last dozen years or so. I know how many vampires and werewolves died by your hand alone. I know you have been asked by the Luna Cult to assist in extracting Simon from a Minor House. House Tremaine, to be exact. He wants you to risk your life, send you into a risky situation in which there is a good chance none of you will survive."

"That's my business," I said, acid on my tongue. I hated that this guy knew so much. I'm used to keeping my business my own.

"All I ask of you is that you join me. Forget the Luna Cult. Forget House Tremaine. They are minor concerns in the greater picture."

I set my bottle on the table. "How so?"

"Tremaine is a mess, the Luna Cult is fractured. They pose almost no threat to the city as a whole, despite what they want you to believe."

I didn't say anything. I wasn't so sure he was right

about the Luna Cult. Any type of organization that large was a threat to someone.

"I could use someone like you," he went on. "I have had enough of the politics, all the bullshit that goes with the Cult and the vampire Houses. With you, we could take down any House we choose. We could make *them* serve us. This city could belong to us."

"High aspirations, I see."

"There is no sense in striving for mediocrity."

"If you wanted me to join you, then why did you send your goons after me?" I asked, unable to keep the anger out of my voice. I leaned forward, clutching my bottle of beer as if I was going to hit him with it. I wasn't so sure I wouldn't.

A faint smile played on Adrian's lips. He closed his eyes and sighed, seemingly unconcerned by my aggression. "Look at your little encounter as if it were a test. I needed to make sure you were who I thought you were. I needed to make sure you could handle yourself in stressful situations, situations that you didn't plan for. You did well against impossible odds."

"I wouldn't call a single wolf impossible." I nearly growled the words. "I have handled more than that often enough."

"But not wolves as special as Eugene, you haven't."

I opened my mouth to ask him what he was talking about, but then it hit me. That wolf had been damn near impossible to kill. Silver hadn't bothered him. He had seemed half crazed, willing to die for the cause, whatever that cause might be. What had Adrian done to him to make him that way?

Before I could pose the question, he turned his dark gaze back to me, pinning me to my chair with the power in his eyes. "Do you accept my proposal? Will you join me against the vampire Houses? Will you cast aside our petty differences, turn away from your current life, and seek to achieve something greater?"

Petty differences? I wanted to laugh in his face. The guy had sent someone to kill me and he called it petty. He was as crazy as the wolf trapped in the cell below the Luna Cult Den if he thought offering me the city would sway me away from my chosen path.

"I don't think so," I said. "You can take your proposal and shove it up your ass. It stinks enough to be right at home." I leaned forward. "I don't make deals with people like you. I kill them."

"This opportunity will not come again," Adrian said. "If you continue down your current path, you will end up dead." He paused and stared long and hard at me before finishing. "Or worse."

"I don't take threats lightly either. Who the fuck do you think you are to threaten me?" I was shouting now. The entire bar was watching us. "You know who I am, what I am. You know what I am capable of."

Adrian shrugged and leaned back in his chair. He gazed out the window as if I no longer mattered. Maybe in his mind, I didn't. He had delivered his proposal and I had rejected it. It seemed like I was no longer a concern.

"It's a shame," he said after a long moment. "We could have done so much together, you and I. You are far more pleasant to look at than they say. Some paint you as a demonic whore with horns and a tail." His eyes flickered over to me and I saw a hunger deep within them. It made me physically ill to imagine what might have fluttered through his sick mind just then. "I am sure we will meet again."

I rose, taking the last as a dismissal. My hand trembled near my gun and I considered risking having Bart blow my head off with his shotgun. Just as long as I got the satisfaction of killing this asshole before I died, it would all be worth it.

I took a deep breath and spun to face the door. No, I couldn't risk getting myself killed over something so petty. I didn't look around at all the gawkers. I stalked out the door of The Bloody Stake, leaving the wolf to sit at the table. I could feel his eyes following me through the window.

I went to my bike and started it up, cursing all the way. I tore out of the parking lot in a flurry of tossed gravel. The night had turned out to be one major disaster. What the hell was I going to do about Adrian? He knew who I was, what I looked like, and I hadn't killed him. I shouldn't have even approached him in the first place.

I knew I could have waited outside the bar for him to come out, but I had a feeling he had no intention of leaving until first light. He was a werewolf. He could wait as long as it took. I couldn't.

I sped down the street as if I were being chased by a pack of demons. I just wanted to get home, to spend some quality time alone with my own thoughts. I needed to figure out what I was going to do now. Tomorrow, I had to deal with House Tremaine. After that, I would need to figure out what to do with my newest problem.

My week was shaping up to be a real son of a bitch.

20

Ethan was waiting on the front stoop when I arrived home. The garage was open and I parked inside before going to meet him. He had a cool glass of lemonade in hand and was staring off in the distance. His face was covered in dried sweat, and he smelled of perspiration and hard labor. His He-Man shirt was stuck to his back.

"How's the work going?" I asked, leaning against the side of the house next to him. I knew he didn't like the outdoors all that much, so it was rare when I got to talk to him under the night sky. I looked to check out his work and was surprised to see nothing different. "Haven't gotten this far?"

Ethan took a long pull from his lemonade glass and shuddered before turning to face me. "I'm pretty much done," he said. "I've got some wiring to do downstairs, but in general, we can get this thing set up."

"Done already? That was fast."

He smiled, though it was a nervous one. He glanced over his shoulder toward the trees. "There wasn't much else for me to do tonight. I figured I could get it done and over with."

I studied the door, searching for any sign that the lock was in place. Everything looked just the same as it had when I had left. "So, where is it?"

"Flip up the doorbell."

I reached out and wiggled the doorbell. The button rested on a matchbox-sized square. It always had, if I remembered correctly. It didn't want to move at first, but then I found a tiny little switch at the bottom of the base. I flipped it to the right and the doorbell base came up with ease. Underneath was the shiny black surface of the fingerprint reader. I lowered the doorbell back in place, smiling at his ingenuity.

"I figured it would be best to hide it," he said. He seemed to almost have forgotten the wide-open world behind us. "If we want to give the impression that two young lovers live here, hi-tech electronics would look out of place." He reddened at mention of our cover story.

"Does the doorbell still work?"

"It does," he said. "The old keys will still fit in the locks, but they no longer unlock the doors. If anyone tries to use a key or pick one of the locks, an alarm will go off in the basement, the lab, and in each of our bedrooms. You should be able to hear it all over the house."

"The wiring you need to do is inside, I take it?"

"Yeah." Ethan used the condensation from his glass to moisten his hand, then wiped the dried sweat from his face. "I so need a shower."

"When did you leave to get all of this stuff?" I asked, checking out the reader. It was just like the back door. I imagined there would be one at the door connecting the kitchen and garage. "I didn't think anyone would be open this late and I didn't hear you leave this morning."

Come to think of it, I had never seen him leave the house. Deliveries were never made to the front door. So where did he get all his supplies? I doubted he had an endless supply of electronics and silver in his lab.

Ethan started at me, mouth slightly agape. The question seemed to have struck him dumb.

I stared right back. Normally, I didn't ask him questions about how he did what he did. I had no idea where he got the illegal silver to work on my weapons, or how he knew how to modify my gun and motorcycle. I had taken him in when he was a teenager. I just figured he was some sort of savant. As far as I knew, he had the knowledge of the world trapped up there in his head.

"Out with it," I said, crossing my arms. After the day I had, I wasn't in the mood to be screwed with.

"I, uh . . ." Ethan looked back toward the trees like he expected something to burst out of them at any moment. "Can we go inside?" he said. The worry was clear in his face.

"No diversions," I said. "Spit it out."

"Um." He ran his fingers through his hair. He looked about ready to explode. "I really think we should go inside for this."

"Is there someone out here? Is that why you are so nervous?" My words came out a bit more heated than I wanted.

"I don't know. There could be." He gave a nervous laugh. "But that's not the problem."

"Then what is."

"I don't want you to kill me."

I froze at that. Kill him? Why in the bloody blazes would I kill him? Without Ethan, I wouldn't be where I was today. He might not want to admit it, but he was as important to what I did as my ability with my weapons. Without him, I doubted I would have survived this long.

Not that I would ever tell him that. He did have a bit of an ego when it came to his work. Telling him how important he was would be like filling an already inflated balloon to well past bursting. I didn't want to have to scrape up the spillover.

I must have had a look on my face that didn't sit well with him because he blanched.

"Really," he said. "It's not as bad as you might think. There's just sort of . . . I don't know . . . an unspoken law against it, you know?" He tried to smile but failed miserably. "Don't hurt me."

"Why would I hurt you?" I asked. I was doing a pretty good job of keeping myself from screaming in frustration. Ethan could be difficult at times, but he never flat out refused to tell me anything. It was beyond annoying.

"Well, see . . ." He turned away, turned back to me, and then settled on staring at the house over my shoulder. "I sort of don't do this all on my own."

Suppressed anger bubbled in my gut. I just barely managed to hold it in check. "You let someone else in the house? Is that why you never let me in your lab? Do you have someone locked up down there?"

"Yes and no," he said, his face flaming. "There's no one down there now and I don't lock them up.

And it isn't a person, so you don't have to worry
about them telling anyone else about us."

"Then what are you talking about?" I couldn't contain it anymore. I was shouting. "Is there or isn't there
someone helping you?"

"There is."

"Who?"

"Um." Ethan chewed on his lower lip. He looked
all the world like a teenager again, worried about
disappointing an already disapproving parent. "Beligral."

"Who?"

"Beligral."

"I heard you the first time. Who the fuck is Beligral?"

Ethan's eyes widened at my language. I rarely
cursed at him, if ever. "He's the one who taught me
how to do what I do."

"That isn't very helpful. Who. Is. Beligral?" I spoke
slowly, hoping he got the point that I wasn't in the
mood to be pissed with.

"A demon."

"A what?" I shouted. I couldn't help myself. "You
have a demon trapped in the basement?"

"He's not trapped," Ethan said, rushing his words.
"I summon him."

"And that's supposed to be any better?"

"Well, it means he goes away when we're done."

I stared at him, shocked to my core. I never would
have guessed Ethan of all people was summoning a
demon. In my house, no less.

"He's pretty easy to work with," he went on. "He
told me how to make the silver weapons, supplies me

with the silver as well. He also brings me the stuff I need. It makes it convenient so I never have to leave."

"And what does he get in return."

"We, uh, haven't specified that part of our deal yet."

I rolled my eyes and fought down the urge to punch him. A demon. He was summoning a god-damn demon in my basement, using demon technology to modify my stuff. Suddenly, I didn't want my weapons touching me anymore. I turned and threw open the front door, fuming.

"Kat . . ." Ethan began, but I wasn't listening. I stormed into the house, tearing off my belt and shoulder holster. I threw them on the couch as I passed. I headed straight for the stairs and went down into the sitting room.

The room was dark, the fireplace cold. I consid-ered lighting a fire, but I just didn't have the energy for it. I threw myself down into a chair and stared into the empty fireplace, trying to make sense of what I just learned.

I couldn't see how it was possible. Ethan had always been a good kid, had always been kind and friendly to me. Sure, he had his issues—we all did—but summoning a demon wasn't something a good kid did.

Of course, he was no longer a kid. It had been years since I rescued him from the vampire's grasp. He was a grown man now, able to make his own de-cisions. Should I really be pissed at him for doing something that has helped me more than anything else had? I mean, without the weapons, the modified gun and motorcycle, I would be barely scraping by. Hell, I would probably be dead.

When had he started? That was a question I couldn't answer, that I wouldn't ask him. He had started modifying my things almost as soon as I had taken him in. He could have been summoning the thing long before I ever met him. Maybe that was why Count Valentino hadn't drained him as soon as he captured him.

"Fuck," I mumbled. I wanted to scream it from the rooftops. I knew I should have. What Ethan had done was irresponsible. And dangerous. He was putting his life, as well as my own, at risk for a few cool gadgets. I wasn't sure it was worth it.

The sound of his tentative footsteps on the stairs came from behind me.

"Kat?" he said, his voice low, abashed. "I'm sorry. I never wanted you to know."

I continued to stare at the fireplace, though my anger was waning. I might not agree with his methods, but summoning the demon had helped. I couldn't deny that.

"If you want me to leave, I will."

"No," I said, "I'm fine."

"Are you sure? You seemed pretty pissed back there."

"I'm fine," I said through gritted teeth. Okay, maybe I wasn't *fine*, but I wasn't ready to punch a hole in the wall. That had to count for something. "I was just surprised."

He breathed a sigh of relief and came the rest of the way into the room. He sat down in the chair next to me, his empty lemonade glass still in his hand.

"I'm sorry," he said. "I don't like having you mad at me."

"I'll get over it."

"I know, but I'm still sorry."

We sat in silence for a few minutes. I could hear him breathing next to me. He sounded frightened, as if he thought my calm exterior was hiding a burning rage that would be unleashed on him at any moment. I didn't blame him. I had to have looked terrifying outside.

"Maybe you should stop summoning him," I said. "We have what we need now. We don't need him any longer."

"I can't," Ethan said. He sounded utterly defeated. I wondered what kind of hold this demon had on him. "I've tried to stop before. It's like a drug. I can't help it. And when I don't summon him, things . . . happen."

"What sort of things."

"I can't talk about it," he said, his voice so low even I had a hard time hearing him. "Bad things."

I wanted to know more but didn't press him. Pressing him would only upset him more. Hell, it would probably upset me too. "All right."

"All right?"

"We move on," I said. "We can worry about Belphagor or whatever his name is some other time."

"Beligral."

"Close enough." I sighed. As if having the Luna Cult asking for help, a rogue wolf sending people after me, and dealing with House Tremaine wasn't enough. I just couldn't handle dealing with a demon. Not then. Maybe not ever.

"So, what now?" Ethan asked.

"We go on as we were."

There was a moment of silence before he spoke again. "Is something else bothering you?"

"I don't know what you mean."

"You're tense. And it's not about Beligral. Did something happen while you were gone?"

"I didn't get the information I was looking for," I said. "My source couldn't divulge what he knew."

"And?"

"And what?"

"And what else? Your source has come up short before. I can tell there is more to it than you are letting on."

I sighed. I really didn't want to drag Ethan into this. Did he really need to know a rogue werewolf had propositioned me? It seemed more my business. What good would it do if he knew?

Of course, I never liked keeping things from him. Even though I was still pissed about the whole demon thing, it *was* Ethan. If I didn't tell him and Adrian showed up with his goons, he would need to know what to expect.

"I might have a problem."

"What kind of problem?"

"The big hairy kind."

"A wolf after you?" he asked. "Someone you couldn't put down?"

"Sort of." I hated talking about it. Just thinking about it irritated me. "He knew who I was as soon as he saw me."

Ethan's eyes widened for a second before he regained his composure. I had to hand it to him, he took the news pretty well. "Did he know your name?"

"No, he knew I would be at The Bloody Stake, though. He was the one who sent the wolf after me last night. He knew I was Lady Death." I cringed speaking the hated name.

"So, if you didn't kill him, what did he want?"

I told him about my conversation with Adrian. I didn't leave anything out. Since I was telling him about it, I might as well get it all out now. There really wasn't much to say. It only took me a couple of minutes to spill the entire story.

"Did you consider his offer?" Ethan asked when I was done.

"No. Why would I? He tried to have me killed."

Ethan relaxed visibly. I hadn't even noticed him tense up. "Good," he said. "It's never good to work with the bad guys."

I gave him a sharp glance. He was grinning.

"Maybe I will send you out to gather information next time," I said. "It might do you good to get out once and a while, to see the world. The world isn't simply made up of good guys and bad guys anymore."

"I would, but sorry," he said, rising. "Agoraphobe, remember?"

"Right." I couldn't help but smile. Just talking to Ethan could raise my spirits. It was why I would never put him out, no matter what stupid thing he did.

"I'm going to take a shower," he said, heading for the stairs. "I smell like donkey doo." He laughed, though it was clear he was still upset about our little spat, but he was at least able to joke. That was good. I didn't know what I would do if ever I drove him away with my anger. I mean, he had survived this long summoning and working with a demon. How bad could it really be?

21

The day came and went, and before I knew it, I was on my motorcycle, heading for the Luna Cult Den. After so many consecutive nights of clear skies and brisk breezes, I was surprised to find a light mist in the air. Dark, heavy clouds obscured the moon, depositing their moisture on the denizens of the sleepless city. It would have been refreshing if it hadn't been such an ominous sign.

I didn't bother parking any closer to the Den than the last few times I had been here. The alley seemed as safe a place as any to park, and after walking the roads a couple of times, I knew it would be futile to attempt to drive them. I didn't mind walking in the light rain. It gave me time to think, to make sure that this was actually what I wanted.

My pace quickened as the rain picked up. The wind was blowing cold, sending a chill straight through my leather and into my bones. It was still early by vampire standards. That didn't make the empty streets seem any more welcoming. In fact, it made the walk that much worse.

I was sure someone was watching me. It held a strange sort of comfort knowing that if something were to jump out at me, someone from the Luna Cult might show up and help me take care of the problem. Not that I thought I needed help. It was just nice to know it was there.

I picked my way through the dark streets, empty alleys, and around rundown buildings until I was finally standing on the green before the Luna Cult Den. It looked as dead and empty as always, though I did see one Cultist hurry into the building at my approach. I never even saw a light shining through the open door before it closed.

The rain pattered on the sidewalk as I made my slow way toward the front door. I knew what I was doing was stupid. As friendly as he seemed, Jonathan was still a werewolf. The closer I came to the Den, the more it seemed like a bad idea. I knew I should turn around, knew it would be the smart thing to do.

Before my fears caused me to change my mind, I was standing in front of the doors to the old library. I didn't even have a chance to knock before the doors opened and two Cultists I didn't know stepped out to greet me. Neither looked happy about the job, but they were at least civil. It was more than I could say about my big Mexican friend the last two times I was there. Thankfully, he didn't seem to be in attendance tonight.

The Cultists led me through the bottom floor to the stairs. I followed them up the stairs and to a pair of large gilded doors on the second floor.

The doors were clearly a new addition to the building. It didn't match the décor of the library at all. They were carved with images of men turning into werewolves, some in the process of shifting. Others were fully human, but something about the way they were carved gave them a definite wolfish appearance. Surrounding them were fully shifted werewolves, their mouths open as if howling at the window at the top of the door. It was circular, and was colored and stained to look just like the full moon.

My Cultist guides bowed their heads to me, though I noted their eyes never left my face, before scurrying off to perform whatever duties they had been assigned. The doors remained closed, and there was no one outside them to direct me inside. The entire Den seemed empty, in fact. I had barely seen anyone on my short trip to the second floor.

I looked around once to make sure I hadn't over-looked anyone, then shrugged. The two Cultists hadn't knocked for me, so I supposed I was supposed to take the hint and go in myself. I pushed open the doors and went in, my right hand lingering near the hilt of my sword.

The doors opened up into a well-furnished room that looked as though it had been yanked straight from some extravagant mansion and dropped into the middle of the old library. Bookshelves lined one entire wall. The books on them were old and leather bound. Large couches faced each other at the center of the room. They were covered in red velvet and silks hung over their backs, giving them a soft, flow-ing look. Pillows decorated the couches, each match-ing the décor of the rest of the room.

I took another step in and the doors swung slowly closed behind me. A wet bar stood to my left in an alcove I hadn't been able to see from the doorway. A man in a tux stood behind the small counter, his hands behind his back. He never even flinched as I entered. He stared straight ahead, not seeming to be aware of anything going on around him at all. He was bald, of course, and the Luna Cult tattoo in the middle of his forehead looked old and faded.

A moment later, doors on the opposite end of the room opened and Jonathan strode through, beaming confidence. His black pinstriped suit was ironed and looked stiff and uncomfortable. He didn't wear his usual hood, and the flat portion of his head and his mangled features stood out in stark contrast to the rest of his garb. Nathan and Gregory stepped out behind him, similarly dressed.

"I'm glad you decided to come," Jonathan said, moving to stand at the center of the room. "I feared you might not show up, or if you did, you would come so late we wouldn't have time to properly dress you." He ran his hand over the silk decorating one of the couches. "I have considered how we might get you inside without setting off anyone's internal alarms. You have this way about you that screams vampire, and I fear Count Tremaine will pick up on it too quickly for us to get in place."

I didn't move forward to greet him. I held my ground at the door, still unsure I was doing the right thing. Even though I loved my leather, I felt extremely underdressed. I had no intention of wearing anything else. This was a kill mission for me, not a banquet.

"What do you have in mind?" I asked, scanning the room. There didn't seem to be any more doorways, though I hadn't seen the one Jonathan had come in until the door had opened. It was worked into the design of the room so that it was nearly invisible.

Nathan and Gregory stood flanking Jonathan. Gregory had his usual grin in place and he gave me a quick, almost childlike wave. It might have been cute if it hadn't looked so awkward on him. Nathan glowered at me, like usual, and I gave him a smile that set his teeth to grinding.

"I was thinking that instead of having you slip in and risk being discovered apart from the group, we can disguise you as one of us."

"You already suggested that. I get a fake tattoo and try to blend in once I meet up with the rest of you. I would prefer to keep my gear on, so if you have a robe or something I can wear over my things, that would do." Nathan smirked as if what I said was amusing. I ignored him. "I'll go in through the window like planned and meet up with you afterward."

Jonathan waved his hand in dismissal. "I don't believe that will work."

"Why not?" Anger flared up in my words. I hated it when plans changed at the last minute. I usually spent a long time working on my plans and kept to them as much as possible. Too many changes too close to go time tended to make things fall apart that much faster. People died when things went wrong. I had no intention of dying.

"There is one detail about you that will not fit in with the rest of the Cult." He ran his fingers through what remained of his hair. "Unless you are willing to shave your head to fit in, you could not pass for one of the Luna Cult. And you definitely would never be able to pass yourself off as a werewolf."

I shook my head. "Not happening." I wasn't one

of those girls who spent hours messing with her hair, but I was still attached to it. I seriously doubted the bald look would suit me.

"That is why I decided to come up with another way." Jonathan took a step forward but stopped as Nathan laid a hand on his arm.

"Don't," the big man said between clenched teeth. "I don't trust her. We should forget about all of this and do this on our own. She is too much of a risk."

"A risk that we must take if we expect to keep our freedom," Jonathan said, never taking his eyes from me. "Let me go, Nathan, or I will be forced to leave you behind."

Nathan's jaw tightened. He looked like he was going to say more, but instead, he simply removed his hand from Jonathan's arm and resumed glaring at me.

Jonathan brushed his sleeve where Nathan had touched him, smoothing out the nearly imperceptible wrinkles. "If you would let me, I would like to cast a glamour on you. I will disguise you so that no one will be able to recognize you as anything but a member of the Cult."

I stiffened. "I don't think so." Magic was something I didn't want to have anything to do with, and with good reason. It wasn't something I could touch, something I could see. Something I could kill. It was the force that defied all normal explanation, something I couldn't fully wrap my head around no matter how many times I thought about it.

Those with the power were able to do things I could only dream about. They had power that could rarely be controlled by normal means. The strongest of the sorcerers could kill with a single word, a flick of the wrist. Those men and women were hunted down, extinguished as soon as possible. They were a threat, a threat that not even the vampires could control.

Some of those sorcerers rose to power early on when the vampires and werewolves originally took over, thinking themselves safe in the changed world. They viewed themselves as equals to the vampires, even wanted to become monsters so that they would share in their supposed immortality.

Instead, they found themselves destroyed by their own magic and the monsters they thought would protect them. Now, only a few scattered sorcerers still existed. Most could only do harmless charms anymore, fearing anything more powerful would draw attention to them. I was sure there were still powerful sorcerers tucked away somewhere, waiting for the moment to strike.

My thoughts drifted to Ethan and his demon. What kind of power did I have lurking in my very own house?

The thought made me shudder. And here Jonathan was, wanting to cast a glamour on me. It was probably one of the simplest and most harmless things a sorcerer could do to another person, and yet just the thought of him working magic on me made my skin crawl.

"It will only be for the night," he said, taking another step forward. "As soon as you no longer need it, you can drop the glamour yourself just by thinking about it. Your will alone can shatter a glamour cast on you. There is no harm in allowing this. The glamour will hide your weapons, as well as your features, allowing you to enter without anyone noticing something is amiss."

I shook my head again. "I don't trust you. I don't trust anyone who can do what you do, let alone anyone who is what you are."

"Understandable."

I wracked my brain for a way out of this. I knew Jonathan would probably demand I go through with it before he allowed me to leave. Something about the way he looked at me, the way he stood with his back straight, face set in a determined stare, said he had made up his mind about this long before I arrived. If I wanted to take down the Minor House with him, I was going to have to accept the glamour.

"What will this involve?" I asked at a near growl. I really didn't want to do this, but what choice did I have?

"All you need to do is relax. When you feel my power flow over you, accept it. If you fight it, it will be repulsed and the glamour will not stick. It is important you stay calm." He smiled. "Think happy thoughts."

Yeah right. I rested my hand on the hilt of my sword just to let him know how little I liked this and closed my eyes. There was no way in the world I was going to be able to relax. I was in a room with three werewolves, and I was actually going to let one of them do something to me. What in the hell was wrong with me?

Jonathan whispered something I couldn't quite make out and a flow of power washed over me. It was like a heavy, wet breeze that left no moisture on my skin, disturbed not a single hair on my head. It flowed over my body, covered me head to foot, and I had to fight to keep from tensing and backing away.

The hair on the back of my neck prickled. It felt like

something much akin to a spider web was brushing against the nape of my neck, over my face and hands. My fingertips tingled and twitched on their own accord. My eyelids fluttered and I opened my eyes to see Jonathan standing before me, a small half smile on his face.

"That wasn't so bad, now was it?" he said, motioning me toward a mirror on the far side of the room.

I gave him a wary look and moved to the mirror. It was built into the wall and was full-length, giving me a good view of myself. I stepped in front of it and couldn't stifle the gasp that rose to my lips.

I recognized my face, or at least part of it. My mouth was pretty much the same, if not a little fuller, a little redder. My eyes were the same eyes I had seen looking back at me in hundreds of mirrors before, but my cheekbones seemed higher, sharper. My dark hair was gone, replaced by a shining, shaved scalp. The mark of the Luna Cult stood out in the center of my forehead like a beacon. The skin around it was red and irritated, as if it had just recently been added. Heavy-looking robes hung around my shoulders, and there was no hint of my weapons within its folds.

"The eyes are the hardest," Jonathan said, coming to stand next to me. "There is something about the eyes that refuses to be changed, especially when the glamour is cast by someone with my limited power."

I questioned how limited his power really was, considering he had cast a glamour over the entire Den, as well as the one now disguising me. I wondered if he had to maintain each, using a chunk of his power to do so, or if once they were cast, they would stay up until dispelled. I thought about asking him but changed my mind. I could ask about it later if we survived.

"And no one will know it's me?" I asked, unable to keep the awe out of my voice. I had never been under the effects of a glamour before, and the results were startling.

"As long as they don't have someone specifically looking for glamours, no one will know."

"And if they do?"

Jonathan frowned and shrugged. "Then we will be found out before stepping through the door."

"And what about my weapons? Are you going to tell me they won't have someone patting everyone down, using metal detectors? Will the glamour protect against that?"

"No." Jonathan looked troubled as he surveyed me in the mirror. "I didn't think of that."

"Then I think our original plan stands." I noted the fall of his features, and for some reason, I felt guilty about it. Had he thought we might go in arm in arm or something? "But the disguise will be good once I am inside. If anyone sees me, I can play stupid and hopefully they will just think I got turned around somehow."

Jonathan nodded, but he still looked disturbed.

We both looked at my reflection in the mirror for a couple of moments longer. Nathan was clearly irritated by the delay. I could see him moving around in the mirror, fidgeting with his suit and tie, glaring at me whenever he thought I wasn't looking. Gregory seemed right at home, content to wait until the end of the world if that was what it took. Did anything ever faze him?

"Why don't you use a glamour on yourself?" I

asked, moving my arms and legs to see how the robes flowed around me. They looked perfectly natural, taking up the same amount of space as my coat. It was eerie how close they matched up. "Aside from darkening the hood you usually wear, I mean. Why not put on a different, unmarred face?"

Jonathan met my eyes in the mirror and held them as he spoke. He was all seriousness, as if the question was one he asked himself a thousand times a day.

"I don't hide who I am. My face reminds me of what I was. If I forget my face, I might revert back to the way I was before. I cannot have that."

His voice was silky smooth despite the slight slurring of his words. I hardly noticed when he drew closer.

"I told you before that you made me who I am today. Your actions changed my life forever. Why should I hide from myself?" His hand rested on my shoulder. "While I hide behind my hood, I do so out of respect for others. Many cringe at the sight of me. I refuse to hide behind a glamour that would make me someone else, something different. I cannot go back to that life."

I wasn't so sure I understood, but I nodded anyway. Regardless of how he did it, he was still hiding his face. Just because one way was veiled in darkness and the other would change the structure of his face, it was still deception. He was the same man, regardless of how he looked. Maybe it made him sleep better at night knowing he could change his features and mingle with the rest of the world and simply chose not to.

I stepped away from the mirror and headed for the door I had come in. Jonathan's hand slipped away.

"So," I said, stopping with my hand on a doorknob carved in a pretty accurate representation of the moon. They took their lifestyle pretty seriously here. "Shouldn't we get this show on the road? Time's a wasting and I would like to get home before dawn."

22

We went over the plan once more after meeting with the rest of the Luna Cult that would be joining us. Aside from Nathan and Gregory, Jonathan was the only werewolf going. I didn't know if that meant they were the only three in the entire Cult, or if they were the only ones he trusted. I kind of hoped it was the former.

The other Cultists were Purebloods, devoted to the Cult and the rescue of their Denmaster. They were the ones Jonathan trusted the most. I just hoped they wouldn't get in the way once all hell broke loose. They didn't look to be trained fighters like I hoped they would be.

I was just thankful Pablo hadn't been included in the group. I'm not so sure I could have held off from killing him if he started making trouble. I was too stressed as it was without having to deal with his attitude. Nathan was bad enough.

The plan was pretty straightforward. The Cult was going to go in through the front door, and I was to wait until the guards were focused on them before making my move to the window. The hope was that they would be too busy making sure the Cultists were unarmed and wouldn't notice me slipping in.

Once inside, I was to make my way toward the sound of the Cult. Jonathan assured me they would be making enough noise that I wouldn't have any trouble finding them. If all went well, they would linger at the staircase they hoped would lead down to my location and I could join them without being noticed.

Of course, there was no telling if they would even pass the right staircase. No one had been inside the actual mansion, so as far as we knew, our paths wouldn't even cross. And it was no sure thing I would be able to get in and to them without running into someone along the way. I had a bad feeling this wasn't going to be as easy as it sounded.

If I ran into someone, I would have to do my killing quietly. It wasn't exactly my forte, but I could manage it if I had to. I doubted our plan would work out like planned anyway. It sounded far too easy for it to work out right. Something always went wrong with any plan, no matter how carefully laid out. I knew that. I'm pretty sure Jonathan did to, but it was better than nothing.

This had all the makings of a disaster.

And it was the Luna Cult's skin that was on the line the most. If they were blasted the moment they stepped through the door, I could just turn around and call it a night. What did I care if the Cult ended up broken and scattered?

That was the dig. For some reason I couldn't quite pinpoint, I did care. Maybe it was the trust Jonathan had shown me, the willingness to let me do my thing even though he knew there was a good chance I would kill him when it was all said and done. Maybe it was the fact I was given this opportunity to take down a Minor House when I would never have stood a chance alone that had me cheering for their success.

Whatever the reason, I didn't like the feeling. I shouldn't be thinking anything but dark, blood-red thoughts about the Luna Cult and its head were-wolves.

We separated and I went to get my motorcycle. I would follow the others most of the way to House Tremaine, then break off once we were close. I would use the same path I took two nights ago to get to the side of the house. From there, I could wait for Jonathan and the others to get to the front door. If anything went wrong, he would shout a warning and I could get away. It was nice he was willing to keep me out of danger like that.

It kind of gave me the willies.

The rain was coming down hard by the time I got to my Honda and found the others in black, unmarked cars. Jonathan, Nathan, and Gregory shared a car, while the other Cultists crammed into two other beat-down vehicles. They started driving the moment I came into view. I fell in behind them, keeping my distance just in case someone from House Tremaine decided to meet them down the road.

The drive was cold and slow. Gregory drove the head car, and he obeyed every traffic law in existence. I was beginning to wonder if he was intentionally stalling when we finally turned on the street where House Tremaine was nestled. I let them drift even farther ahead and parked behind the backstop at the old abandoned ballpark.

No other cars passed as I made my way up the hill and into the trees. The leaves and branches created a canopy that kept most of the rain off me as I worked my way toward my watch point. I was thoroughly drenched, and the leather of my pants had all but glued itself to my thighs, making movement more difficult than I would have liked.

It wasn't until House Tremaine came into view that I noticed I was being followed.

I wouldn't have noticed it at all if it hadn't been for the snap of a branch and the faint glow of a cigarette poking out from behind the edge of a tree. Whoever was following me obviously didn't care if I noticed him. I could almost hear him chuckle from his hiding place.

I pretended not to notice my stalker. I was supposed to be a Pureblooded Cultist, not someone trained in stealth and death. I kept going as I had been, though I allowed myself to make a little more noise than I normally would have, until I reached the large oak that had provided me protection the first time I was there.

I scanned the grounds and saw that the lawn was pretty empty, which was surprising. I thought someone would have been out there by now.

Jonathan had yet to arrive. They had probably stopped a little ways down the road to give me time to get set. When he did get there, I would have only a few minutes to get into position.

There was another snap of a branch, but I kept my eyes on the grounds. I used my peripheral vision to keep an eye out for my stalker, waiting for him to make his move. I closed my hand around the hilt of my sword and wondered how it looked through the glamour.

A moment later, my stalker strode into view. He

didn't even bother to keep himself concealed as he approached. I turned to face him, keeping my hand on my sword, but didn't draw. I didn't want to break my cover quite yet. I still might do this without having to fight him.

"Well, well, well," he said, tossing the cigarette on the ground. He stamped it out with his foot. "Look what I found. I thought I smelled something fishy." He took a deep breath and let it out in a pleasurable sigh. "The things I could do for you would make your toes curl."

The wolf was smiling. He was the same man I had seen two nights ago. He was wearing a wide-brimmed hat now, pulled down over his eyes to keep out the rain. Otherwise, he looked the same as I remembered, right down to his suit.

"No thanks," I said, smiling. "I've had my fill of fat, arrogant men."

His smile faltered and died. "Now, what would a member of the Luna Cult be doing out here like this?" he asked, his voice going cold. "Shouldn't you be with your friends down there?"

I glanced over my shoulder to see Jonathan step out of his car. He was taking his grand old time, adjusting his jacket and tie, talking to each and every Cultist. He was still giving me time, and I would be damned if I wasn't going to be in position when I was supposed to be.

"I'm just making sure everything goes as planned," I said. "I won't get in the way. You can go back to lurking around in the dark."

The stocky man with his little pencil mustache shook his head slowly as he strode toward me. His hand went to his waist and I expected to see him pull a gun or knife. That wasn't what he was going for.

"I think we can do something else to pass the time," he said, unbuckling his belt. "I'm sure Tremaine and your friends can handle things between them just fine without us watching on. There is no reason for us to get wet without reason."

I kept the revulsion off my face and held my ground. My hand shifted from the hilt of my sword to the two daggers at the front of my belt. It probably looked to him like I was reaching for the glamour-made cord around my waist.

The werewolf smiled and unzipped his pants. He ran a hand over his face and used his index finger to smooth down his mustache. It didn't improve his looks in the slightest.

"You barely have a smell about you," he said, sniffing the air. "The rain does that, you know. I would love to see if you smelled like a girl I once knew. You look like her. She died happy."

I let the wolf close on me. It was all I could do to keep from attacking him with every word out of his mouth. Everything about him oozed slimeball.

He left his pants hanging loosely around his hips, thankfully leaving everything else tucked away. He twisted his hat on his head, centering it before stepping in close.

I pressed my back against the oak tree and waited for him. I moved my right hand down to join the left, each hovering just inches from the hilts of my two silver knives. I had to wait for the right moment before acting, or else I might blow the whole plan. If he cried out, the game was over. And if he shifted, things could get ugly fast.

The wolf glanced down to where my hands hovered and he smiled again. "Let's see what's under those robes, now shall we?"

"Let's," I said as I drew both knives. I lunged forward and the wolf opened his arms as if he thought I was throwing myself at him in lust. The satisfied look on his face turned into one of shock as the first knife penetrated his groin. The second came at him from the side and embedded itself in his throat, cutting through his jugular and severing his windpipe all in one fluid motion.

I darted to the side before the blood could spurt out on me. I yanked both knives free as I moved, ducking under his flailing arms. I didn't want to get his blood on me, nor did I want him touching me. Having his scent on my knives was bad enough. Any wolf with a good nose would smell it. I had to hope the rain would wash enough of the scent away to keep them off me until the time came for me to reveal myself.

He looked at me, his mouth working, and he dropped to his knees. He clutched at his groin, ignoring the wound in his neck as if it were unimportant. He gurgled something inarticulate before falling face-first into the wet earth.

He was still alive and it could take him some time to die, but he wasn't going anywhere. Werewolves might be more resilient than normal folk, but that didn't mean they didn't die. He was losing a ton of blood and couldn't breathe. The silver from my knives would effectively paralyze him, make his wounds slow to heal, so that he would die well before recovering.

I didn't have time to sit around and watch him die, however. Normally, I would have cut off his head to be sure, but to do so would mean getting more of his scent on my weapons. I couldn't risk it.

I wiped my knives clean on the wet grass, well away from where the dying wolf's blood pumped out onto the ground. He reached out toward me and I jumped back, barely keeping myself from screaming. His eyes glazed over and he fell limp, though the blood kept coming.

I watched him as I cleaned the knives, waiting for him to move again. I was surprised he had managed even that much with the silver running through his veins. Most of the time, a wolf wouldn't even be able to twitch after being struck by a silver weapon. This guy had been pretty damn strong. I was glad he had never shifted.

My thoughts drifted to the night before and the wolf that hadn't seemed to be bothered by silver. I shook off the thought before it could fully form. I seriously hoped werewolves with a resistance to silver weren't becoming common. If they were, I was in for some serious trouble.

I sheathed my knives when they were as clean as I could get them, wishing I had thought to bring spares. I could have left the dirty ones behind a tree and gone in with fresh ones, but there was no going back now.

With one last glance at the dying wolf, I started picking my way down toward Tremaine's mansion, hoping luck was with me and no one would find him before the real action began.

23

The rhythmic thump of a dryer came from the open window. It was the only sound.

I breathed a sigh of relief as I rested my back against the wall. I had worried the room would turn out to be something other than a laundry room. The smell from the vent was oddly sweet and cloying. It blew warm air on my back, a pleasantry in the chilly rain.

I waited there, crouched down, my hand ready to draw any one of my assortment of weapons the moment someone came into view. I leaned toward the front of the house to better hear what was going on.

Jonathan's voice could just barely be heard over the sound of the dryer. He had to have been close to shouting, because there were pauses in which I was certain someone else was speaking, but their voice was lost over the thumps coming from the laundry room. What were they drying in there? It sounded like cotton-covered bowling balls.

I scanned the yard for movement while I listened. I was pretty sure I hadn't been spotted during my mad dash across the expansive lawn. While I hadn't seen anyone spying on me, there were quite a few windows on that side of the house. If anyone had happened to peek out just as I started running, they couldn't help but have seen me.

Since no one had shouted any warnings, I figured I was safe enough. I turned my attention to the laundry room window as the voices died down. It swung outward and upward, just enough to cool the room inside, but not nearly enough to permit the rain to make much more than a tiny splash on the inside sill. I pulled the window the rest of the way up, wincing in anticipation of its screech.

It went up with ease, sliding up and locking in place with a faint click. There was just barely enough room for me to slip through, but even then it would be a tight fit.

The laundry room was dark. No one moved within the confines of what appeared to be a rather spacious room. It was dark enough that even with my night vision, I couldn't quite make out everything inside. I was reminded of the glamour on the Luna Cult Den and wondered if maybe Tremaine was employing a sorcerer of his own. If so, it was a pretty weak one, since I could still see light coming out from beneath the door on the far side of the room. That was something Jonathan's glamour would have hidden.

I slithered my way through the opening and found the washing machine just under the window. The top was closed, giving me a perfect stepstool in which to get down. I took my time, making as little noise as possible, though I doubted anyone would have been able to hear me even if I had fallen in and crashed down on top of the machine.

I leaped from the washing machine to the vinyl floor, my feet making barely a sound. A laundry basket filled with stained white sheets lay on the floor next to the washer, and about a dozen other similar baskets sat against the far wall. I couldn't tell if their loads were clean or dirty from where I stood, but I could still smell the blood that stained the white sheets nearest me.

My stomach did a flip and I had to fight down the urge to investigate them further. I had no idea whose blood it was, but the smell of it was almost overpowering. More than one person had died on those sheets, that's for sure.

I turned my attention away from the clothes baskets and focused on the door. It was the only exit from the room, aside from the window, and it was closed. The faint light that seeped beneath it just barely illuminated the floor around the door and a hamper standing open to its left, but little else. The light had probably been what had screwed up my night vision, casting just enough of a glow to keep it from kicking in like it should.

I pressed my ear to the door. I couldn't hear any sounds coming from the other side. I listened for a good thirty seconds anyway to be sure, then took hold of the polished doorknob, turning it so slowly it would be nearly imperceptible to anyone not staring directly at the door.

The laundry room gave way to a sort of game room dimly lit by a ceiling light. The light cover was heavily tinted, giving the room a certain ambience that spoke of long nights of curling smoke, beer-stained shirts, and hours of poker or pool. A pair of pool tables sat relatively close together in the middle of the room. The balls were already racked, and a pair of pool cues lay crossed on each of the tables.

There were three dartboards on the opposite wall. The darts speckled the board haphazardly, as if whoever had played last wasn't very good. A pair of arcade games that looked to have come straight from the '80s sat side by side along another wall. Their screens were lit up with flashing title sequences and brief clips of game play.

To my right was a card table with four chairs pushed in around it. Cards lay facedown in front of each chair, as if whoever had been playing had been called away suddenly and had left their cards in place while they took care of whatever needed doing. Piles of chips of varying sizes sat beside the cards, giving validity to the idea.

That meant someone was probably coming back before long. I had no intention of sticking around long enough to meet them.

I didn't have time to completely look the room over. The place was huge. I probably could have fit the entire upstairs of my house in this single room and had space to spare.

There were two other doors in the room. One was to my right, just past the card table. The other was on the far side of the room. Both were closed.

I assumed one of them went down into a basement. My best guess was that it was the one to my right. Just past that door was a stairway leading up to the next level of the mansion. I hurried across the room and took up position by the door. I stopped to listen for a moment; hearing nothing, I moved on to the stairs. I peered around the corner, taking only a quick glance to see if anyone was standing guard, but there seemed to be no one there.

In fact, I saw almost nothing. The stairs were made of polished wood, and there was no carpet or rug to soften my footfalls. Other than that, I could see hardly anything. The room above was far too spacious. I caught a glimpse of a light fixture on the ceiling and that was it.

The sound of footsteps caused me to jerk back. It took me a moment to realize the footfalls weren't coming from above, but rather from the closed door at my back.

"Shit," I muttered as I darted to the other side of the door and pressed myself against the wall. I couldn't tell if the door swung in or out, but I hoped it would swing toward me so it would block me from sight long enough that I could jump whoever was coming before they saw me. If I was forced to fight, I needed to make it quick. A single scream would alert everyone in the mansion that something was wrong.

I drew a knife from my waist nice and slow. The footfalls came steadily nearer. As far as I could tell, it was only one set, which was a relief. If I had to deal with more than one person, I wouldn't be able to keep one of them from shouting out an alarm.

I drew my second knife just in case. There was no telling if what I was about to face was a vampire, wolf, or Pureblood. If it was one of the first two, I could be in for a serious fight.

The footfalls reached the top of the stairs and the doorknob jerked to the side violently as if whoever was coming was in a piss-poor mood. He was grumbling to himself, words I couldn't make out over the loud crash of the door as he threw it open and it slammed against me.

A thick, heavily ringed hand reached around the side of the door, inches from my knife-wielding hand. He thrust the door closed behind him, never turning to look my way.

He started for the stairs but stopped after only a pair of steps. "Goddamn it," he muttered as he started to turn back around.

I shot forward, my knife taking him under the chin, nailing his mouth closed. His eyes widened and he tried to choke something out through the sudden bubbling of blood that filled his mouth. He fell forward into me and I had to brace myself against his weight. He wasn't a small man in the slightest. He had to weigh all of three hundred pounds and was at least five inches taller than me.

I bore his weight, not wanting him to slam me against the door. I doubted anyone would recognize the bang for what it was, especially after the way he had slammed it closed, but I didn't want to take the chance.

The man reached out and grabbed the hair at the back of my head and yanked as hard as he could. My head jerked back, but I didn't relent. I twisted the knife in his jaw and heard bone snap. I struck out with my other knife, ramming it deep into his ample stomach. I sidestepped the gush of blood, not wanting to get any more on me than I already had.

The man's grip loosened and he fell to his knees. I tried to bear as much of his weight as I could as I helped him down to the ground. He still hit with a sizable thump. I jerked the knife in his belly upward, sending his entrails spilling out onto the floor. He grunted something and then fell on his face, unmoving.

I was almost positive the man had been a werewolf. He had fought too hard to be anything else. A normal Pureblood would have gone down after the first knife thrust.

Again, I was reminded of the wolf from the night before. I looked down at my blood-smeared weapon. Maybe Ethan's demon silver wasn't as pure as it used to be.

Of course, I wasn't entirely sure the guy had been a wolf. He hadn't shifted. He could have just been an extremely resilient Pureblood, one the vampires trusted to watch over them during the long days.

I wiped the blade on the man's shirt. He was dead either way. It didn't matter who or what he was.

My other knife was trapped under his bulk, still embedded in his jaw. I considered flipping the big man over, but the sound of a large group moving at the top of the stairs brought my head swinging around. I could hear Jonathan's voice clearly.

I didn't have time to work my knife free. I would have liked to have hidden the body, taken all my weapons, and done my best to remove all the blood. I had to hope that while the Cult was in the house, all hands would be upstairs with the rest of the action.

At least I hoped everything was taking place somewhere upstairs. If that group were to come down here now, there would be no stopping an all-out brawl.

I sheathed my knife and tried to clean my hands on the dead man's clothes. He had died pretty quick. I was definitely leaning toward him not being a wolf.

The blood didn't want to come off, but I did the

best I could. Somehow, the blood didn't get on my clothing, which was a relief. With the way things had been going, it wouldn't have surprised me if he would have gushed all over me, ruining any chance of me slipping in unnoticed.

Still, the smell of blood was going to be strong on me regardless. It was on my weapons, on my hands. I just had to hope the wolves of House Tremaine wouldn't be sniffing around too much. It was going to be hard enough to blend in with the others as it was.

I quickly went back to the base of the stairs, keeping myself well out of sight. The group appeared a moment later, a procession of wolves and Cultists. I didn't recognize the first two men to walk by. They were probably some of Tremaine's wolves. They passed by the stairwell without a pause. Jonathan called out to them to stop, but they acted as if they hadn't heard him and kept walking.

Jonathan stepped into view next. His suit was undone and he had a ruffled look about him. They must have frisked him pretty hard to make him look that disheveled. He glanced almost nonchalantly down the stairs and gave me a quick nod before continuing on at a slow, deliberate pace. Nathan and Gregory were at his heels. Neither looked my way.

I hastened up the stairs, hoping no one could smell me coming, let alone hear me. I stayed low to the ground, taking the stairs at a crouch. My boots made a faint thump on the stairs, but it was nothing compared with the shuffle of feet of the Cultists making their slow way past.

None of the Purebloods looked my way. They were each wearing outfits exactly like mine, though they probably smelled a whole hell of a lot better. I knew this façade wasn't going to last. Not with all the blood.

I reached the top of the stairs just as the bulk of them passed by. I crashed to the floor, making as big of a scene as I could.

"Sorry," I mumbled, just loud enough for everyone to hear. The wolves in the lead had stopped and turned to see what the noise was all about. "Tripped over my robe."

They grunted and continued on. I glanced behind me, doing my best to look abashed, and saw two more of Tremaine's wolves behind the Cultists. It was the woman who had walked the grounds the night before, looking as dainty as ever, and a man I didn't recognize. They glared at me, but gave no indication they had noticed me coming up the stairs.

I fell in with the Cultists and kept my head low, taking in the sights with my peripheral vision.

The mansion was clean from top to bottom and looked as if it had been specially prepared for the occasion. All the lights on this floor were on, and a pair of servants in tuxedos stood against the wall. I knew they were probably the Pureblood staff. Their collars were high and their coats covered their wrists, hiding what I knew would be scarred flesh from countless bites. Light music played in one of the rooms ahead. Large double doors separated us from the music, and it was clear that was where we were headed.

The closer we got to the doors, the more I relaxed, certain everything would work out as planned. At least this part of it anyway. Once we were in the presence of Count Tremaine and his vamps, I doubted things would go as Jonathan hoped. Vampires weren't exactly the most predictable of creatures.

The wolf escorts stopped at the double doors, the rest of us falling in silently behind them. One of the wolves rapped three times on the heavy wood and then stepped back, his hands behind his back. The doors weren't carved like the ones back at the Luna Cult Den, but they were still impressive. It would take a train to knock them down.

A soft voice called out for us to enter and the two wolves opened the way. It looked as though it took all their strength to budge the sturdy doors. Maybe not a train, then. More like a nuclear missile.

The music swelled as the doors opened and we were led into a well-decorated ballroom. Metal rings lined all the walls, sturdy-looking things that had the hairs on the back of my neck standing on end. I knew what they were for. I had seen plenty of vampire ballrooms to know that the rings were where they kept captives, wolf and Pureblood alike.

A half-dozen wolves stood to either side of the door, and a handful of men and women who were clearly vampires of the House stood facing the doorway, making a sort of aisle that led to a thronelike chair sitting on a small dais at the far end of the room.

Seated on the chair was Count Tremaine himself. He was bare-chested beneath a leather jacket that fell all the way to his knees. It covered most of his black leather pants. He wore rings on nearly every finger and had about five or six necklaces dangling on his well-muscled chest. Knee-high boots decorated with buckles and zippers were propped up on the back of a kneeling nude woman who was chained to the throne like a dog. She was clearly a Pureblood. Dried tears marred her delicate features, but she took her role as the royal footstool with more dignity than I could have mustered.

I tore my eyes from the tableau in front of me and chose to examine the two men standing to either side of the throne. The first was tall, unassuming, and dressed in what could only be called a sort of casual formal attire. He had a smug grin on his face that reminded me of Gregory. His lips were stained red from a recent feeding. As far as I could tell, he was just another vamp of the House, though a high-standing one if his position at Tremaine's side meant anything.

It was the other man who caused my breath to catch in my throat, my eyes to widen.

Standing on Count Tremaine's left, his flat-eyed stare examining the group of Cultists ushered into the room, was Adrian Davis, Luna Cult defector.

24

I kept my head low even though I was still veiled by Jonathan's glamour. I didn't know how good Adrian's eyes were. Could he pick me out just by my eyes? We hadn't talked *that* long. Would he even think to look? He knew Jonathan could cast glamours, so it wasn't too much of a stretch to think they had prepared against such a thing at the doors. Was I even safe now?

"Welcome," Count Tremaine said. He didn't budge from where he sat. He looked down on us, his face full of disgust. It was clear he didn't think too highly of the Luna Cult. "Hopefully you have come to a decision in regard to our proposition. I do hope it will be mutually agreeable to both our sides. I would hate to end our talks so . . . suddenly." He grinned, exposing perfectly white teeth.

Jonathan strode to the head of the group. "Where is he?" he demanded. "I will not discuss any treaty with you until I am sure Simon is okay."

"Treaty?" Tremaine laughed. "Who said anything about a treaty? You will bow to me. You will call me

Lord and Master, and you will do as I say when I say without question. You will have some freedoms, in that I will not force you away from your precious Den, but you are still mine. Treaty? No, you will be my servants just like every wolf of this House is mine to call."

Jonathan's jaw tightened, but he managed to keep from saying something that would damn us all. "Just let me see him," he said, his voice as tight as his jaw.

Tremaine sighed and sat up, taking his feet from the back of the nude woman. She visibly relaxed but didn't rise. By the way she moved, I guessed she had been doing this for years.

"Who are you to make any sort of demands?" Tremaine said. "I will not allow you to tell me what to do, even now. Do you agree to join with House Tremaine, to meld our might with your resources? That is all you need to say."

The small gathering of vampires moved around us, clearing space as if they expected a fight to break out at any moment. With the way things were going, I wasn't so sure it wouldn't.

Nathan started to step forward, seemingly empowered by the movement of the vampires. Jonathan waved him back before he could do something that would set someone off. I wouldn't put it past Nathan to initiate the fight before we were ready.

"I only want to see Simon to make sure his blood is not already tainted," Jonathan said. "It is a mere request, one that should be easy for someone of honor to fulfill. I'm not asking you to set him free."

I had to hand it to him, Jonathan had balls. Not many people would talk to the Count of even a Fledgling House like that, let alone the Count of a Minor

House, albeit one of limited strength. Most Counts would kill him where he stood. Count Tremaine only smiled, though it was clearly forced.

"Let's say I show him to you," he said. "What will you do for me then?"

"If he is alive and untainted with vampire blood, I will do what I came here to do."

"And that is?"

"I will do whatever it takes to make sure Simon and my Cultists leave here alive and in one piece. Our lives are more important than my dignity. I will bow to you if that is your desire. I will do whatever pleases you."

"Even take the Oath?"

Jonathan hesitated only an instant before nodding. I heard the sharp intake of breath as if Nathan was about to object, but like a good dog, he held his tongue.

Tremaine leaned back on his throne and propped his feet up on the girl's back again. He stroked his chin with one hand and drummed his fingers on the arm of his throne with the other. A smile slowly spread across his face.

I was itching to act. Diplomacy wasn't my thing. Even though I knew Jonathan was holding face just long enough to get Simon into the room, I still hated the act. How long before Adrian noticed something was amiss? How long before the smell of blood roused suspicions? We were on borrowed time, and I knew if things didn't hurry along, someone would either smell the blood or find the bodies I had left in my wake.

It would only take seconds. If I could just move closer to the throne, I could leap onto the dais and

embed a knife in Tremaine's throat before taking
out Adrian. I was sure Jonathan and Nathan could
handle their own long enough for me to take them
out, as well as any vamps that got in my way. My hand
moved involuntarily to the hilt of my sword. I had to
clench my fist tight to keep from grabbing it.

As if sensing the movement, Adrian's head perked
up. He frowned and scanned the gathering of Cultists,
me included. I dropped my eyes and looked hard at
the back of Gregory's knees. I felt Adrian's gaze pass
over me and glanced up just long enough to see
his eyes fall on Gregory. The corner of his mouth
twitched as if he were concealing a smile.

No one seemed to notice his sudden interest in us.
Hell, I wasn't even sure Jonathan had even noticed
Adrian standing there. It was odd he hadn't reacted
to the presence of the traitor. Had he known Adrian
would be here? If so, I really wished he would have
told me. I'm not much of one for surprises, especially the bad kind.

"No," Tremaine said at last. "I don't think it would
be in my best interest to bring the pup out in the
open where anyone can see him. Things happen
when all the cards are played. Think of him as my
ace in the hole. If you do not swear the Oath, then
he will be tainted and set free at the Den to kill everyone. If you bow now and pledge yourself to me, I will
release him to you. This is not a debate. You will do
as I say or die where you stand."

Tension flowed around the room like a living
thing. Even the Pureblood Cultists could feel it. They
tensed and looked around as if expecting an attack
from all sides at any moment. The wolves along the
walls were dressed to shift, their clothes loose and

disposable. At a single word, they could be on us in the blink of an eye.

Jonathan glanced back at me. His gaze lingered only a moment before shifting to the Cultists. I knew what that look meant, and I didn't like it.

Wait.

He turned back to Tremaine and raised his hands out in front of him, palms up. "You already checked us for weapons. You already scanned us for magic, for my glamours. What can it possibly hurt to let me see Simon? I only want assurance he is alive. In doing so, you will ease my fears, the fears of the rest of the Cult. The others will be more willing to join you if they know they can trust you."

Tremaine closed his eyes and sighed. "I tire of this," he said. "I want my dogs to be obedient. You might pose a problem down the road if I cannot break you of this most annoying habit." He opened his eyes and laid a seething gaze on Jonathan. "But all dogs can be broken. I will give you your bone this time, but I will be taking it out of your hide later. There may be something you can do for me."

Tremaine motioned toward the double doors. The vampire at his side leaped off the dais and stalked past us to the doors, grinning at us like we were sheep.

Shit. If they were holding Simon downstairs, then Mr. Vamp here was going to stumble right into the body I had left lying right in front of the damn door. I should have taken more time to hide the body, found another way to reach the group. I had been careless and my carelessness, might cost us the element of surprise.

I couldn't let him find the dead man. Not yet. We

still could get the jump on them. What did I care if the Denmaster was lost? As long as we killed Tremaine and the vamps in his House, I would call it a win.

I started to reach for my sword and gun, but Adrian's voice rang out over the ballroom, stilling my hand.

"Wait," he said, his voice slow and controlled. He took a step forward, a faint smile on his lips. He glanced back to Tremaine and said something only the Count could hear before stepping from the dais.

"Davin, wait," Tremaine said, leaning forward. He drummed his fingers on his nude footstool's back, giving the gathering of Cultists a withering look.

The vampire stopped at the double doors and turned to face the room. "Count?"

Adrian moved toward the Cultists. They stood clustered around me like meat waiting to be slaughtered. They were going to get in the way, I knew. These weren't fighters.

He didn't even give Jonathan a passing glance as he moved past him to where Gregory and Nathan stood. He sniffed around each of them, though he paid special attention to Nathan, who was growling deep in his throat.

"What's the delay?" Jonathan asked, facing Tremaine. He sounded panicked. "I just want to see Simon, not have my people molested by this turncoat."

Tremaine dug his fingernails into the nude woman's back. She let out a small hiss of pain but didn't recoil from his touch. "You can wait until we make sure everything is in order."

I sucked in my breath as Adrian approached. His eyes scanned the gathering of Pureblood Cultists, lingering on me twice as his gaze swept over us. My hands were already halfway to my weapons, but I was hesitant to draw. If I were to reveal myself now, there was a good chance Adrian would use the Cultists as shields. The Purebloods would die before I could get a clear shot.

Son of a bitch. Why had Jonathan brought them along in the first place? He could have brought tougher looking Cultists, or more wolves, or something. Hell, did he even have to bring so many? They could do nothing but die.

Adrian shoved aside a pair of Purebloods who were making a valiant effort to keep him from working his way into our midst. They stood no chance against him. They staggered to the side and he stepped between them, taking a deep, long breath as he came to stand in front of me.

He closed his eyes for a heartbeat, took another breath, and let it out slow and controlled. He opened his eyes, stared directly into mine, and smiled.

"Hello," he whispered.

My hands plunged into my coat just as he jumped back.

"They have a vampire with them," he said almost casually. He grabbed a Pureblood Cultist and pulled her back with him as he retreated. She let out a cry and tried to fight him, but he was just too damn strong.

My weapons came out and I let the glamour shimmer and drop around me. No sense in keeping it up if I was already made. I wanted them to see their killer, not the bald facsimile Jonathan had created.

There was a heartbeat of silence. No one breathed, no one moved. Adrian stood facing me, his human hostage shielding him. He looked smug, safe.

He didn't know how good a shot I really was.

The air tingled with adrenaline and excitement. I raised my gun and the barrel of my Glock was instantly trained on the center of Adrian's forehead. All I needed was a single instant and I could drop him.

A smile curved my lips.

Now *this* was what I lived for.

25

I pulled the trigger just as someone careened into my arm, throwing off my aim. The bullet whizzed past Adrian's head and struck the wall. The entire room burst into a mass of confusion. Wolves leaped from the walls, shifting and shedding their clothes as they closed in on the group of Cultists. The vampires standing around us fell back, letting their expendable servants take the brunt of whatever damage our ragged looking group might be able to inflict.

I cursed and tried to level on Adrian again, but he vanished in the flurry of action. Nathan shifted as soon as the Tremaine wolves started moving, his suit tearing and falling to the floor in useless rags. He looked far more imposing as a wolf than in his human form, which was quite a feat considering how scary he could be even without all the fur and claws.

Jonathan took a step back and stood as if protecting the Luna Cult Purebloods. He didn't shift or look as though he had any intention of shifting. His eyes roved over the fighting, anger bubbling from every pore of his body, yet I wasn't so sure his anger was targeted at Count Tremaine or his wolves. Gregory was at his side, the smile that was somewhat charming, if not a little goofy, still in place. It was starting to grate on my nerves.

I drew my sword, cursing under my breath. This wasn't how it was supposed to happen, but at least we were getting to the action. I wanted more than anything to get one more shot at Adrian, but he was nowhere to be seen.

"Back toward the doors," Jonathan said. The Cultists started moving as soon as he spoke. They scrambled toward the doors, their robes tripping them up, screaming as the wolves barreled into their ranks. Two more wolves moved to bar the door and their retreat was halted.

I swung my gun around and shot a wolf who was tearing into a Cultist. The bullet from my modified Glock moved with enough force to penetrate his skull, but slow enough so that it went no farther. The wolf dropped almost immediately, his brain scrambled. The Cultist fell from between his claws, the tattoo that once adorned her forehead torn clean away—along with half her face.

Another wolf had hold of one of the other Cultists. He held her between us, peering at me with hate-filled eyes. He snarled something totally unintelligible and snapped at me. I would have tried to shoot around the woman, but she was still alive, struggling weakly in the grasp of her much larger, much stronger opponent. I wasn't going to risk killing her just to get to the wolf.

Instead, I pushed through the stunned Purebloods and dropped to my knees the moment I was within reach of the wolf. I swung my sword at his ankles and it bit into his flesh, striking bone.

The wolf howled in pain, but instead of dropping the woman like I had hoped he would, he dug in with his claws and tore her damn near in two. Her body fell to the ground, a bloody, pulped mess.

I rolled to my feet to face the now unshielded wolf. His eyes were a dark yellow, almost orange in the bright lights of the ballroom. I brought my gun up to bear as he started weaving left and right. He was limping heavily where my sword had taken him in the leg, but he was still moving.

It was then I noticed the scar in the center of his forehead.

I cursed softly and lowered my gun. As the wolf started to lunge for me, I brought my sword up in a sweeping motion. He didn't have time to avoid it.

The silver blade bit into his groin despite his best efforts to avoid the strike and he dropped, clutching at himself and shuddering. Blood poured from the wound, and even though the silver hadn't done its job of paralyzing him, the castration would.

There was a loud roar, and I glanced to the side just as Nathan ripped the head off a much smaller werewolf. A pair of vampires were coming up behind him, and I was about to shout out a warning when Nathan spun around with the dead wolf's body still in his hands. He used the corpse like a club, knocking one of the vamps on his ass. The other vamp hissed and lunged forward, only to have her throat shredded by his claws.

A scramble of sound drew my attention back to the wolf whose life as a male I had just ended. He was back on his feet, blood dripping from his groin, and he was limping my way. A mad grin was spread across his wolfish features. His tongue lolled from his mouth and his eyes were rolling around his head, unfocused, uncaring. Saliva dripped from his jaws in a white foam. His teeth were bared and blood bubbled deep from within his mouth, mixing with the saliva.

"What the fuck?" I said, taking a step back. I knew silver didn't seem to work against the former Cult wolves, but having his family jewels cut almost clean off should have kept the wolf down. I didn't care how crazy you were, you didn't get up from a wound like that.

The werewolf lunged at me, claws bared and ready to tear me apart. I just barely managed to slide around the blow. As I slipped around him, I jabbed him in the ribs with the tip of my sword, opening a gaping wound in his side. He growled with pain but stayed on his feet. He turned back to face me, ignoring the blood pouring from his body in appalling gushes.

Close combat was clearly not working. The wolf made another pass at me and I dodged him easily. The wounds might not be causing him as much pain as I would like, but they were still slowing him down. He staggered to the side and snarled in rage before charging again.

He never even came close to me and he howled in frustration. He sounded weak now, his howl more of a groan than anything. He was panting, frothing at the mouth in a red-tinged foam that splattered the floor at his feet. He glared at me and staggered forward a step. His motions were slow and deliberate, as if he had to think hard about putting each foot in front of the next. He lunged at me, only to come face-to-face with my modified Glock.

"Nighty night."

There was a muffled thump as the bullet buried itself in his brain. He dropped to the floor, and this time, he stayed down.

"Get up from that, asshole," I growled, turning to the rest of the battle raging around me.

By now, half the Cultists were either dead or wounded. The other half were cowering close to the ground, covering their heads with their arms. I saw genuine fear in their eyes. Some of them were probably seeing for the first time the wolves they worshipped so fervently as the monsters they really are. Maybe it would make them realize how foolish they had been to ever worship such beasts.

Nathan was still battling one of the vampires, as well as a wolf that had joined in. The female vamp was lying on the floor in a pool of her own blood, gasping for air. Her arm was severed almost completely from her body, but you wouldn't know it by the look of anger in her eye. If someone didn't finish her off soon, she would heal long before dying.

Just as I was about to step forward and finish the job myself, a wolf grabbed her and tore her head off in what looked to be an uncontrollable rage. The side of his head was flat, and the pink flesh of scar tissue looked out of place against his dark fur.

Jonathan had decided to join the fight. Seeing the Cultists he wanted to protect dying around him probably did it. He stayed close to the remaining Cultists, taking out anyone who came anywhere close to them.

I started forward to assist him but stopped when a sudden movement to my right caught my eye. I quickly swung my gun around and found myself aiming at

Gregory, still in human form. He was moving quickly toward me, his face frantic. His eyes were wide, scanning the mayhem around him. That damn grin was gone at least.

Davin, the vampire who had been sent to retrieve Simon, shot past Gregory and came straight at me. I wasn't ready for the attack and had to drop to my knees and use my forearm to deflect his incoming strike. I just barely kept him from reaching my throat and I used his momentum to throw him over my shoulder.

I got to my feet, swung my gun around, and fired at him before he could fully right himself. He flung up an arm just as I pulled the trigger and the air around him wavered. The bullet struck the rippling air and ricocheted across the room.

"Damn it," I muttered, holstering my gun and drawing my last knife in a quick, fluid motion. Did I mention I hated sorcerers?

Davin straightened and licked his lips as if already savoring the taste of my blood. Not that he would drink it. Vampires got nothing out of drinking another vampire's blood. He would get more nutrition out of a cat or dog than he would out of me.

He kept his eyes on my weapons, but he didn't seem all that concerned. He was clearly older than the vamps I had dealt with at the Fledgling Houses I had taken down. None of them had been able to do anything remotely close to sorcery. No wonder House Tremaine had risen to Minor House status. With a vamp sorcerer, they had an advantage very few could overcome.

"Give me a knife," Gregory said at my side. I just

about stabbed him he was standing so close. I had all but forgotten him.

"No," I said, trying to ignore him. I was reluctant to give up one of my weapons, especially since my other knife was still stuck in the wolf downstairs. The other vamps and wolves in the room were completely content to fight it out with Nathan and Jonathan, leaving me alone with Davin. I wished Gregory would go away and find someone else to bother.

"I want to help," Gregory insisted. "Give me a knife so I can help."

"Why don't you shift?" I said, taking a step away from him. He was seriously crowding my personal space. If the vamp attacked, Gregory would get in the way. "You'd be of more use that way."

The vampire stood his ground and grinned. He seemed to be enjoying our little side banter.

I wanted the vamp to just attack and get it over with. Now that I knew what he could do, I was ready for him. If he wanted to get in close with me, he would have to drop his shield. As long as Gregory didn't get in the way, I could have the vamp down and disabled in seconds. I just needed to get within his reach.

Besides, the longer we stood there staring at each other, the more likely it would be that Adrian or one of the other Tremaine wolves would join in our little standoff, severely tipping the scales in their favor.

At least I didn't have to worry about anyone hitting me with silver. Thanks to the vampire ban on the stuff, I was pretty sure I was the only one packing the illegal metal. It gave me an advantage over everyone in the room. I like having the advantage.

Gregory thrust an open hand out toward me. He

wasn't going to go away unless I gave in and gave him what he wanted.

"Damn it," I said, putting my last knife in his hand, hilt first, careful not to let the silver touch his skin. As long as he didn't cut himself with it, it would only burn him anyway. It would hurt like hell, but it wouldn't incapacitate him.

Davin's grin widened as he took us both in. He looked mere moments from a gale of laughter. He turned his gaze away from us to take in the rest of the fight. It was getting pretty desperate for the good guys.

I took a step toward the distracted vamp, hoping to get in close before he knew I was coming. From what I understood, the shield charm would stop bullets, but something moving slower could get through. As long as I didn't rush things, I could take him down before he knew what hit him.

Before I could go more than a step, a stabbing pain in my back sent shockwaves through my body. My muscles instantly seized. My entire body locked up, and my sword fell useless from my suddenly weak fingers. I fell to one knee, fighting my body as I went down. I would have screamed if I had the breath.

Another stab to my shoulder dropped me the rest of the way to the floor. I managed to hit with my un-injured shoulder and fell over on my back instead of my face. If I was going down, I was going to do it facing my killer.

Gregory stood over me, the knife I had handed him in one hand. It was stained red with my blood. He had that smug grin on his face again and was shaking his head sadly as if he was disappointed in me.

"I wish things could have ended differently," he said.

"Fuck you," I gasped through teeth that didn't want to unclench. It was all I could do to force the air out for the words, but he heard them fine. The silver coursed through my veins, paralyzing me. The poison would eventually run its course and I would be able to move again, but that would take time. Time was something I was quickly running out of.

A scream that seemed to shake the very walls of the ballroom jerked Gregory's head to the side. Whatever had made the tortured sound must have been good for his side, because when he turned back to me, he was absolutely beaming.

He leaned over me and I tried to reach for his throat, though I knew it was useless. I managed only to move my arm a fraction of an inch. I wasn't even sure it was my own muscles that caused the movement or if my arm had simply convulsed. I couldn't feel anything but pain from head to toe.

"Say good-bye, Ms. Redding," he said, pressing my knife to my throat.

"No." Suddenly, Adrian was standing over me. He was still in human form and looked as though he hadn't bothered to take part in the fight at all. His clothes were completely unrumpled, as was his hair. "Keep her alive. Tremaine wants to speak with her."

Gregory scowled and leaned into the knife even more. "No," he said. "This is my moment. Tremaine can go fuck himself if he thinks I'm going to give up the chance to kill her. I'll be a legend."

The edge of the knife bit into my neck, and the pain of silver seeping into my bloodstream caused my eyes to squeeze shut, so I missed what happened next. All I knew was that the bite of the knife was suddenly gone, replaced by what felt like thick, sticky rain and a tearing sound. A split second later, there was a pair of thumps, one hitting so close to my head I felt the impact through the floor.

I scarcely dared to breathe. Not that I was able to breathe all that well as it was, but if I could have held my breath voluntarily, I would have. Had Jonathan managed to save me somehow?

"Get her locked up before she can move," Adrian said, shooting down my hopes of salvation. He gave an annoyed sigh and I heard him walk away.

Rough hands thrust under my arms and around my ankles. I was hoisted into the air, carried between two unseen assailants. I tried to fight against the silver, but it had its teeth in me. I wasn't going to be moving for a long while and I knew it. I could no longer hear the sound of battle and I feared what that meant.

I managed to open my eyes as my captors reached the door where I had left the dead man's body. One of them cursed, but neither stopped to investigate their fallen comrade. They would have more than enough time for that, I was sure. They opened the basement door and took me farther into the depths of House Tremaine.

26

Tremors shook me as the silver worked its way out of my system. It felt like hours before I was able to move my arms and legs, albeit stiffly. I closed my eyes and waited for the moment when the pain would stop, praying that when I opened them again, I wouldn't see the bars surrounding my cell, the cold stone floor, or the inevitable faces that would surround me, pleading for help I couldn't give them.

I could hear them. Muffled whispers and the shuffling movements of those so thoroughly defeated they couldn't move at much more than a crawl. A soft woman's voice, cracked by days without water, tried to soothe someone close to her. A cough that sounded as if it brought up more blood than sound came from my right and then abruptly ceased.

The pain ebbed enough so that I could sit up. I had been stripped of my coat and weapons, and tossed in a cell to rot. At least they left me my clothes, which was more than I would have expected. I opened my eyes and looked around the small cell, and the tremors increased tenfold. It wasn't the silver doing it to me this time.

It was the memories.

I couldn't see the room that contained the cells within House Tremaine. All I could see were the cells of House Valentino, the floors smeared in human and werewolf blood. The whispers of the cells next to me turned into screams of pain, of tortured wails. I was back in hell, back to where my life as a Pureblood ended and the life of a predator began.

I closed my eyes and tried to shut out the memories. I wanted to push them as far to the back of my mind as I could. They refused to budge, refused to be banished back to the dark hole in my mind where all the darkest memories lurked. They taunted me, forced me to confront my current predicament by giving me glimpses of a past I would much rather forget.

Footsteps that sounded hollow on the concrete floor passed my cell, but I refused to acknowledge them. I wasn't even sure I was really hearing them or if it was all still in my head. A cell opened and something was dragged by, a body by the sound of it. I refused to look up, to even peek at what was going on around me out of fear of what I might see. I knew what happened in dungeons like this. I was in one before. I had lived it.

Thomas's face floated before my mind's eye. It was Thomas before the first change, before they turned him into a werewolf. He was smiling, telling me everything would be all right, that we would infiltrate the Minor House, take out Count Valentino, and the rest would fall into place. We would be legends.

Funny how those words tended to come right before disaster. Gregory should have known better.

I should have known.

Thomas's face contorted, shifted into the snarling wolf he would become. He hadn't been able to control the change, hadn't been able to keep his face then, nor could he now in my mind. He lashed out at his captors, killed the vampire, tore him to shreds as easily as he would a newspaper. He knew the consequences of his actions, but he couldn't stop. The beast had him. It would keep him.

And what could I do? I was trapped behind bars that were too strong, too sturdy for my human body. I could only grasp the bars in trembling hands, scream at him to stop before he went too far. I had prayed he would realize what he was doing before it was too late.

Thomas's rage had no bounds. He attacked the wolves that tried to subdue him, ravaged them with a strength born of his newly changed body. He was an animal now, a savage beast who knew only to kill.

But before he could kill them all, before he could escape with what was left of his self, they caught him, buried him beneath their numbers. They forced vampire blood down his throat, made him consume the very vampire he had slain.

They tortured him before my very eyes.

And then they came for me.

My eyes snapped open and I forced myself to take stock of my current situation. Living in the past wasn't going to help. It would only slow me down, force me to confront things I didn't want to deal with. Not now. Not ever again. If I wanted to get out of here alive, I needed to focus.

The room was large, almost as large as the hidden
basement in the Luna Cult Den. The walls were lined
with cells. Most of the ones on the far wall were occupied. The cells to my left and right were empty. A
door three cells down hung ajar. A trail of blood was
smeared across the floor all the way to the stairs.

There were no guards, no one to keep an eye on
the prisoners. A desk sat by the stairwell, but it was
unoccupied. It looked as though no one had sat there
for a good long while. A pile of old magazines and
newspapers rested on the swivel-back chair behind
the desk. The desktop was covered by more magazines. A cattle prod and a whip lay on top of them.

The stench of urine and feces was heavy in the air. I
stood and the floor under me crinkled. I looked down
to find newspaper spread out in the corner of my cell.
The cells across the way were likewise adorned, though
the paper was wet and lumpy where the occupants
had deposited their wastes.

A girl of no more than fourteen crawled to the
edge of her cell and dangled her arms out toward
me. She had a pleading look on her face and made
strange, muffled, chuffing sounds. Her eyes were
wild and bloodshot. Where the whites did show, they
were yellowed and diseased looking.

She wasn't going to live much longer down here.
By the way it smelled, very few would.

I moved to the front of my cell and grasped the
bars in my bare hands. Searing pain jolted me backward and I fell back onto my ass. Hard. My hands
were red and blistered where they had touched the
bars. It was painful but would most likely heal within
an hour or two. It was what the pain meant that was
far more distressing.

Silver. Now that I knew that it was there, I could see the shine to the bars, the way they gave off a certain smell. These weren't the usual iron or steel bars. These were made of pure silver, probably enhanced in some way. The sorcerer came to mind. I wasn't getting out of here unless someone was kind enough to open the door for me.

Fat chance of that happening. This was going to be my prison.

The room was entirely windowless, so when the morning came, I would be safe from the sun. That was something at least. I just had to survive whatever Count Tremaine had in store for me until then. I knew he wasn't going to ever let me out while conscious.

I knew Adrian would push for it. He knew I was Lady Death. I had killed so many vampires and werewolves, I lost count years ago. My skin would be worth more than any number of Purebloods. Letting me out while I could still fight back would be far too dangerous, and Tremaine wouldn't want to damage his prize.

House Tremaine no longer needed the Luna Cult to rise through the vampire ranks. They had me.

I got to my feet and tried to think clearly through the silver-induced pain. I needed to get out of there before anyone bothered to come and check on me. The moment someone came downstairs and found me moving around, they would be all over me. Any hope of escape would be lost.

The people across the room in the other cells weren't going to be much help. Most of them were near starvation, others so dehydrated they were pretty much corpses already. I was surprised the vampires had let them degrade so far. These people were their food, were they not? Or were the captives here useful in some other way?

I wasn't sure I really wanted to know. Normally, a Pureblood kept in a vampire House was kept healthy enough to feed upon, but not kept strong enough to fight back. Even the Purebloods in Count Paltori's basement had been fed and watered regularly. These poor wretches were hardly enough to sate a single wolf, let alone an entire House full of wolves and vamps.

There was a hook above the desk by the stairwell. I assumed that was where they kept the keys to the cells, but there were no keys to be found. There might be spare keys in the desk, I supposed. How I was going to get to them was beyond me.

I started to look away when I noticed the stuff on the floor next to the stairs. My weapons were there, tossed haphazardly away like they were of little importance. If I could only get through these bars, I could make a fight of this.

Of course, that was the problem. How was I ever going to get out of this on my own?

I had to think. Silver bars made leaving the cell a near impossibility. My gear might be in the room with me but was too far away to reach. The weapons wouldn't do me much good if I was still locked up anyway. The floor was solid concrete. So were the walls, and I imagined there was nothing but cold, hard earth on the other side.

I turned my head slowly and scanned the cells once more, my breath catching in my throat.

Where were Jonathan and Nathan? Where were the other Luna Cult members who had survived the fight? Had anyone else survived? I seriously doubted I was the only one who had been captured.

So then, where was everyone?

My eyes traveled to the smear of blood on the floor. It went right past my cell and up the stairs. It was still fresh enough that I could smell it if I took a deep enough breath. Whoever had been dragged by had still been alive at the time.

The door at the top of the stairs opened and three sets of footfalls echoed throughout the basement prison. The Purebloods cowered in the back of their cells, whimpering and pleading in soft voices.

Count Tremaine, flanked by two other vamps I didn't know, stopped in front of my cell, his face a mask of hatred and anger.

Tremaine looked me over, taking his time as if he were trying to remember my every feature. "Who are you?" he demanded, his eyes finally falling on my face.

I stared at him, ignoring the other two vamps entirely. They were probably high-ranking members of House Tremaine, ones who managed to avoid all the fighting upstairs if their flawless appearance gave any indication. Tremaine himself looked as though he hadn't taken part in the fight either. Not a hair was out of place.

"Who sent you?" Tremaine asked. His nostrils flared, and a trickle of blood slid from between his lips.

I licked my own lips out of reflex. Tremaine grinned, exposing his teeth. His gums were bleeding, his fangs slowly extending. We were but a night from the full moon, and already he was losing some control over his change. I could feel it, too. It would make his rage more acute, send him over the edge that much faster.

If it came down to the vamps torturing me and a quick death, I would gladly play on their lack of control to get it over with quickly.

"What House do you belong to? Are you a rogue?" he went on, licking the blood from his lips. "If you tell me, then perhaps I will give you something to feed upon." He gestured toward the caged Purebloods. "They aren't much, but people in your predicament can't be too choosy, now can they?"

I barely heard the last. My mind was running races going over what he had said.

He didn't know who I was. How could he *not* know? Adrian had more than enough time to tell him by now. There was no way the wolf would keep it to himself, not if he had sworn the Oath and was a part of House Tremaine.

Would he?

I kept my mouth shut and straightened. If Count Tremaine didn't know who I was, then there was still hope. He had no idea what I was capable of. One mistake and I could be all over him. All I needed was a single instant and I could use the silver bars to my advantage. I knew he was probably vain enough to fear the scars the silver would cause him. Just one more step toward me, one ill-advised movement within my reach and I could have him.

Tremaine shook his head as if disappointed in me. "You really should talk," he said. "I want to know how and why you became involved with the Luna Cult. Are they already sworn to another House? Was this whole thing some sort of elaborate ploy so they could get you inside to finish me off? I have claimed the Cult. They are mine now, as are their wolves."

I tensed at that but said nothing. He was just

trying to get to me. I had stood behind similar bars and listened to the same sort of banter before. I was sure Jonathan wouldn't have already declared his loyalty to House Tremaine. Even under duress, he would fight them.

I couldn't help but glance at the smear of blood on the floor and wonder. Whom had it belonged to? Could I really be so sure Jonathan hadn't already caved? It could be his blood for all I knew. Or Simon's. If Tremaine had given him the Denmaster, then what was stopping Jonathan from bowing down now that I was behind bars?

"The weapons you carry are forbidden," Tremaine said. "How did you get them past our security? Then again, how did you get them at all?" He looked thoughtful a moment and I was certain he was working out who I was in his head. "Were you the one who killed Edgar?"

I smiled at him, hiding my relief. The longer he was oblivious to who I was, the longer I would live.

Tremaine nodded as if my smile told him everything he needed to know. "I imagine you were the one who was snooping around my property the other night. How did you get past Zane so easily? No one gets past his notice."

"Check the morgue," I said, unable to hold my tongue any longer. I figured Zane was the horny wolf outside.

Tremaine's smug look faltered and the rage slowly returned. His hand started forward, inched closer to me. He jerked it back before I could act on the mistake, his smile returning.

"Do you like your accommodations?" he asked, tucking his hands behind his back as if he was afraid they might ease forward on their own if he wasn't careful. It was clear by the look in his eye he wanted nothing more than to wrap his fingers around my throat and squeeze until they popped through the back of my neck. "The cells on this side are made of pure silver." He glanced down at my hands and the smile widened. "As I see you have already discovered."

"Fuck you."

"Perhaps later. Although it is kind of you to offer." More blood dribbled from his lips and ran down his chin. He was definitely losing control. I wasn't sure if that was a good thing or a bad thing. "It was quite hard to procure so much pure silver, as you might guess," he said, eyeing the bars to my cell. "It isn't something we can boast about to other Houses."

"I'm sure they will be thrilled when I let them know."

Tremaine laughed. "I think I might send pieces of you to each Count, see if any of them recognize your scent, the taste of your flesh. Someone sent you here, and it seems they don't mind breaking the rules. I want to know who."

"Remember what I said a moment ago?" I said, sneering. "I think it applies here as well."

Tremaine's jaw tensed. The two vamps at his side were having just as hard of a time controlling their emotions as he was. Their eyes gleamed with hunger, and I knew they would love nothing more than to tear me apart limb from limb.

"Your wit leaves much to be desired," Tremaine said. All evidence of his smugness was gone. All that remained was his anger. "Who sent you? Why are you here? You must have known you could never defeat me with only a mere trio of wolves and useless Purebloods at your side."

"Who says I was being witty?" I took a step forward, putting myself closer to the bars. If only Tremaine would reach out for me, I would have him. Antagonizing him might not be the best idea in the world, but it was all I had. "I'm going to fuck you up seven ways to Sunday. We'll see who will be sending pieces of whom to the other Houses. I'm sure some would appreciate the gesture."

A chill settled over Tremaine's features. He stared at me with eyes burning in near fever. "They are all dead, you know?" he said at a near whisper. "Those you came with. Their blood stains my floor, taints the very air I breathe. You are alone here and you *will* tell me what I want to know. You have no other choice."

My stomach seemed to fall straight through the floor. Jonathan and Nathan were dead. Why did the thought bother me so much? They were werewolves. They were the enemy. I shouldn't care one way or another what happened to them.

But I did care. They might not be my friends, but they were the next best thing to it. What did that say about my life that I looked at other monsters as friends? They were strangers to me, wolves who came to me for help, not friendship.

And yet the thought of their deaths hurt. They had trusted me for some reason I couldn't quite fathom. I had even gone as far as to trust them to come along with them. They could have turned me in to save their own skin, told Tremaine who I was, but they hadn't.

"I will give you time to think about it," Tremaine said. "Tonight will be busy as we prepare for tomorrow's full moon. You have until then to make your decision. Either you tell me what I want to know, or you will become part of the celebration. We shall see how you like being the focus of attention during tomorrow's festivities."

I glared hard at Tremaine. I wanted to throw myself at the bars of my cell and rip his throat out, silver bars be damned. I knew he wasn't going to let me walk whether I talked or not. If I gave him what he wanted, he would just throw me to the wolves. He was probably planning on doing that anyway.

"Think about it." Tremaine and his vampire flunkies turned and left, leaving me trapped in my silver cell, his last words lingering in my ears.

27

I wiped my hand across my mouth. A smear of blood shone bright on the back of my hand. A dull ache in my gums told me that my teeth had started to push through, though I wasn't quite sure when exactly it had happened. The moon was getting to me just like it was everyone else. By tomorrow, things were going to get pretty damn violent. It might make what happened earlier look like a slap fight in comparison.

I dropped down on the floor and tried to formulate some sort of plan. I knew chances were slim I would get my hands on Tremaine or any of his men while still behind bars. I also knew I wasn't getting out of there unless someone came and broke me out. The full moon was coming, which meant the wolves were going to go completely bonkers. The vampires wouldn't be much better. I really needed to get out of there by then.

I ground my teeth in frustration. I had no idea how I was going to get out of this one. Unless some moon-hopped wolf went nuts and accidently tore the doors off my cell, I was as good as dead. Hell, maybe sitting there wasn't such a bad thing. The silver should keep anyone out, just as it kept me inside. Maybe I would be lucky and the vampires and wolves would kill themselves off in a moon-induced rage.

The night just kept getting better and better. With Jonathan and Nathan presumably dead, there was no one who could help me. There was always a chance Count Tremaine had lied about the fate of my companions and they were cooped up somewhere else. Maybe there was still a chance one of them would break free and help me escape.

And maybe I was grasping at straws made of pure silver. Even the thought burned.

Contemplating my fate wasn't going to get me anywhere. As far as I was concerned, things couldn't really get much worse. I just needed to wait it out and hope a moment presented itself in which I could make good my escape. If all went well, I could take out a few vamps and wolves on my way out. I refused to die down here.

The door opened and heavy footfalls descended the stairs, bringing my head up. As soon as I saw the sharp features and square shoulders of the man approaching, I realized that my night could indeed get a whole hell of a lot worse.

"Hello, Adrian," I said, my voice even, although I was a total mess inside.

Adrian knocked the magazines and newspapers from the swivel-backed chair and wheeled it over to my cell. He eased himself down, resting his arms on the backrest. He smiled, displaying his pointed teeth.

"We are alone," he said. "No one else is listening, and as long as you cooperate, no one will have to know about our conversation." He glanced back at the Purebloods cowering in their cells before turning back to me. Obviously, he didn't view them as important. "I think it time we had another little talk, don't you?"

"What do you want?" I asked.

Adrian glanced toward the stairs, his shoulders tense. He looked as alert and as imposing as ever. He also seemed detached, if it was even possible to be both alert and detached at the same time. It was unsettling.

"Do you remember our last conversation?" he said. "I might have told you that my offer would not come again. It appears I had been mistaken. I think now would be an opportune time to reopen dialogue on that matter, don't you think?"

"What makes you think I am any more willing to listen now than I was before? I don't think much has changed since then." Okay, maybe I was stretching the truth a bit there; but hey, I really didn't want to talk to this guy, no matter what he might have to offer.

"Nothing," he said. His gaze never left mine. He was in complete control of himself, totally unfazed by the coming full moon and the night's activities. We could have been sitting and having a nice talk over beers in The Bloody Stake for all the emotion he was showing. "But I am here nonetheless."

I crossed my arms and faced him without expression. I wasn't about to sell my soul to the devil again. Once was enough.

"You are quite an amazing person." Adrian allowed himself a slim smile. "You managed to dispatch my test without so much as a scratch."

"My Honda would disagree." And my knees and hands, but he didn't have to know that.

He frowned. "Pardon?"

"My bike, asshole. Your fucking wolf wrecked me and scratched my bike all to hell. You owe me for that."

Adrian's left eyebrow twitched. I couldn't tell if it was due to amusement or irritation. I was betting the latter.

"Regardless, you are unharmed."

One of the Purebloods edged toward the front of his cell. He made hardly a sound, yet Adrian's head snapped around like someone had slammed a couple of pots together behind him. The caged man froze where he was, eyes full of terror, and then slowly slipped back the way he had come.

"What's your point?" I asked, pulling Adrian's attention back to me. I didn't like the way he looked at the scrawny man. He had definitely looked hungry there. I wasn't about to sit back and watch him snack on some guy who thought it might be a good idea to eavesdrop on our conversation. "I have come out of worse scenarios unharmed. What makes you think you or one of your grunts are any better than every other wolf who has ever tried to take me out?"

"I have you now."

"Your boss has me now."

His eyelid twitched again. Definitely irritation.

Adrian took a deep breath and let it out slowly before going on as if our little exchange had never happened. "You handled yourself well at the Stake when you found out I was asking about you. I would have expected you to act much more violently. I was almost hoping for it."

"I was having an off day. Let me out and I would

be happy to oblige you with as much violence as you could ever want."

"You walked right in the Luna Cult Den even though you knew it could be a trap," he went on, unperturbed by my interruption. "You met with Jonathan and his wolves and came out, once again, unscathed."

"He didn't threaten to throw me in a cage," I said. "What's your point?"

"And here you are now. You walked right into a Minor vampire House, knowing full well there was a good chance you would be forced to fight. In fact, I believe you were counting on it. My source had been quite vague as to what was going to happen. He could only tell me Jonathan had a plan and it involved outside help. Imagine my surprise when that help turned out to be you."

"Gregory." I spat the name.

Adrian blinked once as the name crossed my lips. That was all the reaction he showed. "He was useful for a time, though his information was quite limited. It was frustrating, to say the least."

"Where is he now?" If I could get my hands on Gregory, I think I could die content. Screw Tremaine. Just give me the traitor and I would be happy.

"Which part?"

I hesitated a second before nodding. I guess that explained what had happened when my eyes had closed back in the ballroom. I had pretty much figured it out already anyway. There weren't too many wet, sticky liquids that could have fallen on me back there.

I looked down and saw I still had his blood on me. There wasn't as much as there should be. I imagine my coat had taken the worst of it. I was going to have to throw these clothes away.

"I guess that means there is one less asshole I need to kill when I get out of here."

"Perhaps." Adrian shrugged noncommittally. "But I really think you should stop and consider my offer before deciding who needs to die. I have updated it if you care to listen."

I mimicked his shrug and kept my face carefully blank.

"House Tremaine might gain power by bringing the Luna Cult into the fold, but they are still just another vampire House. They will make a mistake somewhere down the road, and someone much more powerful will destroy them. I don't plan on sticking around long enough to see it happen. Not from the inside anyway."

A scream came from somewhere above, muffled by at least a few floors. I kept my gaze on Adrian, refusing to so much as flinch at the sound. Adrian did likewise. He looked as though he hadn't even heard it.

"Then why are you here at all?" I asked. "Once the vamps have hold of you, it isn't exactly easy to break away."

"Because I needed to establish a base, obtain power of my own. Do you think those that followed me did so only because they thought my ways were better? They did so because I promised them a way out, a way to take control of their lives. We will not hide in the shadows like the Cult. We will not bow down to anyone—werewolf or vampire—who thinks they can own us."

"So you led them here? That doesn't seem like the way to go if you wanted to go your own way." I laughed. "Tremaine probably forced you to swear the Oath." From the look on his face, I knew I was right. "How exactly do you plan on getting out of that one?"

"Once he is dead, my Oath will be broken. I will be able to do as I please. I will take the wolves from the wreckage of the House and from there . . ." He shrugged. "The world is a large place."

I stared at him long and hard. The Oath was a supernatural bond between vampire and werewolf. A vampire couldn't bond another vamp, just as a werewolf couldn't bond another wolf. It had to be a werewolf swearing fealty to a vampire. No other combination worked as far as I knew.

I had never seen an Oath sworn in person, never planned to, but I knew it had something to do with blood and magic older than the world itself. The Oath is what keeps the wolves in line once they enter service with a vampire House. They are bound and incapable of harming the vampires who rule them, no matter how much they might want to.

How all of this affected me, I had no idea. Whatever Adrian truly wanted, he was being pretty damn evasive about it. I couldn't very well kill Tremaine for him if I was stuck behind bars, and I doubted he would just open the doors and let me walk. He had to know he was pretty high on my to-be-killed list.

"There is one thing I am missing," Adrian said. "One thing a man of my stature needs if he wants to rule his people absolutely."

"And that is?"

"A mate."

My throat closed up. If he was implying what he thought he was implying . . . I shuddered.

His eyelid fluttered and his upper lip lifted in a sneer. "I can see the mere suggestion disgusts you."

"It's nothing personal," I said. "I just don't make a habit of dating anyone whose blood could turn me into a raving lunatic." Not that I was dating anyone at all. He didn't need to know that either.

"I never said anything about dating." Adrian squared his shoulders and sat up in his chair. He had an ultra-alert look about him that set me even more on edge. "And just because our blood doesn't mesh, doesn't mean other things do not."

"No thanks."

"I would bond to you. I would take the Oath. I will let you free from here and lead you straight to Count Tremaine. I will let you kill him, dismember him, revel in his blood, and stand by your side as you do it."

I blinked at him a few times. Did he really just say what I thought he said? "You'd what?" I asked to be sure.

"I haven't told him who you are. He thinks you are just some vampire from another House who has infiltrated the Luna Cult. I have done my part in making sure that is what he continues to believe." Adrian almost smiled. "Jonathan refuses to give you up. He stands fast that he knows nothing of you, that you joined his ranks unnoticed."

"He's still alive?" Relief washed through me. It warmed me from head to foot.

"Yes, so is Nathan if you care to know. They have taken the Oath. They belong to House Tremaine now, as does the Luna Cult. They cannot help you."

The warm feeling was washed away by a flood of cold. "They wouldn't have done that."

"They had little choice." His face went utterly blank once again. "It was either swear the Oath or be executed in a most unorthodox way." I definitely heard the disgust there. "Count Tremaine threatened them with the mixing of blood. He would have sent them back to the Cult where the Madness, as well as the insanity caused by mixed blood, would cause them to tear the Cult apart in one bloody orgy of death. They would kill everyone."

My mouth went dry. I had no idea what I could possibly say to that. I knew I couldn't simply agree to Adrian's terms. For one, I didn't trust him. For another, there was no way in hell I was going to sleep with him. Just the thought made me want to vomit.

And even if he did hold up his end of the bargain and release me, how could I ever trust him not to do to me what he planned to do to Count Tremaine? He had turned against everyone he had ever sworn allegiance to. What was to stop him from doing it again?

I still couldn't figure out how it would benefit him. If he were to swear the Oath, he would become subservient to me. I could kill him any time I wanted and he couldn't raise a hand against me. It made no sense. What did he get out of it?

"You really have no choice," Adrian said. "Either you join with me or you will suffer unbearable torment. I will tell Tremaine who you are, will make sure he understands what tainting your blood would really do to you. If you refuse me, tomorrow night will be your last."

"Then when tomorrow comes, I'll be sure to let Tremaine know what you really think of him. I'm sure he would be interested to hear how you are interested in bedding his captive to secure your own powerbase."

Adrian snarled and leaped toward my cell. I never even flinched. He slammed his face up against the bars, wrapped his hands around them as if he were going to tear the cell door straight from its moorings.

I waited for him to cry out, to flinch from the silver bars, but he held on as if it didn't bother him in the slightest.

"I will tear your heart from your chest," he said. "You do not know who you are dealing with. I am capable of doing so much worse than anything Tremaine could ever dream of. I always get what I want."

I hardly heard what he was saying. I should have been thrilled to finally get a real reaction out of him. I just couldn't focus. I stared at his hands, at his face pressed against the bars that should have scorched his flesh, left him writhing in agony. There wasn't even a hint of pain on his features.

I should have known it wouldn't have bothered him. It *was* his wolves that seemed impervious to my silver, so why should he be any different?

I had to admit, I wasn't on my game. Getting stabbed in the back with your own weapons tends to do that. I really needed to get past all of that or I definitely wouldn't be getting out of here alive.

Adrian eased off the bars and took a step back. His face was whole, his hands unaffected by the silver. He took a deep breath and composed himself.

"I gave you a chance," he said. "Two chances, in fact. Your pride stands in the way of common sense. You are a vampire. You need to live like one and quit acting like you are human. It is a shame you will not live long enough to reach true enlightenment."

He turned and stormed out of the basement, slamming the door behind him. I watched after him, stunned into silence.

Time passed. The temperature in the basement dropped. The rain outside had picked up. Even in the basement, I could hear its patter. The Purebloods cowered in their cells, curled into balls, trying to keep the warmth from leaving their bodies. Some of them wouldn't survive the night.

I was cold to the bone, though it had little to do with the plummeting temperature. I was trapped down here with what was clearly a madman holding his secret close to his chest out of some insane belief that in doing so I would join him and become his mate. If he ever thought I would go through with it, he was even crazier than he seemed.

I sat and pressed my back against the cold stone wall. I had no idea how I was going to get out of this. What I really needed was a miracle.

I pulled my knees to my chest and did the only thing I could do.

I waited.

28

The morning came and went. I could feel the sun through the heavy stones and the soft earth separating me from freedom. My strength waned and then gained force as the sun began its slow descent. I searched every corner of my cell, tried to claw at the walls, use my vampire-enhanced strength to tear at the stones, but it was no use.

No one else came to see me during the day. I was left alone with the Purebloods who moaned and begged me for help. I didn't know what they wanted me to do, trapped as I was. It was all I could do to keep from screaming myself.

As the sun finally went down, to be replaced by the full moon, I felt myself giving way to my baser instincts. Blood covered my chin, pouring from the wounds inflicted by my incisors pushing from the gums. My breathing picked up, and at first, I had no control over myself. If anyone would have been in the cell with me, I would have torn them to shreds.

It took a good long time for me to calm myself

enough to think. I knew it was the moon playing on the taint in my blood. I could control it. Barely.

The door at the top of the stairs opened and I rose to my feet. It was time to meet my fate, and I was going to do it standing. If by some miracle they made the mistake of coming in after me without pacifying me first, I would make them pay. Tremaine had better have sent a dozen wolves and vamps to contain me.

I watched the stairs, waiting to see whom he had sent. Since it was the full moon, it was unlikely the wolves would be coming for me. Not unless he wanted them to ravage anything they could sink their claws into. The Madness would have its teeth in them by now.

Nathan appeared at the foot of the stairs, causing me to start in surprise. His face was concealed by the darkness shrouding the room. I could just make out his form, his features, so I knew who he was, but I couldn't quite make out what kind of expression was on his face. The full moon did that, weakened some of the basic senses, fueling baser instincts instead.

He hurried over to my cell. "Hurry," he said, producing a set of keys from his pocket. "They don't know I'm down here."

"How?" I asked, stunned. I was so happy to see him, yet afraid at the same time. Nathan wasn't exactly one of my favorite people.

Nathan got the door open with a hiss of pain. It was somewhat a relief to see someone else affected by the silver after Adrian's show the night before.

"I took the Oath," he growled, his voice deeper and darker than usual. "Tremaine is conceited, so

full of himself, he thinks that it is all it will take to
ensure our loyalty."

I stepped out of the cell the moment the door
swung open. I was so happy to be free, I just about
hugged the big man.

That would have been a mistake.

Nathan stepped back from me, eyes wild. Now that
I was closer to him, I could see he wasn't quite himself.
Sweat rolled down his face, his cheeks were bushy, as
if he had grown a full beard in a matter of hours. Actually, that wasn't too far from the truth. Dried blood
speckled his new beard. I could see his sharp, pointed
teeth every time he opened his mouth.

The change was upon him. It was only a matter of
time before it took complete control of his senses.

"We have to get moving," he said. "I don't have
much time."

"What's the plan?" I asked, moving toward the
corner where my things lay. My back itched when I
turned it to the big wolf. If he lost control now, I was
as good as dead.

My sword, both my knives, and my gun were all in
the corner. My belt and shoulder holster had been
tossed on top of the pile, but my coat and packets of
silver dust were missing.

"I know where Simon is," Nathan said. "You get
him and I will get Jonathan. We kill Tremaine and
get out of here before the place erupts." His voice
sounded decidedly animal-like now.

"What about them?" I motioned toward the caged
Purebloods as I slipped on my shoulder holster. Its
weight felt comforting.

"They are safer in there than they will be out here."

One more look at Nathan and I knew he was right.

He was barely holding on to his humanity, and I knew that most of the wolves around the city wouldn't be trying to exert so much control as he was. Letting them out would only be condemning them to death. Nathan would last minutes more, if that. The Madness would soon consume him, and I would need to be as careful of him as I would Tremaine.

And I was feeling it, too. I could feel the hunger in me fighting to get out. If one of those Purebloods was bleeding and I came too close . . .

I snapped my belt around my waist and sheathed my sword. I checked my gun and found, to my surprise, they hadn't removed the bullets. I jammed it in its holster with a satisfied smirk. My spare magazine was in my coat, however, so I would need to be careful with the remaining bullets.

"Let's go," I said, nodding to Nathan. The Purebloods could wait. Once the fighting was over, I would make sure they were freed and safely escorted back home, even if I had to do it myself.

We started for the stairs, Nathan in the lead.

"They are holding Simon upstairs. He is in the last room on the top floor. Count Tremaine sent me to gather him and I came here instead. I will deal with Tremaine myself. You shouldn't have too hard of a time getting Simon out of here while I have him distracted."

I grabbed him by the arm, stopping him halfway up the stairs. He spun on me, eyes flashing animal yellow. Course fur sprouted around his ears and he looked so feral, so ready to kill, I took a step back.

"What about the Oath?" I asked. "You can't go up there and kill Tremaine. The Oath won't allow it.

How do you expect to get Jonathan away from him if you can't fight him?"

He snarled at me in what I took to be a grin. "The Oath might stop me from killing Tremaine myself, but it won't stop me from killing his wolves. And who is to say what will happen once I fully succumb to the Madness. Not even the Oath can stop me then." Saliva dripped from his jaws. "I suggest we get upstairs and separate before then."

I couldn't agree more. I motioned for Nathan to keep going and we continued up the stairs. The caged Purebloods didn't even cry out for help as we left them behind. They weren't stupid. They knew their freedom wouldn't mean much if they were torn apart the moment they were free of their cells.

The game room looked empty at first glance. It took my eyes a moment to adjust, and when they did, I noticed the blood on the walls and the pair of bodies lying crumpled under the card table. Their throats had been torn open. Their blood covered a vast majority of the floor.

Nathan, I supposed. I glanced to where I had last seen him, but he was gone.

I moved to the stairs, checked once to make sure no one was there, and took them by twos, keeping my body low. A scream erupted from somewhere deeper in the house. None of the servants were within sight. Hell, no one was. I wasn't so sure that was a good sign.

I paused for an instant to consider my options. I could go find Simon like Nathan wanted me to and hope that he was heavily sedated. He *was* a werewolf. The full moon was going to affect him just like any other wolf. He would kill me whether I was there to help him or torture him.

I could also go after Tremaine. Nathan couldn't take on the vampire himself. Not with the Oath. If I found Tremaine, I could plant a bullet between his eyes before he even realized I was there. As far as he knew, I was still locked away in that basement cell. From there, it would only be a matter of making sure the crazed wolves didn't get me before I could escape.

Or I could run. The front door was just down the hall. This wasn't my fight. I could leave Nathan and Jonathan to take care of Tremaine. They could kill each other off, and I could clean up the remaining mess later.

Cursing, I turned toward the second-floor staircase. Maybe it was the bloodlust that did it. I didn't know Simon from Joseph. What did I care if he survived this or not?

But he was the reason I was here, whether I liked it or not. I might have come along just to kill some vamps, but Simon was the true goal of this mission. I couldn't betray Jonathan and Nathan by turning my back on them.

Then again, maybe I just wanted my coat back.

As soon as I set foot on the second floor, a vampire stepped out from an open doorway. He was dressed as though he were preparing to go out to dinner at some fancy restaurant. His suit had been pressed, its lines sharp and clean. A rose was pinned to his lapel.

I didn't hesitate. I drew my sword and slashed at his neck. He had only enough time to flinch before the silver blade bit into his throat. That flinch saved him from being beheaded, but it didn't save him from receiving a mortal wound.

The vampire grasped at his throat. Blood spurted between his fingers in gushes. His eyes twitched and a glazed look came into his eyes. He crumpled to the floor, twitching. The silver had done its job, and all he could do was lie there and watch as I stepped over him and headed farther into the mansion.

I ran down the hall, keeping my eyes peeled for any more company. Most of the doors were open, their rooms empty. The few closed doors I passed could contain a wolf or vamp, but as long as they didn't get in my way, I needn't bother myself with them.

I turned a corner and saw another staircase at the end of the hall. I flew up the stairs as more screaming came from below, followed by a spine-chilling howl that had all the hairs on my arms standing on end.

The next floor looked to have come straight from a museum. Paintings and statuettes ran along the walls. The doors were lined in iron, and I knew I had found Tremaine's safe floor, though leaving such valuables out in the open seemed silly considering a rampaging wolf could easily destroy everything.

I moved quickly down the hall, ignoring most of the doors as I passed. Like below, almost all of them were open and empty. I didn't have to linger long to see that. Mirrors lined every wall, giving me a fun-house look at every room as I passed. It was almost surreal.

The door at the end of the hall was closed. A rose dripping blood was etched into the design of the door. I hastened to it and tried the doorknob, fully expecting it to be locked.

It turned easily in my hand.

I pushed the door open and drew my gun, bringing it to bear. I would hate to have to shoot Simon, but I wasn't about to let a moon-crazed wolf tear me to shreds just because I was careless. It didn't even cross my mind to question why the door supposedly holding back a crazed werewolf was unlocked.

The room was dark, and while my night vision wasn't what it usually was thanks to the full moon, I still couldn't miss the large, looming shape that seemed to be coming right at me.

I just barely stopped myself from squeezing the trigger as I realized the shape wasn't actually moving. It wasn't even standing. It looked to be floating there, hovering a foot off the ground. It wasn't until my eyes adjusted to the gloom that I realized what I was seeing.

A partially shifted wolf hung from the ceiling, his hands bound by a rope laced with silver dust. His wrists were red and raw from trying to fight against the stinging bindings. His head was down, but I could see dried blood on his muzzle, caked to the fur. His chest was torn open, heart and entrails lying on the floor at his feet.

I crept forward, my breath caught in my throat. I scanned the room, ready to fire the moment I saw movement. As far as I could tell, I was alone with the corpse. I eased forward, certain I would find Jonathan's face looking out at me from the dead thing. The head shape wasn't right, but I just couldn't get the thought out of my head that it was him.

I slowly reached out, uncertain if the beast was truly dead. He smelled it, for sure. My fingers brushed the hair on his head and he didn't make a move. I lifted the dead wolf's head gently by the hair, bringing his face up.

The crescent moon of the Luna Cult had been roughly carved into the corpse's forehead. It had bled quite a bit, so it had been done while the wolf had still been alive. His eyes had been plucked from his skull and stuffed into a muzzle that had partially extended during his attempted shift. My silver dust packets rested in the empty orbs of his eye sockets. They had been slashed open, dumping their contents into his head.

I swallowed hard as I released his hair. His head fell back hard against his chest. I knew this had to be Simon. There was no one else it could be.

I scanned the rest of the room, but as far as I could tell, when the room wasn't being used to display dead werewolves, it was just another bedroom, perhaps Count Tremaine's own.

It didn't make sense. Nathan had been sent up here to retrieve the Denmaster. If Tremaine had eviscerated the wolf ahead of time, then why send Nathan after him? Was this some sort of message? Or was something else going on?

A cold chill ran up my spine, and I knew with a sudden certainty I had made a huge mistake. I ran out the door and down the stairs, hardly paying any mind to the still-dying vampire as I raced past him and back down to the main floor.

There were no other vamps to stop me. No one appeared out of a dark corner, no wolves came charging at me. The entire mansion had gone deathly quiet. The body had been planted there for Nathan to find. I was sure of it. There was a reason the whole place seemed empty now.

I skidded to a stop at the foot of the stairs, debating on what to do. I could just turn around to leave, forget about this whole thing. Simon was dead. Nathan was probably dead as well. There were no wolves to stop me, no vampires to fight.

But I couldn't leave Jonathan there to deal with Tremaine on his own. It was stupid of me, especially now during the full moon. Nathan had risked his life to come break me free, had most likely paid for it. Could I really turn around and walk out on them?

"Fuck," I grumbled under my breath. The full moon had to be clouding my mind, making me do things I would never do without its influence. It was the only explanation for what I did next.

I hesitated for a heartbeat before I started for the closed double doors leading to the ballroom where this whole mess had started. It was the only place that made sense. I knew beyond a shadow of a doubt that Tremaine would be in there.

It was time to end this.

29

A hushed silence fell over the ballroom as the heavy double doors swung open and I stepped inside. They really were as heavy as they looked. I had expected fireworks right away, werewolves and vampires alike lunging at me. Instead, I was met with a wall of silence, of smiling faces, and a whole hell of a lot of fur.

Count Tremaine stood at the center of the room. He was flanked by four other vampires of the House, each staring at me with knowing smiles. The rest of the mansion was so quiet, I was almost positive everyone still breathing was in that very room.

If this was all the vamps left in House Tremaine, then things would be a lot easier than I could have ever hoped. I guess Mikael had been right when he said Tremaine had recently been weakened. There should have been a whole hell of a lot more vampires here than the small group facing me.

Tremaine smiled, displaying fangs that had punctured his gums long ago. They were stained red as if he had recently fed. For an instant, I thought I saw surprise on his face, but it was quickly swallowed by the bloodlust and glee in his eyes.

Along the wall to my right were chained were-wolves. The heavy rings embedded in the walls held the chains, keeping the wolves from lunging too far from where they stood. Almost every single one of them was fully shifted. The rings were just far enough apart so that they wolves couldn't reach other and tear the head off its neighbor.

I recognized Jonathan and Nathan at once in the mass of fur. Jonathan had yet to shift, though his eyes were wild, teeth bared and extended. Nathan was fully shifted, his coat matted with blood.

A growl erupted from a throat at my side and I took a quick step forward into the room. Two wolves were chained just inside the doors, one to either side of the wide opening. If I hadn't walked directly in the center of the doorway, one of them could have easily snatched hold of me and began tearing me apart bit by bit before I even knew they were there.

"So glad you could join us," Tremaine said, his smile never wavering. His eyes betrayed the calm tone of his voice. Underneath the cool façade was a building rage, accentuated by the full moon.

I brought my gun up to bear and Davin stepped in front of the Count. I felt a thin flow of power and saw the shimmer in the air. He had lifted his shield. As long as they stayed huddled together like that, my gun was useless.

"I won't ask how you managed to escape," Tremaine said, glancing toward Nathan. "But my question would be as to why you are here instead of choosing to flee while you had the chance."

As one, the wolves started thrashing in their chains,

pulling the links taut to the point they should have snapped. They gnashed their teeth at each other, at the vampires in the middle of the room, at their own bindings. One wolf began to smash his head against the wall as if he thought he might be able to bash his way through before his brains splattered out his ears. Blood was already running from his nose, and I could hear the crunch of bone as his skull began to fracture.

"Maybe someone was feeling generous," I said, taking another step into the room. I didn't feel comfortable with the wolves at the door that close behind me. "Maybe I offered him something you couldn't."

Tremaine's smile deepened, though his eyes hardened. "Or there is more to this story than I have been told. No one seems to be willing to talk about how you managed to be here, who you really are. There is definitely something about you that brings out their loyalty. It would be fascinating if it wasn't so aggravating."

I took another step forward and two of the other vamps moved in front of Davin and Count Tremaine. I stopped and glanced at the raging wolves chained to the wall. Something was missing. It hadn't hit right away, but now that I was farther into the room, something was definitely not as it should be. Or should I say someone?

Where was Adrian?

I looked over each face and tried to determine whether any of them might be the Luna Cult defector. If he was here, he was already shifted into full-on wolfman, and since I had never seen him in his wolf form, I wouldn't be able to pick him out with certainty.

But if he was there, wouldn't his wolves be there,

too? Not a single wolf in the room bore the scar on their forehead that would indicate their ties to Adrian. Had he already jumped ship, knowing what was to come? Or was he being held back in reserve, Tremaine's proverbial ace in the hole?

I glanced over my shoulder to check the wolves by the door. Neither of them had the bulk to be Adrian, nor did they bear the scar. The doors were still open and I could see out into the hallway and into the next room. No one lurked out there as far as I could see.

"I was going to send someone to fetch you anyway," Tremaine said. "I sent a wolf after the former Den-master, but he seemed to have gotten distracted." He glanced at Nathan again. "I suppose while you are here, we can commence the festivities. Perhaps you might be willing to talk now that you can see you have little chance of success. I would hate to have to sick my wolves on you before I learn what I wish. They would tear you apart."

"Your wolves could try," I said. I still had my sword in hand. I was loath to rush right in and use it. I didn't know what kind of abilities the vampires had, especially Count Tremaine. Davin was obvious. The others, I wasn't so sure about. The older they were, the more power they could have gained over time.

The last vampire moved to stand on the other side of Count Tremaine. The wolves on the walls began thrashing even more as he neared. A loud crack jerked my eyes toward the one who had been beating his head against the wall. He hung limp in his chains, his skull smashed in. Brains and blood clung to the wall, pooled on the floor.

"Perhaps it is time to release them," Tremaine

said, as if in reflection. "The wolves grow restless and their meal has finally arrived. I had planned a hunt, giving you a chance to show your skills, though I hadn't planned on allowing you weaponry. You could serve well as entertainment for the evening. I always enjoyed seeing a member of another House fight for their lives. It is quite relaxing."

"Where's Adrian?" I asked, my eyes roving over the ravenous wolves. Jonathan was almost fully shifted now. It was clear he was trying to fight it, but it was a battle he would never win. "Has he already been set loose? Did you leave him to hang with his entrails spilled out on the floor like the wolf upstairs?"

Tremaine's smile faltered. "You saw that, did you?" He shrugged. "It's no matter. I left him there for my newest wolf to find. I had hoped the sight of him like that would break his stubborn streak. I see I misjudged how stubborn he really was."

Jonathan's head swung toward Tremaine, his eyes glowing fiercely. A few wolves down, Nathan struggled even more against his bindings, his eyes trained on Tremaine as if he could kill him with a stare. He gnashed his teeth, tore at his restraints with his claws. Whatever the vampires had used in their chains, it was pretty damn strong stuff. Not many metals could stand up to the brute strength of an enraged werewolf.

"Why do it?" I asked, inching closer and closer to the gathering of vampires.

Tremaine glanced toward Jonathan and then back to me. The smile had returned. He was so smug, so sure of himself, yet I could see the doubt behind that smile. This wasn't how he planned things to go down. That meant he was no longer in control. A man like him needed to be in control, craved it.

"Because I could," he said. "A wolf who refuses to act in the name of his master is useless to me. I found those strange packets in your coat to be quite effective in dealing with him, by the way. They are rather ingenious, really."

"So, then, where is Adrian? How does he factor into all of this?" I felt naked without my coat, exposed. It bothered me my own weapons had been used against Simon.

"Adrian can take care of himself. He is no concern of yours."

"Did you know he was coming to me?" I took another step forward. I needed to get closer if I wanted to have any chance against them. I just needed to get to Davin. Once his shield was down, I could finish off the others before they could react.

Or so I hoped.

"He came to me before tonight even, asked me to join him," I continued. "He has no intention of sticking with you. He believes your House is done. He only wanted the power you could provide him, the resources he would need to gain power of his own. He was recruiting your wolves right out from under you."

The doubt thickened in Tremaine's eyes. His smile slipped and finally fell away for good. "You lie," he said. "Adrian is bound by his Oath, just as are all my wolves. Even your precious Luna Cult werewolves are now mine. They have sworn the Oath."

I think he expected me to flinch at the last. I only smiled. "They swore the Oath, yet here I am. How do you figure that happened?"

The two vamps in front of Tremaine eased slowly to the side, spreading out. Their faces had not changed since I entered. They watched me warily, though it was clear they felt they had the upper hand. They did have the numbers on me, but I had the weapons. A few more steps away from Davin's shield and I could put a bullet in both their brains.

Tremaine closed his hands into fists. His upper lip lifted into a sneer, and for a second, I could have sworn his ears and eyebrows got just a little bit fuzzier. What the hell?

"The Oath is binding."

"So are handcuffs and rope. They can be broken."

"Not the Oath."

"But it can be worked around." I moved forward another step. The two vamps sliding around the side moved with me, though they kept close to Davin and his shield. "I ask again, where is Adrian? Shouldn't he be here protecting you with the rest of your wolves?"

Tremaine took the slightest step back. The movement was so slight I almost didn't notice it.

"I think he has left you here on your own because he knew your time had come. He knew you were done, that tonight, your House would be at an end. He knew what was to be unleashed here, and he wanted no part of it."

"No one leaves," Tremaine said. "Whatever you think you know, you are wrong. Adrian is hunting with his wolves outside the estate. It is his reward for being so faithful to me."

I took another step forward. "And the man upstairs? What did Simon do to be eviscerated like that?"

Tremaine stared at me, hatred burning in the depths of his gaze. "He was an example, nothing more."

A roar came from my left that caused me to jerk back. The chains rattled and Jonathan lunged for-

ward. He was yanked back well before coming close
to anyone. The rage in his eyes was so wild, so strong,
I feared what would happen if he actually did break
free. I knew I wouldn't be safe from his rage, not with
the moon being full and the Madness taking hold of
what was left of his sanity.

Tremaine laughed at the seemingly futile display.
His confidence was back in full. I had given him what
he wanted. I had told the Luna Cult wolves that their
Denmaster was dead. In Tremaine's mind, it proved
his superiority over them. He didn't realize how wrong
he really was.

Another loud snap came from the wolves, this one
so loud it sounded like a bomb had gone off in the
room. A crack like a hundred-foot whip, followed by
a crash like thunder, shook the very foundations of
the mansion. The wolves were in full rampage mode
now, thrashing in their bonds, howling and gnashing
as one, fueled by Jonathan's rage.

A howl of triumph came from Nathan's direction,
and it was echoed by the rest of the wolves down the
line. He heaved forward with all his might and a large
chunk of the wall tore free. Another wolf lunged and
his chain snapped as if whatever strength had been
holding it weakened with the breaking of the first.

Wolf after wolf began to push forward, their chains
breaking, mortar and stone falling from all around
the metal rings. It sounded like a dozen gunshots
went off in quick succession, and the entire house
shook as the werewolves finally broke free of their
bonds.

30

Jonathan's chain snapped and the vampire closest to the wall went down under his rending claws. His scream was cut off before it could truly be voiced.

More chains snapped and the wall shook with the strain.

Within seconds of the first snapped chain, the wolves as a whole were free.

Claws and fur flew as they fell on each other, lost in the grip of the Madness. Howls and cries of pain echoed through the mostly empty house. Blood fell from torn, shredded flesh. The wolves fought friend and foe alike, desiring only to kill.

And to feed.

The vampires were moving almost immediately. They needed to contain the wolves as fast as possible, to minimize the damage. Each wolf that fell beneath the claws of another was one less wolf for House Tremaine to use.

They were so intent on what was going on with the werewolves, the vamps seemed to have forgotten me. Either that or they thought me a lesser threat. These were moon-crazed wolves they were dealing with, after all. Perhaps they thought I would help them in subduing the insane shifters.

I didn't hesitate. The moment the vampires turned their backs to me, I moved.

The first bullet took one of the vamps in the side of the head. He dropped without a cry, the bullet lodged in his brain. He shuddered on the floor, his body convulsing with the silver poisoning his body.

All eyes turned toward me at the sound of the gun going off. Everyone seemed frozen for a split second, as if they were so shocked that I actually shot someone, they didn't know what to do.

Davin was the first to regain his composure. He spun to protect himself, as well as the Count, with his magical shield. The third vamp stayed close, waiting for me to make my move before deciding what to do. He kept glancing at the wolves, his eyes wide, waiting for the moment when they might pounce.

I took a step toward Tremaine but was forced to turn away from him when a handful of wolves charged me. Blood mixed with saliva splattered on the polished floor as they charged. There was nothing in their eyes but the Madness. They knew only that I had made the big sound and were intent on ending me.

Cursing softly, I backed away. I didn't have enough bullets to deal with all the wolves, as well as Tremaine. I shot one wolf in the head in the hopes it might make the others change their minds about me, but it seemed only to enrage them further. They came on without missing a step.

I was forced to backpedal as they advanced. I had my back to the far wall, which was thankfully empty of wolves, but there was no way out there. I kept firing, counting the bullets, knowing at any moment it would be my last. I dropped one wolf, then another, but they were coming too hard, too fast. I would never drop them all before they got to me.

The third vampire started forward as if he thought he could join in on the kill. He must have forgotten what had happened to the last vamp who got too close to the wolves.

A pair of wolves leaped on him, ripping his throat out before he could so much as scream. Within seconds, he was a mass of blood and guts, strewn across the floor. The two wolves quickly fell on one another, fighting over the remains.

I dropped another wolf as it lunged for me, barely stepping aside as its body flew past and slammed into the wall at my back. I only had time to pay it a quick glance to make sure it was going to stay down before I was forced to contend with the remaining wolf.

I raised my gun, hoping I had at least one bullet left, and was about to pull the trigger when I realized who it was that was coming. Nathan's eyes were yellow, almost fully dilated, and there was absolutely no recognition in them. I jerked my aim away anyway, cursing under my breath, and tried to sidestep his leap.

I wasn't fast enough. His full weight hit me in the chest and we both went down hard. My gun went spinning out of my hand, landing somewhere out of sight. I landed on my back, the full weight of the fully shifted werewolf on my chest. Blood trailed down his face. One ear was almost completely torn from his head. His breath smelled of gore and death.

I fought under him as he snapped at me, barely

getting my forearm up under his chin before his teeth closed around my face. He fought hard and it took all my strength just to keep him from biting my nose off. There was no way I was going to get him off me by pure brute strength. My sword was still in my hand, but I wasn't going to be able to stab him without dropping my guard first. He would probably kill me before I could get the angle right to break his skin anyway.

"Nathan," I gasped, my breath pressed from my chest by his weight. "Stop."

He snapped at my face, then suddenly jerked back, eyes wild. He seemed to look me over, panting and growling deep in his throat. It was almost like he was having some sort of wolf-language conversation with himself. I only hoped the sane part of him that was buried deep within the depths of his brain would win out in the end.

I struggled beneath him, trying in vain to push him off me. All I needed to do was stab him and he would be paralyzed by the silver. I wouldn't have to kill him. I just needed to get him off me and get the hell away from him before he regained control of his body.

My breath was coming in harsh, painful gasps. Even vampires needed air. I wouldn't die from suffocation, but I sure as hell could suffer from it. His weight pressed down on me, pushed the air from my lungs and I gasped for breath.

Nathan howled, mere inches from my face, and I froze, certain he was going to finish me off. I couldn't hold him off much longer. My arm was trembling. The lack of air was causing my strength to wane.

Even my moon-hyped strength was no match for Nathan's all-out rage.

He opened his mouth wide, his tongue a bloody mess in his mouth. His lips pulled back from his teeth, his eyes bulged from his head. He growled deep in his throat, then turned his head and leaped off me, charging back into the fray.

I got to my feet the moment he was gone. I sucked in large gulps of air and had to steady myself a moment before acting. I held my sword in both hands as I scanned the fight, trying to make sense of what I was seeing.

Werewolves were fighting each other all over the room. I hadn't even realized how many wolves Tremaine had at his disposal. The pair that had been chained by the door had broken free, but were fighting right in front of the doorway, blocking off any escape. It was a mass of fur and death everywhere I looked. The vampires were standing close to the dais, watching it all in rapt fascination.

And Nathan was going right for them.

I didn't bother looking for my gun. It was probably out of bullets anyway. I raised my sword and charged right in behind him. In the tumult caused by the fighting wolves, neither of our approaches could be heard. Both vampires stood watching the fight, most likely thinking me dead already. Davin still had his shield up, but he was facing the wrong way.

Nathan hit Davin full in the back, sending both of them flying across the room. Davin screamed once and then fell abruptly silent as Nathan tore out his throat with his bare hands. Before he could finish the job, another wolf attacked him from the side and they went tumbling head over heels together, slamming against the wall.

I came in next, not bothering to watch the fight. Nathan could take care of himself, I was sure. I swung my sword with all my might, hoping to catch the distracted Count unaware and lop off his head with one swing. He ducked as if he felt the strike coming and rolled forward, nearly crashing into a pair of wolves with a death lock on each others' necks. Tremaine flowed to his feet and turned to face me, rage contorting his features.

Or I thought it was rage at first. He sloughed off his leather jacket like a second skin. Thin, membranous wings sprouted from his back before the jacket even hit the floor. Bone cracked and groaned as they unfolded behind him, spreading out a good five feet to either side of the vampire. His face twisted, fur sprung from the tops of his ears, thickened on his face. His nose snapped and folded in like an accordion, as if someone had hit him square in the face with an invisible piano.

A full-fledged shapeshifter. Fuck!

I charged Tremaine before he could take flight. His transformation had taken only a few seconds, and had stopped at the wings and altered facial features as far as I could tell. He looked like some sort of giant bat-man. If he were to live for a few hundred years more, he might even learn to complete the change, though he would never be able to lose mass to shrink to the size of a real bat. I wasn't going to give him that chance.

Tremaine kicked his coat into the air, aiming for my face. It forced me to hesitate for an instant to bat it down, but that instant was enough.

He lifted off the ground and coasted upward above the melee, his wings beating the air. He let out an ear-splitting shriek and hovered just out of reach of my sword.

I didn't have my gun to shoot him and he seemed to know it. It could be anywhere, including in the clutches of a crazed werewolf. I expected to be shot in the back at any moment.

Tremaine flew around to flank me. I kept my sword high, refusing to relinquish my guard. If he was going to attack, he was going to have to get through my defenses. He didn't have a weapon other than his teeth and hands. He would have to get in close to fight me, and all I would need to do was prick him.

Tremaine shrieked again, this time louder. The sound of his call was like fingernails on a chalkboard, amplified over a hundred speakers all turned up to ten. I fell back a step, wincing in pain. I nearly stepped on a werewolf who had just finished off another wolf. He looked up at me, one eye glistening with Madness.

I immediately recognized the caved-in features of Jonathan's head. He got to his feet, wobbled ever so slightly, and took a threatening step toward me. Blood caked his fur, and the eye on the bad side of his head was swollen shut.

It was then I remembered my knives. I had come to rely too much on my gun and the longer reach of my sword during the frantic fight.

I grabbed one of the knives from my belt and flipped it over in my hand so that the silver touched my fingers. The burn was nothing compared with what I would feel if Jonathan were to lock his teeth around my throat. I reared back and let the knife fly. Jonathan jerked back, but I wasn't aiming for him.

The knife hit Count Tremaine in the membranous portion of his left wing. He let out a shriek and flapped his wings frantically. He was just barely able to keep himself aloft. He glowered at me, seemingly impervious to the silver of the knife.

It didn't matter. That wasn't my goal anyway.

I pulled my second knife and flipped it over in my hand. Jonathan watched me warily but didn't attack. Even with the Madness, he still held on to some semblance of control. He was far stronger than I ever would have imagined.

Tremaine's wings increased their beat. He shrieked again, this time in panic, as he tried to fly away. No matter how frantically he beat his wings, he couldn't gain altitude, couldn't propel himself forward and away.

The second knife took him in the other wing, puncturing a hole clear through it. He cried out and plummeted to the ground. He hit hard, one of his useless wings bent under him. It snapped like a twig.

"He killed Simon," I said, staring hard into Jonathan's one good eye. "Take your revenge."

Jonathan howled and charged Count Tremaine just as the vamp regained his feet. Jonathan hit him square in the chest, his claws embedding themselves on either side of the vampire's head. The enraged wolf squeezed with all his might, muscles bulging. Tremaine's features shifted from bat to human and back again. He beat his broken wings frantically, tried to pummel Jonathan with them, as well as with his hands.

"The Oath," he said, his voice coming out contorted from his batlike mouth. "You swore the Oath."

Jonathan snarled at him, unable to form words in wolf form. I'm pretty sure he told him to fuck off.

"You can't do—" Tremaine's words cut off as his skull caved in. Blood and brains shot everywhere, splattering all over the front of Jonathan, over the fighting wolves. One of his eyeballs rolled across the floor and came to a stop at my feet.

I didn't wait around for the aftermath. As soon as Tremaine's headless body hit the ground, I made for the door, hacking away at any wolf that came anywhere close to me. One of the wolves that had been blocking the door was dead, and the other was off fighting elsewhere. I made straight for the exit, not bothering to snatch up my knives or search for my gun. I could come back for them later.

I ran for the front door. The fighting went on behind me, wolves howling and snarling as they fought. None of the wolves followed me. I burst through the front door and was standing beneath the angry light of the full moon within moments of Count Tremaine's death. No clouds were in the sky. The night seemed as bright as day.

I paused for only a moment before taking off running again. All I wanted to do was get home and take a shower. I was covered in blood and gore, and wanted to be rid of it before it somehow found a way into my bloodstream. There probably wasn't enough to taint me, but I wanted to be sure. I felt sick from having it all over me, and after what I had witnessed, I couldn't stand to have the stuff on me any longer.

A long, mournful howl lit up the night, and I turned long enough to see a very large werewolf standing on top of Tremaine's mansion. His eyes were on me, and in the moonlight, I could see his teeth glistening. I could have sworn he was smiling.

"Adrian." The name slipped through my lips and a chill coursed throughout my entire body.

He seemed to hear me despite the distance. He nodded once and then turned, vanishing over the rooftop. I stared after him wordlessly, my body cold as ice. Seconds passed and Adrian didn't appear again.

Part of me wanted to go after him. Part of me knew if I did, I wouldn't live through the encounter.

Without waiting to see if anyone else would appear, I turned and fled from the massacre raging on behind me, wondering if I would be the only one to survive.

31

I sat idling outside The Bloody Stake. The parking lot was full. Laughter drifted out when a young couple opened the doors and walked out, arm in arm. No one followed them.

I watched them get in a car and drive off. I considered pulling out right after them and going home. I didn't want to be there. I knew what waited for me inside, and I really didn't want to have to face it.

Five nights had passed since the events at Tremaine's mansion. Adrian hadn't come for me, nor had any of the wolves. I didn't even go back for my weapons or in search of my coat. I had others. I didn't need them.

But then the letter arrived, placed on the front stoop. I never saw who left it, but I had a good idea. It wasn't too hard to figure out, what with his signature and all at the bottom of the page.

I shut off my Honda and frowned. After tonight, Ethan would get to work on repairing it. The scratch looked obscene to me now. It was a constant reminder of a week I sorely wanted to forget.

"What the hell," I said. What did I have to lose? I

would just go in, see what he wanted, and get out. I needed some downtime, time to relax before starting all this craziness again.

The inside of the Stake was loud and obnoxious like always. Mikael was in his usual spot; he winked at me as I came in. It was a telling gesture. He knew I was responsible for the fall of House Tremaine, though he didn't know how close I had come to failing. If I had anything to say about it, he would never know.

I scanned the crowd until my eyes fell on a certain hooded form sitting alone at a booth. I picked my way across the floor, an old coat I had stopped wearing years ago dragging on the ground behind me. No wonder I had shoved the thing into my closet and bought a new one. The damn thing was too long.

I slid into the booth, unsure what to say. Jonathan kept his head down, staring into a beer he hadn't even touched. Another beer rested in front of me. The silence hung over us like a cloud, waiting for the first word to blow it away.

"So," I said, first to breach the silence. "House Tremaine is truly dead." I took a sip of the beer. It was warm. It had sat there for quite a while. I set it aside, not liking the taste of it. I was hungry for a drink of another kind, though I hadn't been able to bring myself to hunt. I had seen enough blood lately. I didn't need to spill more.

"The sorcerer survived," Jonathan said, never lifting his head. "We have him locked away for now. He isn't talking. We'll break him eventually." He took a sip of his beer. "There might be one or two more that survived. I'm not sure."

"They might know my face."

"They might," he said. "But they still don't know who you really are. I never told them. No one did." The last came out pained.

In his letter, Jonathan had told me the results of our raid on House Tremaine. None of the Pureblood Cultists survived. Nathan and Jonathan lived, but that was all out of our little group. The Purebloods in the basement were freed, but they would probably die anyway. They had endured so much, there was little hope of recovery for most.

"What of the mansion?" I asked. "Did you burn it?" I felt ashamed asking. That was the sort of thing I should have known. I hadn't been out of my house since the battle.

Jonathan shook his head. "The mansion is already occupied. It was claimed just after I went through the place with the Cult, making sure no one else was hiding somewhere in its depths."

"Figures," I said. Vampires were quick to capitalize on the fallen. "Do you know who is there now?"

Jonathan took a deep breath and looked away. "Adrian has taken up residence with a few of his wolves. He didn't take part in the battle. He wanted us to kill Tremaine. We did his job for him."

I tensed, waiting for more. I could still feel that last lingering glance on me, the power of his eyes. He was still loose and *he* knew who I was.

"But I see no reason to go after him," Jonathan finished.

I just about choked on my tongue. "Even after what he did?" I had to fight to keep from shouting. Bart glanced in our direction, then turned his back to us to polish a glass I was sure was already clean.

"He is one of my kind," Jonathan said. "He could

have taken part in the battle, but he didn't. He gave us the chance to take down Tremaine without getting involved himself. I think that gives him the right to make a life for himself."

I wasn't so sure I agreed. The bastard had nearly gotten us killed. "But he defected from the Cult, knows where your Den is located. What happens if he decides to come finish you off?" And there was that whole bit about being resistant to silver. I wasn't so sure I was ready to divulge that information just yet.

Jonathan shrugged. "We will keep an eye on him. If he tries something, the Luna Cult will step in. Just promise me you won't go after him unless he does something worthy of your attention."

I cursed softly under my breath. Why the hell should I promise anything to him? Jonathan was a goddamn werewolf. He may have promised in his letter never to reveal my location, reveal who I was, but he was still the enemy. I had to keep reminding myself that, and it was really starting to piss me off.

"I can't promise that," I said. "If he steps in my way, I will be forced to take care of him."

Jonathan and I sat quietly at our table for a long time. I tried the beer once more but gave up on it. It wasn't sitting well in my stomach. I felt like I was going to puke and I didn't know why.

"I have your things," Jonathan said. He reached down beside him and picked up a bundle. "I think this is everything."

I took the bundle from him and glanced at its contents. My coat was there, as was my gun and two knives. Damn it. He was making it even harder to hate him with every moment.

"Thanks," I muttered setting my things beside me.

We stared at our beers, refusing to meet one another's eye. We had barely survived a fight for our lives together, and yet this seemed to be the hardest thing we had ever done. Why the hell was I feeling so awkward?

"Thank you," he said after a while. "For everything you have done."

"I did it for myself. Not for you, not for the Cult, and sure as hell not for Adrian Davis."

"Still," he said. "The Luna Cult as a whole owes you our thanks. We wouldn't be here if it wasn't for you."

I shrugged off his thanks and resumed staring at my beer. Why was I still there? I had my things back, and it seemed like we had both said all we needed to say. I could up and leave anytime I wanted. I could put all of this behind me. My life would be the better for it.

But I sat there, unable or unwilling to move. It didn't feel right to turn my back on him. Not now. Maybe not ever. We had worked well together, as much as I hated to admit it. Sure, things could have gone better, but in the end, we had won. House Tremaine was no more. The Luna Cult was safe and intact.

And more importantly, I was alive.

Eventually, Jonathan pushed away from the table and stood. He favored his left leg slightly, leaning to the right. I didn't ask him what had happened. He would heal eventually. I might be grudgingly accepting of him now, but that didn't mean it would stay that way forever.

"If you ever need anything from the Cult, feel free

to get in touch. You will always be welcome in the Den as long as you don't bring violence with you. No one will stop you, not even Pablo." I could hear the smile in his voice as the last.

Jonathan took a deep breath and looked around the room. No one was watching us. He turned back to me, head lowered, and then pulled back his hood. I couldn't stop the gasp that rose to my lips.

His head was whole, round like it should. It was the same face I remembered, just complete. His glamour hid his bruises, hid the hideous scar on the right side of his face. Seeing him like he was meant to be was like looking at an entirely different person. I had to admit, he looked good that way, though a deep part of me wasn't so sure I liked seeing him as a real person.

He smiled and it looked genuine. "Thank you," he said as he lifted his hood, covering his face. "You have shown me more than anyone what I should be. I can never thank you enough for the life you have given me."

I sat speechless. What could I possibly say to that? I wasn't a hero or someone's savior. I was a killer. Deep down, I knew eventually I would lose my humanity because of what I did. It was only a matter of time.

But right then, it didn't matter. His praise felt good, though I would never admit it.

Jonathan's hand fell on mine, and even though I knew I should, I didn't move it. It felt warm, solid. "I hope to hear from you again," he said. The calluses on his palms felt strangely exhilarating against the back of my hand. "May peace find you, Lady Death." He whispered the last so softly I almost didn't hear it.

He turned and walked out of The Bloody Stake without another word. I watched him go, wanting to say something, but incapable of speech. When he was gone, I found myself alone, fingering the back of my hand where he had touched me. The sensation of his hand on mine was gone, vanished like moonlight at the dawn, but the memory of his touch lingered, scored itself deep into my mind.

That couldn't be good.

I gathered my things and walked out of the bar, knowing that even though Count Tremaine was dead, things were definitely not okay.

I wasn't so sure they would ever be right again.

Please turn the page for an exciting sneak peek of
the next Kat Redding novel,
TAINTED NIGHT, TAINTED BLOOD
coming in July 2012!

1

The body lay crumpled in the driveway, a heap of cloth that could have been anything if not for the distinctive smell that drifted on the light breeze. If I had simply been driving by, minding my own business, I might not have even noticed it. It was halfway up the paved drive, almost blended in with the darkness.

But I *had* been looking for it, and the corpse assured me I was in the right place.

Countess Telia was known for her cruelty. She hadn't been active very long, at least as a minor power of her own. She was the head of one of the newest Fledgling Houses, a vampire who tortured dozens of Purebloods to the point of insanity just for the fun of it. Once she was done with her playthings, she would release them, letting her victims return to their families to suffer their final days crippled and mindless.

It appeared this time she had gone too far.

I parked my modified Honda DN-01 just off the road and hid it behind some trees. The motorcycle was completely black, including the piping, so it would be hard for anyone who wasn't expressly looking for it to see it. Even a vampire would have a hard time picking it out of the shadows.

A dog barking in the distance was the only sound as I slipped into the brush. I crouched down, listening and watching for any sign of pursuit. House Telia was deep within vampire-controlled territory, so the chances of someone spotting me were actually pretty good. I wanted to make sure none of the local vamps or wolves decided to follow the girl on the motorcycle, looking to have a little bit of fun.

As far as I could tell, no one had followed me. I breathed a sigh of relief and drew my sword. The demon-crafted blade shone in the moonlight, but I was pretty sure it wouldn't matter now. By the time Telia saw me coming, it would be too late.

The gun came next. My modified Glock 17 fit comfortably in my hand. The bullets were made of silver, and thanks to Ethan's modifications, they wouldn't pass all the way through a supe's body. They moved too slowly for that.

I rose from my crouch, careful not to let my leather creak in the all-too-silent night. I was dressed in full-on black. It was my usual work attire. It just wouldn't do to run around fighting vampires wearing a white T-shirt and jeans. I had an image to keep up.

I slipped from the cover of the trees and started up the driveway. The body was just a hump on the paved surface, barely discernible as anything other than a pile of bloody rags. I could smell death on the air and knew this victim had been tortured to the point where there would probably be little left.

I approached, wary nonetheless. Even though I

was pretty sure the victim was dead, I nudged her with my foot and touched the silver blade to her flesh to be sure.

Nothing happened.

The dead girl's shirt was shredded in the front, and there was blood everywhere. She had been torn from groin to sternum by what looked to be werewolf claws. It wasn't exactly Telia's style, but I wouldn't put it past her to give a young girl like this to one of her wolves. She had to keep her minions loyal somehow.

Countess Telia was new, a recent break-off from one of the Major Houses. Mikael Engelbrecht, my snitch, hadn't been able to tell me which Major House she had come from, but he implied it was one of the biggies. He would have told me more, but he was in the pay of the Count or Countess Telia once belonged to, so he refused to divulge any more than he had to. I didn't like it, but I had to respect his loyalty to his customers, especially since I was one of them.

Still, that didn't stop him from telling me about Telia's exploits, how she had cut the arms and legs off one of her victims and dumped him outside his home, his wounds sewn closed so he wouldn't bleed out. His tongue and eyelids had been removed, as were his nipples, ears, and any other dangly bits that she could get to with a knife. He survived in body, although his mind was long gone.

Why she hadn't been killed by the Major House she ditched was beyond me. Vampires didn't like it when their underlings defected. A vamp thinking she could leave a Major House to start her own usually turned up dead within an hour of making her claim.

But there Telia was, torturing victims and reveling

in their blood just like any other baby vamp, albeit a more violent one. I was there to put a stop to it.

I left the body where I found it and started up the drive, keeping close to the trees so anyone who would happen to glance out a window wouldn't see my approach. I moved in near silence, my vampire-light feet barely making a sound on the pavement. I'd even learned to minimize the sound of leather with my walk. Being a vampire had its advantages at times.

It wasn't until I was halfway up the driveway that I noticed the other bodies. All of the lights in the house were blazing, including the outside light. It spilled out over the corpses, illuminating them like actors on a stage. I could see the dark stain of blood against the black pavement.

I froze and gave the house a good long look. One body, I expected. Three was a bit much.

I hadn't noticed it before because I hadn't really looked, but the front door was torn nearly off its hinges. The window beside it was intact, but the curtains were hanging at an angle, as if someone had tried to tear them down.

And there were no sounds, no moving shadows that told me where Telia or her minions were. Had her little torture party turned into something much more deadly? I had no idea what she did in there most nights. It was entirely possible she had set three Purebloods loose, sicking her wolves on them for pure entertainment.

If so, then where was she? I should have seen a flicker of a shadow, heard the howl of a wolf. She would have wanted to watch the events as they took place.

I approached the two other bodies, keeping my

gaze on the house as I went. They could be in there, watching me. The night was still young, so I was sure they hadn't bedded down for the day.

The first corpse turned out to be another Pureblood, this one male. He had been stripped naked and lay in a pool of his own blood. His ribs showed through flesh pulled tight, as if he had been starved before being released. His stomach had been ripped open and his throat slashed.

I nudged him like I had the other corpse to make sure he was really dead. Sometimes it was hard to tell between a Pureblood and a young werewolf or vampire. It was possible this was some sort of initiation rite that Telia cooked up for her newest recruits. Torture them, let them bleed a while, and then take them in.

But this guy was definitely dead. If she had tried to turn him, she had started the process far too late.

The last body was a few paces away, and at first, I thought he was wearing a fur coat. As I got closer, I realized that wasn't the case and alarm bells started ringing in my head in earnest.

The werewolf was lying facedown, his head a few inches from his body. The cut was ragged, as if it had taken a few hacks to cut through the wolf's thick neck. There were marks on his arms and shoulder where he had tried to protect himself.

It hadn't helped. The wolf had been hamstrung, making him an easy target for whomever had done this. I wasn't sure if Telia had done it herself or if someone else was involved. Either way, I didn't like it.

I hurried to the front of the house and pressed my back to the wall. The place wasn't large by vampire standards. It was bigger than where I lived, but not

by much. Countess Telia still had a ways to go before
she could move up to the mansions the other Counts
and Countesses preferred.

I crept along the wall to the nearest window and
peeked in. Furniture lay strewn across the room. A
mirror had been smashed, leaving shards of bloody
glass all over the floor. A glass coffee table had been
shattered as well, adding to the destruction.

And there was blood everywhere.

My stomach rumbled as my inner demon made
itself known. I hadn't fed for over a week and it was
starting to get to me. I really should have hunted
before coming. Then again, I hadn't expected to
find bodies lying around with blood splattered all
over the walls.

I fought the urge to feed, pushed it as deep as I
could. The blood was probably tainted anyway. To
taste it would be to risk contaminating myself further.

I slipped past the window to the door. I still had
yet to see any movement from within. It was entirely
possible Countess Telia had been attacked by a rogue
wolf or two and was out chasing down the last of
them. She could return at any time.

Or she could be inside, bathing in the blood of
her victims. It was hard to tell with vamps, especially
ones like her.

I stepped around the corner and into the house,
my gun leading the way.

There was blood on the floor just inside the door,
but there were no bodies. One of the dead outside
could have been wounded here before staggering
out into the driveway to die.

Either that or whoever had been injured here was
somewhere farther in the house, wounded and angry.

I worked my way deeper, checking each room as I passed. The living room I had seen from the window was to my left, and I paid it only a casual glance as I passed by. The dining room and kitchen were likewise empty, though I did find what looked to be an ear lying on the kitchen counter. Whomever it belonged to wasn't anywhere to be found.

There were two other rooms on the ground floor, but I had yet to come across any sign that anyone was alive inside. I still had the basement and the upstairs to canvas, yet something told me I wouldn't find anyone in the house. For whatever reason, Countess Telia wasn't home.

Still, I headed for the stairs. I would check the place over first, freeing any Purebloods I found, and then would wait for Telia to return. I couldn't let her continue her torturous ways. Not in my town.

From the bottom of the stairs, I could see what appeared to be a man's boot resting beside a bloody wall. I slowly made my way up the stairs sideways, keeping my gun trained just above the boot in case the guy sat up.

I needn't have bothered. The boot turned out not to be connected to anyone. The hallway behind it was empty of everything but blood. I stepped around the boot and just happened to glance back at it as I passed.

There was a foot inside.

The alarm bells in my head weren't just ringing now; they were clanging so loudly, my ears rang with the phantom sound. Something was definitely wrong here.

The first room on my right turned out to be a bathroom. The owner of the foot was inside, lying on the floor, a bloody mess. His head lay in the tub, severed from his body much like the wolf's had been. The job had been sloppy, most likely performed with a dull blade. The dead man's mouth was wide, exposing two extended fangs.

I looked around the bathroom in the hopes of finding something that wound identify the victim. I didn't know what Telia's lone vampire minion looked like. If this was him, then something truly bad had happened here, and by the smell, it hadn't happened too long ago.

I left the bathroom, body thrumming with excitement. Had the Major House come down on Telia after all? Or was it someone else? Could another House have decided they'd had enough of the Fledgling vamp and her torturous ways? Or another Fledgling House could have come after her, looking to make themselves stronger.

A surge of anger coursed through my body. If Mikael held out on me because he knew Telia's old House was coming after her, I was going to be pissed. What if I had shown up while the killing was going on? I might have been caught in the middle of a fight between vamps and wolves from a Major House and Telia's own. I could have been killed.

I wasn't positive that was what happened. Most vampires didn't fight with swords, let alone dull ones. They would have sent werewolves to finish the job. A few well-placed bullets would have wounded Telia and her minions; then the wolves could have torn them apart at their leisure.

This was different somehow. I wasn't quite sure how, but I knew something else was going on. Had

Telia tired of her House? Had she killed everyone in an orgy of blood and torture?

I crept down the hall, checking each room as I passed. There was no one inside, and I had yet to hear the slightest sound. I could taste blood where my fangs had started pushing through in my excitement.

The door to the last room of the house was hanging open. As I neared, I could smell the blood coming from inside. Someone was dead in there. More than one someone by the smell of it.

I neared, and as the massacre inside came into view, I knew things had definitely gotten out of hand.

Countess Telia lay sprawled across her bed. At least most of her did. One of her arms was lying on the floor just inside the door, and her head was lying under the window. She was naked and was propped atop the dead Pureblood tied to the bed beneath her.

I stepped over the arm and another body, this one a werewolf, came into view. The wolf was fully shifted, but his body was nothing but a bloody pulp of entrails and muscle. It looked like something had fed on his intestines.

"What the fuck?" I said, scanning the room. Now that I was farther in, I could see what had killed the Pureblood under Telia. His face was gone, having been chewed away by something. I had a feeling he'd been alive when Telia had been riding him.

I slowly approached Telia's headless body. I was pretty sure she had been beheaded by the same weapon that had killed the others. Whoever had done this had somehow snuck up on her and the first blow had severed her spine. With all the dead lying around, I have no idea how that was even possible. She should have heard something, should have known things weren't well within her House.

A strange feeling crept up my gut. I didn't believe this was an inside job. I was almost positive it wasn't done by a Major House either. This looked a lot like something I would have done years ago, before I was changed, before I had silver weapons.

I hurried out of the room and headed for the basement. If anyone was still alive, it would be down there. Vampires usually kept cages there where they held their Pureblood prisoners. If someone was trying to copy my earlier work, then there was a chance they left the Purebloods down there.

I threw open the basement door and nearly ran down the stairs. I almost stepped on another were-wolf corpse as I hit the concrete floor. I staggered to the side, bringing my gun to bear, just in case the wolf wasn't dead.

It didn't take more than a glance to know he wasn't getting up again. He didn't have a head.

I took a deep breath and immediately regretted it. My fangs pushed the rest of the way through my gums and I started panting. There was so much blood down here, it was intoxicating.

My gaze roamed the room and my shock was all that kept me from giving in to my demon.

The Pureblood prisoners were mostly still in their cages. Those who had gotten too close to the bars had been torn apart, pulled through the bars piece by piece. Arms and legs looked gnawed upon, and someone's jawbone lay against the wall.

Those Purebloods who had managed to huddle far back in their cages hadn't been able to escape the hungry jaws of the beast that had fed here. The bars of their cells had been ripped open and they had been killed where they cowered, easy prey to the wolf who had done this.

My hunger warred with my disgust. I couldn't figure out who would have done this. Why would a were-wolf need a sword when he would have his claws? None of this made any sense.

I turned and fled up the stairs, knowing I was wasting my time here. House Telia was no more, but it hadn't been by my hand.

I slipped in a pool of blood at the top of the stairs and nearly fell. I growled deep in my throat and bolted for the front door. I could feel the urge to feed so strongly it nearly had a hold on me. I couldn't give in. Not now. Not like this.

I hurried out of the house, down the driveway, to my Honda. The fresh air did me some good, cleared my head, but it did nothing to stop the anger that came bubbling forth.

Mikael had to have known this was going to happen. It was the only thing that made sense. Why else wouldn't he have told me everything he knew?

I started up my motorcycle and sped away from the house. Everyone was dead inside, even the Pure-bloods. Whoever had done this was just as dangerous as Telia had been. They had to be stopped.

And I was going to be the one to stop them.